A DARKNESS IN SEVEN DIALS

CAPTAIN LACEY REGENCY MYSTERIES
BOOK SEVENTEEN

ASHLEY GARDNER

JA / AG PUBLISHING

CHAPTER 1

March 1820

"A person to see you, Captain." The cool words of Barnstable, my wife's butler, cut into the enjoyment of my newspaper and morning toast.

Barnstable paused on the doorstep of the dining room, his face frozen in an expression of disapproval. His use of the word "person" told me that he considered whoever it was to be no gentleman or lady, or even a respectable member of the lower classes.

That he announced the visitor at all was odd. When Barnstable didn't like the look of someone, he turned them away at his discretion. My wife had given him that power, which Barnstable used without hesitation.

I finished my slice of toasted bread slathered with sweet orange marmalade, a luxury from my father-in-law's hothouses in Oxfordshire, and reluctantly set aside my paper. The details of the Cato Street Conspiracy, as it was now being called, filled the pages. Radicals had planned to incite a revolution after murdering everyone in the cabinet but had been thwarted by diligent Bow Street Runners, including my former sergeant, Milton Pomeroy and his rival, Mr. Spendlove.

"Who is it?" I asked, keeping my question calm. It never did good to upset Barnstable, who was clearly unhappy he'd had to interrupt me.

"He claims his name is Gibbons," Barnstable replied.

Gibbons. It took a moment to connect the name with a face, but it came to me like a slap. Dry, papery, dangerous. Gibbons was the butler of James Denis and had once been a hardened criminal, possibly still was.

Curious. Whenever Denis summoned me, he'd send a note of one line, using a whole sheet of expensive paper to do so. Or he'd send word via Brewster, who'd become my permanent bodyguard and, I hoped, friend.

"A strange but intriguing event," I said as Barnstable hovered. "Send him in, please."

"Perhaps you would speak to him in the foyer, sir."

Barnstable's frosty tone and the fact that he did not meet my gaze guided me to the correct way to receive another man's servant, whether former criminal or not.

Barnstable had been very patient with me as I learned to navigate the world of the aristocracy. I was a man of property, but my father's small, rundown estate in Norfolk hardly compared to Donata's elegant townhouse in South Audley Street or her eight-year-old viscount son's vast home in Hampshire.

I eyed the remaining pieces of toast and the slab of beef awaiting me, laid aside my napkin, and rose, smothering a sigh as I motioned Barnstable to precede me out.

The dining room, a grand chamber with high ceilings and a long table, was located on the main floor of the house. I descended to the ground floor, following Barnstable down the curved staircase with graceful railings.

Gibbons, a thin man with gray hair in a subdued dark suit,

awaited me on the cross-hatched parquet floor of the lower hall. He wore a greatcoat against the March rain and clutched his hat as though he'd been reluctant to remove it upon entering.

Before I could greet him as I stepped off the stairs, he strode forward and barked a command.

"You will come with me."

Whenever I visited Denis in his luxurious house on Curzon Street, Gibbons rarely said a word. He'd usher me to a chair, serve me a beverage in cold silence, and then stand behind me to prevent me escaping the room.

Today, Gibbons spoke rapidly, his eyes black pools of agitation in a hard face.

My brows rose. "What does Mr. Denis wish me to do for him this time?"

"You will see when we get there. *Now*, Captain."

As much as I bristled at being ordered about, my very inconvenient curiosity awoke. I often landed myself in great trouble letting my long nose lead me, a fault I'd not tried very hard to correct.

"Barnstable," I said to the disapproving butler. "Will you please fetch my greatcoat?"

———

GIBBONS HAD ARRIVED IN A COACH PULLED BY MATCHING BAY horses of fine conformation. He wrenched open the carriage door once I, bundled against the rain, exited the house, and brusquely motioned me inside.

"Perhaps I should send for Brewster," I said in belated caution. I'd come to trust Denis—in some situations—but I'd never warmed to Gibbons. He was a hard man working for an even harder one.

"He's already there," Gibbons said, impatient. "We need to hurry."

In spite of my misgivings, I heaved myself into the coach, unsteady on my bad leg. Brewster or one of Denis's other minions might have lent me a hand, but Gibbons only stood stiffly and waited for me to struggle inside.

Once I was on the seat, he sprang in behind me with an energy that belied his years and waved for the coachman to drive on.

My attempts to persuade Gibbons to enlighten me as the vehicle jolted down South Audley Street went unanswered. He kept his stare on the wall of the carriage behind my head, and I turned to the mist-filmed window to avoid it.

We did not halt in Curzon Street, where Denis lived, but turned to a narrow lane and so into Piccadilly. Carts and wagons filled this wide thoroughfare, and I heard the coachman's curses as we wove through traffic. Piccadilly took us to Haymarket, and from there we entered the Strand.

At St. Martin's Lane, the coach turned north, passing the elegant church of St.-Martin-in-the-Fields. My misgivings mounted as the area beyond the church became more insalubrious as we went.

"You really need to tell me where the devil we are going, Gibbons," I said.

Gibbons did not answer. My fears were confirmed when we entered the dark and vile environs of Seven Dials and creaked along to a tiny street there.

I was in a dangerous neighborhood with a man from an underworld gang, without Brewster to guard me. I'd foolishly hopped into this coach with no regard as to where it would take me, assuming we'd arrive at Denis's elegant home in Curzon Street. Gibbons had no loyalty to me and no liking for me either.

The man remained stone-faced and silent, his unnerving gaze never wavering.

The coach pulled to a halt near a tall house whose facade

wasn't as crumbling as those around it. It did not look occupied, and I had no idea why we were here.

Gibbons wrenched open the coach's door and climbed down, motioning me to descend behind him. He hadn't lowered the step, so I scrambled out without much dignity, nearly falling when my bad knee gave way upon my landing.

I managed to remain upright, swallowing any savage words, and limped behind Gibbons toward the house. The front door opened, and I was relieved to see the broad form of Brewster filling the small foyer.

I relaxed only slightly as I entered the cold interior. Again, I'd been brought here for who knew what reason, and no one in my own home knew where I'd gone.

"It's bad, Captain," was Brewster's greeting. "We're trying to decide what to do."

He waved me into the sitting room, which was as gloomy as the March morning. No fire had been built in the hearth, and my breath misted in the dank air.

Gibbons, having delivered me, disappeared without a word into the back of the house. I did not believe he'd gone to prepare tea for his guest.

"Where is Denis?" I asked. "Whose house is this, and where is mine host?"

Brewster's grim expression told me it was not the time for humor. "Belongs to His Nibs," came his gruff reply. "His Nibs himself is in Newgate. Was arrested early this morning."

I gaped as his words penetrated my bewilderment. "Arrested? *Denis?*"

Denis was the most careful man I knew. He ran a successful criminal organization, and he was very, very cautious. He made certain that the men he employed were scrupulously loyal and that no evidence would ever be found to incriminate him or anyone who worked for him.

I would have believed this some elaborate joke at my

expense, but for the involvement of Gibbons, who had no use for me, and the anxiety on Brewster's face.

"'Tis true, Captain," Brewster said. "Taken by none other than Timothy Spendlove, Bow Street Runner. Didn't he rub his hands in delight?" he finished bitterly.

My jaw remained slack. "How the devil did Denis let Spendlove arrest him?"

Timothy Spendlove, the man with red hair and brows so light they faded into his freckled face, had been after Denis for years. He'd tried in every way to pin something on Denis or his men, but Denis had evaded him with efficient ease.

Brewster answered in some despair. "Because Spendlove's patroller caught His Nibs standing over a dead man, right there in the street." He pointed out the window with a blunt finger. "The man in question was dead as a stone, and His Nibs was holding a knife with the bloke's blood on it. Spendlove couldn't believe his good luck. He carted His Nibs off to Bow Street Nick before Mr. Gibbons could do damn all about it."

CHAPTER 2

*A*t some point, I would have to close my mouth, but I was so astounded by this news it took a moment.

"How did Spendlove orchestrate that?" I demanded. "Denis would never let himself be caught over a corpse, brandishing the murder weapon. *Was* it the murder weapon?"

Brewster shrugged. "I suppose it must have been. Spendlove and his patrollers whisked it to Bow Street along with His Nibs, who was up before the magistrate first thing this morning. No question it's Mr. Denis's knife. Magistrate made short work of things. Sent His Nibs to Newgate, where he is now awaiting trial for murder."

My leg gave a painful throb, and I had to drop into the nearest chair. It was straight-backed and plain, but like everything in Denis's dwellings, comfortable. "I still don't believe it. James Denis would not walk into the street in front of his own house and stab a man to death. He'd have one of his lackeys take the unfortunate person someplace very private and do the deed for him. Wouldn't he?"

"He has in the past, that is true," Brewster confirmed.

"Even if Denis decided to settle the matter himself, why in

the street, where any witness can look out their window and see them? And why wasn't he surrounded by his own men?" Denis never went anywhere without at least four to guard him.

"This is Seven Dials," Brewster pointed out. "None here will admit to seeing anything. They won't risk standing as witness at the Old Bailey, because too many should be in the dock there themselves. As to where his guards were, I don't know." He spread his hands, unhappy.

I tried to picture the scene—Denis, cool and efficient, walking outside with his victim, or meeting him in the street, stepping up to him and thrusting a knife into his chest. Then standing over the man's body, waiting for Spendlove and his patrollers to surround him and take him to Bow Street.

This was madness.

"Who was he meant to have killed?" I asked.

That should have been my first question, I supposed, but Denis was a complicated man with a complicated past. Perhaps an enemy had come upon him, and he'd had to defend himself. It was the only explanation as to why he'd openly dispatch a man in the street.

I had seen Denis kill before, truth to tell. In that situation, both of us had been in dire danger, and Denis's nerve had saved us. The villain he'd shot had been doing his very best to murder us, and I'd not tried very hard to prevent the violence. Battle was about survival.

"Bloke called Pickett." Brewster shook his head. "Never heard of 'im."

Neither had I. "Did you recognize him? Even if you haven't heard the name?"

"Didn't see him, did I?" Brewster said mournfully. "By the time Stout—he's one who works for His Nibs—found me, they'd already taken Mr. Denis off and carted away the body. I went to Bow Street and told a lad I know to see what was happening, but the magistrate had already sent His Nibs off to Newgate by then. Place I'm not going to darken the door of."

As a former thief, Brewster stayed well away from prisons and courts of law. "What did you do after that?" I asked.

"Came back here and poked around but found nothing. Gibbons was here, in a right state. I said we should send for you. He didn't want to but saw the sense in it. Wanted me to stay here and guard the place while he went to fetch you."

"Guard it? Why?"

"In case there's evidence lying about to clear him, I suppose. Not that I've seen anything one way or the other."

"And what am I to do?" I asked in perplexity. "Gibbons hardly trusts me, and I'm no solicitor to convince a magistrate there is not enough evidence for a trial. Spendlove has his claws into this and wants his reward." Which he'd receive if a judge at the Old Bailey convicted Denis of murder. Likely it would be a large amount. "He's waited years for this."

Brewster rubbed his upper lip. "Both Gibbons and me have watched you tumble to the right person enough times that even Gibbons thinks you can help. Gibbons is a cold fish, but he knows a thing or two about the law, having run from it all his life. We need to find a witness, or better yet, the real bloke what did it. Then we can have His Nibs snug at home again in no time."

My dismay at their confidence rose. "You said no one in Seven Dials will admit to seeing anything. How do you propose I find a witness among them?"

Brewster eyed me steadily. "You have your ways. They're odd sometimes, but you get your result in the end."

With luck, mostly. A person said a wrong word at the wrong time and gave himself or herself away. I supposed I was good at noticing such things, but I hardly knew where to start.

"Your optimism is flattering," I said dryly. "You'd better tell me exactly what happened."

"Wasn't here, was I?" Brewster sounded angry, as though blaming himself. "I was home with the wife, as you hadn't been up to anything too dangerous lately. Taking my ease."

"You could not have anticipated this event," I said. "You work for me now, in any case, and couldn't be expected to have prevented the trouble."

I'd hired Brewster directly after Denis sacked him, as Denis had mostly assigned Brewster to look after me anyway. When Denis had tried to hire him back, Brewster asked to stay in my employ instead. My wife approved, as I tended to land myself into treacherous situations, and she was happy for Brewster to get me out of them.

However, Brewster's loyalty to Denis was vast. Denis was very good at keeping the men in his pay free from prison, and he also rewarded them well. Brewster, a former pugilist, had found work for his fists with Denis without risking his neck. He'd not been happy when Denis had first tasked him to look after me, but Brewster had been a great help on our many adventures since then.

"His Nibs has done a lot for me," Brewster said. "I'm that ashamed I wasn't here to lift him out of this trouble."

"There was nothing you could have done," I tried to reassure him. "Spendlove would have arrested you as an accomplice if you'd been anywhere near. This fellow, Stout. I don't recall him, do I?"

I'd once had to question every single one of Denis's men, when he'd been looking for a traitor in his midst. They'd on the surface seemed all of a kind—fighters, boxers, hired ruffians—but had proved to be quite complex and individual. I'd learned surprising stories from them.

Stout had not been on the list.

"His Nibs picked him up in Rome." Brewster scowled. "Bloke had been hanging about there, petty thieving from tourists, trying to save enough for passage back to England. Seems His

Nibs took pity on him, or some such." He rumbled in disapprobation. "He legged it the minute there was trouble, didn't he?"

"To raise the alarm," I said, attempting to be fair. "He couldn't have prevented the arrest either. He was wise to run and fetch you."

"Suppose." Brewster lifted his shoulders, not ready to give the man the benefit of the doubt. "Denis usually has more than one bodyguard with him. What happened to the others?"

"If any others were here, they legged it too." Brewster spoke with reluctance. "His Nibs would have told them to. If we're spotted by a Robin Redbreast, we go separate ways and lie low a few days."

I did not point out his inconsistency in condemning Stout for doing exactly what Denis had trained him to. "I'd like to speak to Stout. Also, to anyone who was in this house at the time. Do you know why Denis was here?"

Brewster relaxed a fraction. "You're going to help, then?"

"Well, of course I am going to help," I said in irritation. "I'd be churlish to dust off my hands and walk away, wouldn't I?"

"I thought maybe you'd be happy to."

I started to retort to the contrary but conceded Brewster's point. "When I first met Denis, yes, I would have. I despised him and what he did. However, I've learned that he is more honorable than many who are supposed to have said honor, and more honest than they are as well. He became who he is through circumstance, not evilness of heart."

While Denis didn't like to show his emotions, I'd become aware that he felt things deeply. He'd learned how to hide such vulnerabilities well, and for good reason.

"Suppose that's true," Brewster agreed.

"Besides all that, I refuse to believe he'd be this foolish. Everything Denis does is carefully calculated, often years in advance."

Brewster gave me a nod. "As you say, guv."

"Then I have no choice but to find out what really happened."

Brewster blew out a breath. "Good."

Gibbons appeared in the doorway in time to hear the last part of our conversation. "Are you going to get on with it, then?" he asked both of us coldly.

I hauled myself to my feet. "Of course, Mr. Gibbons. Please show me the scene of the murder."

———

THE HOUSE WAS SITUATED IN A SMALL CUL-DE-SAC OFF TOWER Street, which itself lay between the X formed by Little Earl and St. Andrews Streets, in the heart of Seven Dials.

Once upon a time, Seven Dials had been a luxurious development, with seven avenues meeting in a neat central square that held a statue and a fountain. However, larger, more sumptuous townhouses in Mayfair soon drew the wealthy from this area, and the neighborhood decayed swiftly. Both fountain and statue were long gone, leaving only broken pavement in their wake.

Seven Dials had already been a maze of small lanes and inlets not found on any map—a mapmaker had to be brave to enter this area and make his notes. Now the neighborhood was a warren of tiny streets holding houses divided into rooms to let, cramming too many into cramped spaces. The formerly elegant main square boasted gin rooms and taverns and had become a well-known meeting place for those who preferred communion with their own sex.

Occasionally there were pockets that weren't so rundown, such as this lane, and in particular, Denis's house here. He did not keep it pristine, which would cause it to stand out, but the windows were whole, the shutters attached and working, and the doors fitted with stout locks.

The street was deserted, rain pattering on my hat as I wandered the pavement where Gibbons directed me.

Brewster dogged my steps, ready both to look for any evidence leading to the true killer and beat off any attackers who might spring from the shadows. Gibbons remained under the small portico at the door, gazing at the rain as though it personally offended him.

There was no blood on the street. It had been pelting rain most of the night, and it still fell in a thin but steady stream. The body had lain a few feet from Denis's door, but either the unfortunate Mr. Pickett hadn't bled much, or the rain had washed his blood away.

I straightened from where I'd crouched to scan the cobblestones and then the columns flanking Denis's front door.

I indicated the area with the tip of my walking stick. "No spray."

Brewster squinted where I gestured and even Gibbons turned his head to look.

"None I can see," Brewster agreed.

"Means the wound was small," Gibbons stated. "The killer didn't slash the man's throat or disembowel him. Probably a single stab to the heart."

"A deep one," I said. "Those can sometimes emit very little blood. The man dies from bleeding inside, or the pierced heart stopping."

Gibbons nodded. "'Appens."

I had formed my conclusion based on my experiences on the battlefield. I didn't like to think about where Gibbons had come by his knowledge.

"It was probably quick," I continued. "Fortunate for the victim, though not for Denis."

Brewster filled in the rest. "Because if the man died messy, and His Nibs had no blood on him, magistrate wouldn't have been in such a hurry to hold him."

I surveyed the houses lining the small street. These were not the charming, half-timbered Tudor dwellings found in some of the oldest parts of town—those that hadn't been gutted by the Great Fire. These had been built from brick maybe a hundred and fifty years ago and stuccoed over. The stucco had crumbled away in many places, and the roofs sagged. The inhabitants on the top floors likely required many buckets to catch the rain on a day like today.

Most shutters were open, but no faces appeared at the windows. If any watched, they knew how to keep themselves hidden.

"Not much left of any evidence," I said to my two companions and for the benefit of anyone listening. "I will have to speak to Denis and hear his side of the story."

"You mean you want to go to Newgate," Brewster said darkly. "I've told you before, guv. You go in there, you might not come out again. On your own feet, I mean."

"I do not require your presence, Brewster," I assured him. "I can run this errand on my own."

"You do require it, guv, at least to the front gates. Your lady wife would not be happy if I didn't watch over your steps from here to there."

That was true. I straightened my hat. "As you wish. Very well, let us go put ourselves in the lion's den."

"Bad thing even to joke about." Brewster shrugged his jacket closer and began to trudge along the lane, making for the waiting coach that had brought me here.

I expected Gibbons to follow, but he remained on the portico like a stone sentinel, guarding the empty house.

CHAPTER 3

*D*enis's coachman drove us out of Seven Dials to Holborn and thence to Newgate Street and the prison that nestled in the corner between that street and the Old Bailey.

Newgate was a grim building, made grayer and more forbidding by the morning's rain. Clouds obliterated the sky, and the curtain of rain shut out the rest of the city. The only flashes of color came from the occasional flick of a woman's bright skirt or man's knitted scarf, but most people hurried past muffled in drab coats, heads bent.

As I approached the gate in the high wall, I reflected that Brewster was right to avoid this place. He remained in the coach, close enough to defend me if I was attacked in the dozen feet between carriage and gate, but he'd pulled back into shadow. Like the denizens of Seven Dials, he was expert at watching while staying out of sight.

The last time I'd yanked on the bell pull at Newgate Prison was to visit one of Denis's employees, who'd been accused of stealing valuable artwork from the then Prince Regent. Before that, it had been to speak to my regimental colonel, whose stubborn streak had landed him in serious trouble.

The turnkey who answered the gate was a stranger to me, but his sullen demeanor fled when I told him who I wanted to visit.

"Feather in our cap, havin' 'im in our little inn." The man grinned, revealing a mouthful of broken teeth. "Famous, ain't 'e? Leastways, to those in the know. Runner what brought him here will be a rich man with 'is reward, won't 'e?" The turnkey's laughter died, and resentment took its place. "Won't be sharing it with the likes of us, I'll wager."

Spendlove share his reward money? Most assuredly not.

The man ushered me inside, and another guard, also cheerful in nature, took charge of me. I followed this guard, who whistled a merry tune, into the dank, stone building.

The interior passageways held more cold than the brisk wind outside. A chill must have settled in here when the prison was built and never left it.

As I'd expected, Denis hadn't been put into the main cells, which were large open spaces, with the commoners. If a man was wealthy enough, he could pay for a private room, in which his valet dressed him every morning and his chef brought him his meals.

Denis had commandeered a suite. When the turnkey took me inside—after politely knocking first—I found a spacious sitting room with a bedchamber beyond it, that chamber containing a well-hung bed against a blank wall. A few of Denis's lackeys were setting up furniture they'd carted in, including a desk and a chair.

Denis stood out of their way, studying a sheaf of papers in his hand. He was younger than me by about a dozen years, had regular features, sleek dark hair, and a trim physique that carried off his well-tailored suit better than did those of many society dandies.

A look into his eyes, however, showed the weight of a past most people would never understand.

I knew a little of Denis's history—what he'd chosen to tell me—and was aware that he'd struggled mightily as a child simply to remain alive. His cleverness and ability to organize others had been the making of him. He'd become a leader in a world his Mayfair neighbors knew nothing of.

"You have a visitor, sir," the guard announced.

Denis did not look up. He completely ignored the activity around him and only deigned to notice me once the guard had gone, closing the door behind him.

Only then did Denis turn to me with his usual deadpan calmness. "Captain. What brings you here?"

I stopped short at his question and reined in my temper with effort. "I happened to be passing and thought I'd look you up," I began in a sarcastic tone then discarded it. "What the devil do you think brings me here? You've been arrested for a murder you didn't commit, and I came to help."

Denis raised the paper in his hand ever so slightly. "I have people taking care of things for me. I will return home soon."

"If that is the case, why are you moving in and decorating?"

Denis's cool blue eyes flickered as one of his men shoved the desk into the middle of the room—it was cold by the walls. The desk was small, unlike the large Hepplewhite affair in his elegant house. It bore the cabriole legs of an earlier style and had shell motifs carved on the drawers. It was a fine piece of furniture, possibly brought out of Denis's attic where it was stashed for emergencies.

"Admittedly, the machinery of the law can take some time," Denis conceded. "Why are you so certain I didn't kill the man?"

"You'd never be so careless," I answered without hesitation. "I have seen you enraged before, but even then, your choices were calculated, not rash."

The ghost of a smile touched Denis's mouth. "I am pleased you believe in me."

I wasn't certain whether he was being sincere or sardonic. "It matters little what I believe. It only matters what truly happened, and how you will prove this to a judge and jury."

"I doubt I will stand trial." Denis lifted one shoulder the slightest bit, as though he had no worry in that regard. "As I have said, there are those working to release me, hopefully without a stain on my character. At least, not for this." The smile flitted across his face again.

"I am pleased you are enjoying yourself. Spendlove, however, is out for your blood, as well as the rich reward he will obtain when you are found guilty and condemned to hang. No doubt he plans to retire to the country with the funds, to tend his garden and paint watercolors or some such."

"Even a determined Runner must have evidence," Denis said. "Mr. Spendlove has none."

A lackey pushed the chair into place behind the desk. Denis thanked him with a nod and seated himself, laying his papers on the surface before him. If the stone walls had melted into warm, rich paneling, and windows materialized with a view of nearby mansions, we might be in his study at his Curzon Street house. At any moment, Gibbons might appear with a cup of steaming coffee or a goblet of brandy to set at my elbow.

"Spendlove will twist heaven and earth to make the evidence appear and be damning," I stated. "You have surprising faith in the law."

"Not surprising." Denis rested his hands on the desk's top. "The legal system grinds slowly but it grinds predictably. There are sticklers for the rules who will insist the trial be aboveboard, and a judge will be careful in his conviction of me. He won't risk the humiliation of his decision being overturned by the Lord Chancellor."

"If you are already dead before the conviction is overturned, that will not help you," I pointed out. "The gallows do a brisk business here, if you hadn't noticed."

The other men in the room paused in their business to watch me grimly. Not because they were angry at my pronouncements, I saw, but because they agreed with me.

I wondered why Denis was being so obtuse about his chances. He must be very certain no evidence would be found to point to him, even him standing over a body with a knife. Either that or he'd already worked out how he'd escape this prison and not be caught and brought back.

"Who was this man you were supposed to have killed?" I asked. "Pickett, Brewster said his name was."

"I have no idea," Denis answered without hesitation. "I'd never seen him before."

"No? And why were you out in the rain in Seven Dials to stumble over a body in the first place?"

"Why I was there is my business. As you say, I more or less stumbled over the body. It was quite dark at five o'clock this morning, and I nearly trod on him."

"So, you leaned down and picked up a blood-soaked knife?"

Denis at last showed a touch of impatience. "I first nudged the man to ascertain if he was conscious, and then I tried to see who he might be. I'd never have simply leaned over him, in case he was an enemy poised to attack. But he was, indeed, dead. I noted that he was a middle-class man or one of the gentry—someone with no business in Seven Dials. I recognized my knife and held it up. That, I agree, was foolish."

"Spendlove sprang from the shadows at the critical moment?" I asked.

"He and his patrollers did. I imagine he'd been following me. He is quite skilled at it." He sounded, for Denis, impressed.

"Then Spendlove knows about your house in Seven Dials," I said.

"Anyone who looks up records of sale would know. I am

listed as the owner of several properties in London. I do pay my taxes."

I did not think I'd heard Denis make so many witticisms so close together in the years I'd known him. I could not decide if he found the situation comical or he was covering up fear.

"How was the man killed with your own knife?" I asked. "Did you notice it was out of your possession?"

"I did not. It was a paperknife, one I use in the Seven Dials house to open books and letters."

"Which means someone who'd been in the house killed Pickett with it."

The men in the room sent me angry looks. "Leave off, Captain," one declared. "None of us would have." This man's name was Robbie, and once upon a time, he'd shoved his huge body in front of me to keep me from having a go at Denis.

"I am only citing possibilities." I knew that even here, deep in the bowels of Newgate prison, I wasn't safe from Denis's ruffians if they took against me. "The alternative is a thief entering the house and stealing a single knife from your desk. Why would they?"

"To fit up Mr. Denis for it," Robbie continued. "Why else?"

"Why else, indeed." I nodded at him. "Which returns me to the question, who was Mr. Pickett? Why was he in Seven Dials to be murdered at the convenient moment? A man you'd never heard of?"

"I did not say I had not heard of him," Denis corrected me. "I said I'd never seen him before, which is true. Mr. Bernard Pickett wrote to me about a week ago, asking for my help. He wanted to meet, and I set the appointment with him for yesterday evening, in Curzon Street. Other than that, I have no knowledge of him. I only learned the dead man was Mr. Pickett when the magistrate told me."

"So, there *is* a connection," I said heavily. "That is unfortunate."

"I have many witnesses to state I never met the man. He did not turn up for the appointment in Curzon Street. I concluded that he had decided not to pursue the matter, whatever it was, as sometimes happens. I went about my business and thought no more of it."

A person might well have misgivings about dealing with a man of Denis's reputation. I certainly had at one time, and still did, though I'd come to realize what I could trust Denis with and what I could not.

Denis, however, had the annoying habit of withholding as much information as possible in any given situation, from even those closest to him. A wise habit for him, but a difficult one for me.

"What sort of help did Mr. Pickett require?" I asked.

Denis met my gaze squarely, which meant he'd choose what details to give me. "He did not tell me the extent of it. I assumed he'd explain during his appointment."

"Why did you agree to meet *him*, in particular?" I went on. "You must receive dozens of letters asking for your assistance. You could not possibly answer each one. Why him?"

"Hundreds a year, yes," Denis said. "Many inquiring, some demanding. Mr. Pickett asked politely and offered a high fee. I decided to speak to him and see if he could indeed afford such a sum."

"You took him on based on whether he could pay the fee?" I heard my incredulous tone and tried unsuccessfully to curb it. "Regardless of what he wished you to do for him?"

"I agreed to *meet* him based on the fee," Denis said with a touch of irritation. "Whether I pursued the matter for him remained to be seen. I do select my clients with some care."

I forced myself to concede the point. "It would be helpful if I could read his letter. Unless you destroyed it?"

"Gibbons files my correspondence. If you call at the Curzon

Street house, he will give you what you require. You will likely find it no more enlightening than I did."

I was surprised he agreed to let me read the letter, by which I concluded that it would not tell me much.

"Perhaps you could write a note to Mr. Gibbons instructing him to let me read it. He might not hand over a letter based on my word alone."

Denis gave me a small nod and neatly tore off a blank part of the paper in front of him. He opened a drawer in the desk to extract pen, ink bottle, and a blotter—his lackeys had provided him with everything.

He dipped his pen, scribbled a sentence, blotted the ink, and handed me the sheet. The message was brief, similar to the ones he wrote to me.

Give Captain Lacey the letters he asks for. Denis.

He'd fully intended for me to read the line, or he'd have hidden it from me. I made certain the ink was completely dry before folding the paper and tucking it into my pocket.

"I know you wish to ferret out a solution," Denis said. "But there is no need. As I say, I will be cleared of this charge before long. Others are working on the matter."

The men in the room exchanged another round of dark looks, not as optimistic as their employer.

"I truly don't believe you killed him," I said to Denis. "So, there remains the question of who did, and why?"

"Seven Dials is an insalubrious part of the city," Denis answered. "A middle-class stranger would be lucky to reach its other side unscathed. He met with misfortune, which happens every day. Will you look into all murders in the area?"

My jaw tightened. "It is different when a murder was done with a knife taken specially from your house for the purpose. Was Pickett robbed? A middle-class gent would be lucky, as you say, to retain even the clothes on his back in that rookery."

"This I do not know," Denis said. "You will have to ask your Runner friend."

"He had all his gear," Robbie interrupted. "Nothing taken, I heard one of the patrollers say."

"Curious, do you not think?" I asked Denis.

Denis regarded us both with indifference. "There was hardly time for him to be robbed. He must have been dead only a minute or two before I found him. What I think happened is that my arrival interrupted the robber or robbers, and they fled before they could finish the job."

Possibly, but there were too many questions yet to be answered. "What about your man, Stout?"

Denis's brows rose. "What about him?"

"According to Brewster, he fled as soon as he saw you being arrested. He accompanied you to the Seven Dials house?"

Denis gave me a nod. "I'm not such a fool as to travel about London on my own. I brought him to make certain the house was safe for me before I entered it. Rather ironic, as the outside of it proved to be less safe."

"He was on the spot," I continued. "In position to take the knife and do the deed while you were not looking."

Denis's gaze returned to his papers. "That is doubtful."

"Mr. Stout is new, is he not? Brewster said you hired him in Rome and brought him home with you."

Denis glanced at me as though reluctant to drag his attention from the page he read. "I'd not have hired him if he weren't trustworthy. He had nothing to do with this." He returned to the papers once more.

I looked to Robbie and the other two who were busily making the room comfortable for His Nibs. I suppose I expected resentment toward the newly hired Stout, but all three gave various shrugs or nods that corroborated Mr. Denis's statement.

Robbie emitted a grunt. "Stout's all right."

Brewster did not seem to think so, but I didn't argue. "Where can I find Mr. Stout? I'd like to hear his version of the tale."

"Who knows?" Robbie answered before Denis could. "We all have our haunts, don't we?"

"He will return to Curzon Street when it is safe," Denis said without concern. "Was there anything else you wished to ask me, Captain? While I have these quiet hours, I would like to catch up on my correspondence."

Denis appeared uninterested in my assistance at all. If he had not done me good turns in the past, and if I was not convinced Spendlove had it wrong, I'd have walked away and let him take his chances.

I gave him a stiff bow. "If I can help in any way, please send for me."

Denis had already resumed his reading. "Very well. Good day, Captain."

He'd dismissed me many times in this way from his pristine study in the Curzon Street house. Only Gibbons was missing to usher me to the door.

Robbie did it instead. He was a huge man, who'd have to stoop under the low-linteled portal to leave the chamber. When he opened the door for me, he quieted his voice to a mere earth-shaking rumble. "We'll look after him," he said. "Don't you worry."

Robbie's reassuring words were marred by the anxiousness in his eyes. I had no answer to this, so I nodded to him and departed.

The door clanged closed behind me, and I heard a key turn firmly in the lock. Denis's lackeys were shutting him in them-selves, not to help the jailers imprison him, but to keep him safe from the other denizens of Newgate.

The rainy cold of the March morning engulfed me as I strode out of the gate to the street, thanking the turnkey who let me through.

I inhaled the air of freedom as I stepped away from Newgate and found it sweet.

———

Denis's coach with Brewster awaited me up the road. When I reached the carriage, I instructed the driver to take me to Bow Street before Brewster could haul me inside.

Coachmen were paid to convey their passengers wherever commanded, but this one glared at me, his face a granite sliver between muffler and hat. "What ye want to go there for?"

"To speak to the Runners," I said. "And the magistrate, if possible." When the man merely stared at me, I continued, "Do you not want your master to be cleared of the charge?"

"'Course I do. But I'm letting you off in Covent Garden. Ain't going no closer to the nick."

Like Brewster, he wanted nothing to do with courts of law. "That suits me," I assured him.

Brewster pulled me in just as the carriage lurched forward, nearly sending me to the floor. I gained my seat with only a minimum of cursing, while a kindly passer-by slammed the door for us.

I told Brewster what Denis had related as the coachman trundled along Holborn to Drury Lane. Brewster only shook his head, as though agreeing with Robbie and the other men that His Nibs was in more danger than he supposed.

We turned from Drury Lane to narrow Russel Street and went along it to the main square of Covent Garden and its market. Denis's coachman halted just inside the square as promised, to the consternation of a few carters trying to transport their wares through.

Brewster also had no intention of accompanying me further, and I slid to the pavement alone. I noticed the carters recognize the coach, close their mouths over foul words, and swerve around the motionless carriage.

I kept rooms off Russel Street in a tiny alley called Grimpen Lane. If the rain continued, I'd consider stopping in them after I sought Pomeroy. I always kept a fire laid and kindling waiting, and the landlady's strong coffee would not be unwelcome.

I was close enough to Bow Street that I could walk there without much trouble. Five minutes and much soggy rain later, I entered the magistrate's tall house, which encompassed numbers three and four.

The main corridor was full this morning, with the magistrate still hearing cases. Minor offenders queued to enter the courtroom—those accused of major offenses would be held in a cell across the street.

Denis's case must have been one of the first heard this morning. Spendlove would have insisted, of course, plus Denis's dangerous reputation likely inspired the magistrate to move him on as quickly as possible.

It was not difficult to track down Milton Pomeroy, my former sergeant turned Bow Street Runner. His voice boomed at me soon after I'd entered the house.

"Well met, Captain. Have you come about the arrest of Mr. Denis? Quite a coup for Spendlove, ain't it? Damn the man."

CHAPTER 4

*P*omeroy strode through the interested crowd toward me, as big and bluff as he'd ever been. His very blond hair was starting to thin and his stomach to further expand, but he'd looked the same wading through the chaos of a battlefield, greeting me cheerily amidst the carnage.

"Is Spendlove here?" I asked Pomeroy.

He bellowed a laugh. "Not a bit of it. He's grilling his patrollers and searching for witnesses so he can put together a tight case. He's not letting *this* fish slip away."

"I hoped he could tell me—or the magistrate could—exactly what happened?"

The men and women who awaited their hearings, dressed in everything from rags to finery, wanted to know as well, based on the way they focused on us.

"*I* can do that, Captain," Pomeroy said with confidence. "Spendlove won't breathe a syllable, but I'm chummy with one of his patrollers. Come with me. I'll regale you with the entire sordid tale."

Our listeners melted away in disappointment as Pomeroy headed for the stairs. I slipped a penny to the boy I thought the most destitute-looking before I followed. The lad stuck out his tongue at me then winked, the penny disappearing into his grubby coat.

I trailed Pomeroy up the stairs, my leg aching from trudging through cold rain and climbing into and out of coaches. I'd vowed to never become the man who couldn't stray from his house without a valet or other servant to steady him, but I might have to swallow my pride if I continued to have such days.

Pomeroy led me past the magistrate's office to a room that was little more than a closet crammed with shelves of boxes and sheaves of papers. Pomeroy shoved his bulk inside this and seated himself at a small desk, waving me to the rickety chair next to it.

"Busy morning." Pomeroy stretched out his long legs, crowding mine as I sat down. "I and my fellows will have to work hard to find someone who brings in as high a reward as James Denis. I raise my glass to Spendlove. He's a right bastard, but he's determined, I must say."

"From what I understand, he did not witness Denis actually stabbing the gentleman," I said, breaking through Pomeroy's annoying good-naturedness. "Spendlove only saw Denis standing in the street with a knife in his hand."

Pomeroy shrugged. "Amounts to the same thing."

"Not entirely," I said.

"Does to Spendlove. To be sure, he'll have a hell of a time gathering the evidence. He wants an unquestionable case and a judge who will convict. No doubt he'll have it all in the end."

Pomeroy's confidence in Spendlove contrasted sharply with Denis's cool assurance that he'd soon be cleared and released. I had to wonder why Denis was so certain he'd find his way out of his predicament, when I knew Spendlove would be merciless.

"Who *was* Mr. Pickett?" I asked. "From what I understand, not a usual denizen of Seven Dials."

"Indeed, no. Seems a respectable gent. Recently inherited a small house in Bedfordshire from an aged uncle or cousin or some such. Other than that, we don't know much about Mr. Pickett. A complete stranger to any I've asked."

Pomeroy was thorough in his own way, so I had no doubt he'd interrogated anyone he could find about Mr. Pickett.

"Was he married?" I asked. "Who is his family? This aged relation, for instance?"

"Don't know. Spendlove and I have patrollers walking about with a drawing of the man's face, asking if any know him. He had no handy letters about his person addressed to someone we could speak to, no bill from his tailor, no book he'd taken from a lending library. Had five shillings in his pocket and a scrap of paper with the address of Mr. Denis's house in Curzon Street."

"Nothing to indicate why he was in Seven Dials?"

"Nothing at all."

I pressed my fingertips together. "How many people were you able to ask about him? It hasn't been many hours since the crime was committed."

Pomeroy looked smug. "I have me resources. Seven Dials is closed to most, but I know those who will pass me information. None of them recognize the blasted man, though, never heard his name. As I say, my patrollers and Spendlove's are fanning out through the City, trying to find his place of employment, if he had one."

"A daunting task, I should think."

"Never you worry about that. We'll find our answers. The key, Captain, is diligent pursuit, plus a large team at our disposal. You might sit back in your comfortable chair in your Mayfair home and ponder, but my men *act*."

I said nothing as I recalled the maze of ruins I'd recently run through in Pompeii as well as the tunnels under the Colosseum in Rome in pursuit of a killer. Pomeroy might believe my living was soft these days, but I still experienced plenty of uncomfortable moments.

I'd learned long ago, however, that I'd never win an argument against Pomeroy. He took orders well, but one had to be firm with that order and not allow him to undermine it.

"I wish them well in their search," I said without challenge. "I wonder—would you be willing to let Grenville cast his gaze over Mr. Pickett's clothes? Even better, Grenville's valet. They'll know exactly where the suit came from, down to the tailor's assistant who sewed it."

"Unless our gent obtained it secondhand," Pomeroy pointed out.

"Even so, a tailor will know who owned the suit, and that owner—or his valet—will know to what secondhand shop it went to. That shop owner might recall selling it to Pickett."

"What will that tell us?" Pomeroy asked. "That a man purchased a suit in a secondhand shop and walked away with it?"

"It might give us an address in Town for Mr. Pickett. We might find a household who is waiting for him, neighbors to ask about him. What do the people in Bedfordshire say?"

"Won't know until the lads I sent to inquire return." Pomeroy shrugged. "But if you want to play your game, very well. I'll bundle up his clothes and send them to you so you and Mr. Grenville can have your gander. As long as I have them back before the magistrate demands them."

"Of course." I was grateful for this concession, though Pomeroy obviously thought Mr. Pickett's personal effects held no importance. He'd never let me examine them otherwise.

"Don't let Spendlove get wind of it either," Pomeroy said.

"I would not dream of it," I promised.

"Knife that killed Pickett belonged to Mr. Denis," Pomeroy went on. "The accused admitted that himself."

For opening letters and books, Denis had told me. "Anyone can steal another man's paperknife."

"Ah, but would they steal it from a bloke like Mr. Denis?"

"He has many enemies." My logic was weak on this point—an enemy of Denis who had access to his house wouldn't stop at stealing one slender knife. He'd ransack the place, or set a trap for him, or some such villainy.

Then again, Denis had been betrayed by a man he'd believed loyal before. I itched to speak to Mr. Stout, the newcomer.

"Are you looking at any other culprit for this murder?" I asked without much hope of it. "I know Spendlove is convinced, but suppose Denis is telling the truth? He bumped into the body, recognized his own knife, and pulled it out before he thought about it."

Pomeroy shook with silent laughter. "Bumped into the body mighty hard, I'd say. Left the poor cove with a hole in his chest, didn't he?"

I regarded him coldly. "Does your answer mean that only Denis is being considered for this crime?"

Pomeroy's gaze was almost pitying. "Stands to reason he did it, Captain. No one else on the street, was there? Spendlove wants Denis, yes, but he does have his principles. He wouldn't risk the conviction being overturned, so if he'd seen someone else do it, he'd say so. But according to him and his patrollers, there was none to see."

I thought of how I'd left Denis so calmly perusing correspondence in his prison room, confident he'd soon be home. Pomeroy was telling me the opposite—that no one else could possibly have killed Mr. Pickett besides Denis himself.

I had to face the fact that Denis might have lied to me and truly done the murder. Perhaps he had faith that a judge who owed him favors would let him off, hence his unruffled demeanor.

But this felt wrong to me. Denis was a careful man—if he

wanted Pickett dead, he had many better ways to quietly do away with him. The drama of being found over the body was unnecessary.

Denis wasn't going to help me, and neither was Pomeroy, and least of all, would Spendlove. Pomeroy had promised I could look over the clothes, but only because he saw no point in it.

I pressed my walking stick to the floor and rose. "Send Pickett's things to South Audley Street, please. The sooner, the better."

Pomeroy gave me a mock salute. "Yes, sir, Captain, sir."

So he'd done during the Peninsular Wars when he'd thought I was being a high-handed fool. I'd been in command of him there. Here, I was nobody.

"Thank you." I forced a cordial nod and carefully slid out of the tiny room. "Good day."

"Good luck to ye, Captain," Pomeroy boomed behind me. "You'll be needing it this time, I'm thinking."

———

BREWSTER JOINED ME AS I LEFT BOW STREET FOR RUSSEL STREET. I waved off Denis's coachman who'd started for us from Covent Garden market, electing to make my way to Grimpen Lane on foot.

I wanted very much to read Pickett's letter to Denis, but I reasoned that Gibbons might not have yet returned to the Curzon Street house from Seven Dials. I might as well rest in my old rooms for a few minutes.

"Well met, Captain Lacey." My landlady, Mrs. Beltan, greeted me as she emerged from her bakeshop below my rooms. "High time you ceased flitting about the world and visited me."

"Haven't had many moments to myself since I returned," I told her apologetically.

Which was more or less true. Since we'd returned from
Rome, Donata had me accompanying her to different gather-
ings every night, as the Season had already begun. Gabriella had
come home with us, her fiancé returning to his family in France
for a while, and I'd wanted to spend as much time with her as
possible.

"See that you gain some," Mrs. Beltan chided me good-
naturedly. She insisted Brewster and I took mugs of coffee and a
cruller each.

"Thank ye kindly," Brewster said to her. "None better in
London, Missus."

"Go on with you, now." Mrs. Beltan flushed at Brewster's
charm and turned to greet her next customer.

We carried our repast to my cold rooms upstairs, and Brewster had me sit while he lit the fire. I sank into the armchair in
which I'd spent many a lonely evening upon my return from the
Peninsular War, wondering if my life would be worth getting on
with. An injured officer with no money or prospects, who'd
barely avoided losing his commission in scandal, hadn't much to
look forward to.

If I'd known then that I'd be married to a beautiful widow,
reconnected to the daughter I thought I'd lost, and the father of
a new daughter as well as a hearty stepson, I'd never have
despaired.

"Who has a key to the Seven Dials house?" I asked Brewster
as he climbed to his feet. He sank into the straight-backed chair
I used at my desk, its wood creaking with his bulk.

"Besides His Nibs?" Brewster lifted his cruller he'd set on the
table beside him. "Gibbons. Probably Mr. Floyd, what keeps the
accounts and notes on the art His Nibs collects. Mr. Denis ain't
free with handing out keys."

"He also employs plenty of former thieves who could easily
pick a lock," I said.

"True. But he knows about locks and don't use the flimsy ones most folk do, like the ones on your wife's house."

This information gave me a qualm. "Have you been assessing our house for its prospects?"

"I've reformed," Brewster assured me. "But if I needed to get into your house because you or your family was in danger, I could do it, sharpish."

"I am pleased to hear it," I said, though I decided I'd have Barnstable consult with a locksmith. "Even so, experienced lock pickers could open Mr. Denis's doors."

"True. But none of them would."

I agreed that a person would be foolish indeed to break into Denis's home and try to rob him.

"You seem to believe Mr. Stout might not be trustworthy," I reminded him.

Brewster shrugged. "I don't know him, do I? I was working for you when His Nibs picked up Stout in Rome. I know nothing about him. How did he latch himself onto His Nibs and convince him to cart him back to London?"

A question I'd been pondering. "Denis would never bring home someone he didn't trust. Robbie seems to think Stout is all right."

"Huh. Robbie don't mind most men, because he knows the instant they annoy him, he can put his fist through them. Blokes understand that, so they're respectful to him, like."

I had to concede his point. "I would like to speak to Stout, in any case. Do you know where he'd go to ground?"

"No idea. Gibbons might. Gibbons is a cold cove, but he knows the most about what goes on in His Nibs' household."

"I would like to have a long conversation with Mr. Gibbons, as well, if he will bother to speak to me." I took a bite of my cruller. It was crackling on the outside and soft on the inside, as a cruller should be. I licked crumbs of sugar from my fingers. "The gist of the matter is that someone entered Denis's house in Seven Dials, stole one letter opener, waited in the street for Mr. Pickett, stabbed him to death, then fled the instant before Denis walked outside to find the body very near his doorstep."

Brewster nodded. "Timing the murder so the Runner and patrollers saw His Nibs instead of the real killer."

I heaved a sigh. "An unlikely scenario. Spendlove will tear many holes in that theory."

"He will that," Brewster agreed.

"I need to discover who would have had the opportunity to commit the crime so speedily and efficiently. Was it deliberately planned? Or did someone seize the moment? And why on earth kill Mr. Pickett? Who the devil was he?"

"None of us know," Brewster answered.

"So you said." I spread my hand, to which sugar crystals still clung. "Denis didn't know him either. Apparently, Pickett wrote to ask Denis's assistance on some problem, but what sort of problem? Denis is willing to let me read Pickett's letter, from which I conclude I'll find no information there. Pickett wasn't robbed, so it couldn't have been a random murder by a footpad of Seven Dials."

"Maybe it were," Brewster offered. "And the killer didn't have time to rob the bloke before he heard Denis come out of his house."

Denis had posited that opinion as well. "That is possible, but it doesn't explain how he came by Denis's knife."

"There is that." Brewster didn't look troubled by our lack of information. His method of catching a criminal was to shake a man until he confessed, but I needed to be more certain before I could present the solution to Spendlove.

"I suppose I had better find out all I can about Mr. Pickett," I said. "Who were his enemies? Would one want to kill him, and how did this enemy accomplish it? I wish I could believe Denis accidentally dropped his paperknife in the street, and one who wanted Pickett dead came upon it and used it to do his terrible deed. But I can't."

"Maybe His Nibs is mistaken, and it ain't his knife."

"I doubt that." I lifted the coffee I'd set aside and took a long sip, and then another bite of the cruller. As distraught as I was about this crime, I'd not let Mrs. Beltan's baked goods go to waste.

Footsteps sounded on the stairs and then came a tap on the door. I recognized Mrs. Beltan's knock, and when I told her to enter, she craned her head around the door. "Begging your pardon, Captain."

I came to my feet, and Brewster, belatedly, followed suit. Mrs. Beltan waved for us to sit again.

"I didn't bring it to mind until after you'd gone upstairs," she said apologetically as she came all the way into the room. "But a young lady called 'round to see you, Captain, a few days ago now."

My brows rose. "What young lady?"

The only young women of my acquaintance were my daughter and those few who made polite calls on her in the presence of their mothers or aunts. None of them would seek me out in Grimpen Lane. The fact that Mrs. Beltan said *young lady*, in a deferential tone, meant it wasn't any of the game girls who used to follow me about.

"She didn't leave a name," Mrs. Beltan said. "I gave her your address at South Audley Street and told her she might write to you about any business. She thanked me and went away, and I never saw her since."

CHAPTER 5

*M*y curiosity mounted. "Can you describe her?"

"She was bundled up against the rain, so I can't tell you much about what she looks like. Well spoken, though. Kind eyes, which I think were brown."

Not very helpful, but that wasn't Mrs. Beltan's fault. It had become known that I sometimes aided people in solving their problems, so the young woman could be a complete stranger to me.

"If she returns, will you send word?" I asked. "She might not be comfortable writing to me in Mayfair."

"Of course. Now, you enjoy those crullers, Captain. I had quite a number coming out of the oven this morning. Too many to sell before they went stale."

Mrs. Beltan's way of assuring me she hadn't given them to me out of charity. I had once been touchy on that subject.

"You're a fine baker, missus," Brewster told her. "You have more going begging, I'll take them off your hands."

Mrs. Beltan shook her head at him, though she always accepted praise when it was due. "Good morning, Captain. And to you, Mr. Brewster."

She retreated, leaving us to finish our treats.

"Shouldn't mention to your lady wife ye have a young woman seeking you here," Brewster suggested.

"Most likely she needs assistance," I said. "But no, unless she does write to me, there's no need to discuss the matter."

I was married to the most comely woman in London, but Donata had it in her head that there were any number of ladies in the metropolis willing to steal me away from her. Very flattering, but quite untrue.

Brewster chortled. "Ye've learned wisdom, guv."

"Prudence, perhaps. Now then, I must decide how to move forward to prove Spendlove wrong. Is the answer in Seven Dials or in Pickett's letter?"

"Neither one, if Mr. Spendlove fit up His Nibs for this murder. You need to put Spendlove through it, I think."

Spendlove had been trying to land Denis in the dock for years. He wouldn't be the first thief-taker to forge evidence or manipulate events to bring a criminal to trial.

"Spendlove has always struck me as a scrupulous man," I said. "Scrupulous to a fault. He wants Denis legitimately."

"Everyone's got a weakness, guv—that one thing they want so much they'll do anything to have it."

Brewster was no doubt right. "I will certainly speak to Spendlove," I assured him. "The magistrates will be careful with this case, though."

"Maybe. Maybe not. There's some as think that if one like Mr. Denis is hanged, all crime will halt in London." Brewster became morose. "It won't though. It will leave a gap, and all sorts of bad 'uns will race to fill it. Won't be safe going out of doors anymore. I wager it's starting already."

Whenever a powerful leader was eliminated, what usually followed wasn't peace and prosperity, but a vacuum there was a battle to fill. I'd seen it in Mysore, and I'd witnessed it with the rest of the world at Bonaparte's fall. So many wanted to grab the power he'd held, and the squabbling was ongoing.

London could become a hotbed of criminal leaders fighting to take over what Denis had controlled. Any wanting vengeance on Denis and his lieutenants might take this opportunity to seize it.

I realized that as my own name was associated with Denis's now, those repercussions might come home to me, my friends, and my family. At one time, one of Denis's enemies had thought to reach him using my stepson. I was still angry about that.

I put aside my empty cup and rose. "Let us uncover this killer, then—even if it is Spendlove himself—and restore Denis to his throne."

"Hope you don't think he'll reward you," Brewster warned as he joined me. "His Nibs likely won't thank you for interfering."

So Denis had already told me. "I don't seek his favors," I said. "I never have, as much as he's thrust them upon me. I want peace and quiet on the streets I walk—if that is possible in this city—and the correct man to be punished for murder. If I can tweak Spendlove's nose at the same time, then so be it."

Brewster chuckled as I closed and locked the door. "As long as I can be witness when you're doing the tweaking, guv. It's all I ask."

—————

I RETURNED THE CUPS TO MRS. BELTAN, THANKED HER AGAIN FOR the repast, and struck out with Brewster into the street.

The rain that had pounded us all morning had lightened a bit. I didn't spy Denis's coach around the square of Covent Garden, and I assumed the coachman had become fed up with waiting for us and departed. I decided to return to Seven Dials on foot, as it was a near enough walk, and see if I could discover anything to help me.

Brewster trudged beside me up St. Martin's Lane, not happy with my choice but not hindering me.

Seven Dials was as dismal in the late-morning drizzle as it had been in the earlier pelting rain. Brewster and I made for the lane off Tower Street as quickly as we could, neither of us wanting to become prey to those who roamed these streets even at this benign hour.

Denis's house was closed, shutters pulled over the windows. Gibbons must have locked it down, taking no chance of a break-in now that its master was gone.

I knocked on the door. If only Gibbons and Mr. Floyd had keys, then we would not be going in if Gibbons had returned to Curzon Street.

We waited for a long time, no echo of footsteps within. I thumped again, the sound ringing hollowly.

Just as I was about to give up, the front door was yanked open by a stocky man about two thirds my height, with dark hair going gray and a face that had once been battered.

He glared at me but subsided a bit when he saw Brewster. "Wot?"

"Let us in, Stout," Brewster demanded.

I'd suspected this was the elusive Mr. Stout. "Is Mr. Gibbons here?" I asked him.

"Naw. 'E's gone, ain't 'e?" His words were delivered in a thick Cockney accent.

Which meant either Stout also had a key, or Gibbons had let him in before he'd departed.

"Open the door," Brewster growled. "The captain is to be given run of the place."

I hadn't heard this from anyone, but I did not argue.

Stout continued to study us with belligerence but finally moved aside to admit us. He slammed the door as soon as we were inside and shot the bolt.

"Mr. Denis told me to clear out the 'ouse," Stout said.

"'E did, did 'e?" Brewster asked. "Ye visited him in the nick, did ye?"

"He sent a message," Stout said sourly. "I'm to shut up the 'ouse, let none in, and take 'is effects 'ome."

"Mr. Stout." I stood in front of him and addressed him as politely as I could. "What exactly happened this morning? I don't believe for a moment that Denis killed that man, but I need corroboration."

Stout peered at me suspiciously. "Gibbons said you might turn up. Told me to talk to ye." His tone suggested that he'd never have spoken to me if he hadn't been commanded to.

"Did you see Mr. Pickett arrive?" I knew better than to ask Stout directly what *he* had been up to at the time of the murder. He'd be evasive, and I'd save much time having him tell me about the movements of others.

Stout rubbed his nose with the back of his hand. "Nobody about, were there? Not in the rain in the dark of morning."

"Why did Denis leave the house?" I asked doggedly. "Do you think he was going out to meet Mr. Pickett?"

Stout shrugged. "Dunno, do I? I got on with my business and didn't have time to stand and look out of the winders. Nuffink to me what a bloke does outside his own house."

Brewster's patience ran out. "You must've seen *something*. Heard something. Else, why'd ye leg it?"

"'Eard the door open and close. Might have been Mr. Denis walking out. Then lots of shouting and feet pounding. I look out th' winder again, and there's a Robin Redbreast and 'is 'enchmen surrounding Mr. Denis and tellin' 'im 'e's nicked. The Pickett bloke is a'lying on the cobbles, dead as a stone. Didn't wait around for them to storm the 'ouse and nick me too, did I?"

"Likely wise of you to run," I said soothingly. Spendlove would have scooped up Stout as well, hoping to threaten Stout into saying he'd witnessed the crime. "Though I'm sorry you weren't looking out the window at the crucial moment."

"None of my business, were it? Never saw the cove before in me life."

I wondered very much whether Stout *had* turned away and seen nothing or if he was exercising the caution all Denis's men had about dealing with magistrates. If Stout admitted to being in the house, he might be forced to stand in the witness box, where a Crown prosecutor would make mincemeat of him.

But if he *had* seen someone else murder Pickett, why would he not admit this to save Denis's life?

"Why were you in Rome?" I asked abruptly.

Stout jumped. "Eh?" His truculence returned. "Whatcha want to know that for?"

"Answer the question," Brewster rumbled threateningly. He was much larger than Stout, though I had the feeling Stout could hold his own.

"Ain't much work in London, is there?" Stout answered. "Not after Waterloo, when all the soldiers poured back into England, me being one of them. Nothing to eat either. No wonder them in Manchester banded together, not that it did them any good. Sending cavalry to break 'em up and trample women and little kiddies." Stout looked me up and down. "You're cavalry, says Gibbons."

"It has been a long time since I drew my saber and charged at anything," I said. "And I certainly wouldn't have at St. Peter's Field if I'd been in the regiment ordered to storm the crowd. I agree, it was an outrage."

"Aye, well." Stout scowled, not appeased. "Gathering in a field to listen to a well-fed cove bleat about our troubles ain't what I call useful, anyway. I'd been on the Italian Peninsula in a break from fighting Boney the Bastard, and thought I'd go back there, try my luck. Did all right, but then I wanted 'ome. Mr. Denis offered me a way, so I took it."

I knew much had been left out of the narrative, but I did not pursue it. "What regiment?" I asked instead. "Infantry?"

"I weren't no officer like yourself. Barely became a corporal, didn't I? And only because too many of 'em got popped full of bullets. Sergeants didn't like me none."

I understood why a platoon sergeant would become impatient with someone like Stout, who likely obeyed an order only when he felt it expedient. Also, I wondered what he'd been doing on the Italian Peninsula, when Austria had led most of the battles against Bonaparte there. I also noted he didn't name his regiment.

He might have deserted, though Stout didn't have the shamed, defiant countenance of deserters I'd encountered. I concluded he truly had traveled to Italy, likely during the Peace of Amiens, either to see the world or to take advantage of the confusion of stolen goods that had gone up and down that area. But if he'd stepped onto battlefields against Bonaparte's determined troops, which at times had been hell on earth, I could respect him for that.

"Sergeants can be strong-willed," I said, thinking of Pomeroy. He'd never shied from telling me when he thought my orders were wrong-headed.

"Huh." Stout unbent enough to snort a laugh. "Ain't it the truf."

"It was kind of Mr. Denis to employ you, to help you come home," I said.

"Ain't nuffink kind about it," Stout retorted. "He needed somefink done, and I did it."

He immediately snapped his mouth shut after he uttered this, as though he hadn't meant to impart too much.

I pretended not to notice. I'd inferred that Denis hadn't offered Stout a way back to England out of the softness of his heart. Whatever service Stout provided, Denis had trusted the man enough to do it and also to be alone in this house with him on a rainy Tuesday morning.

"Why did Denis decide to come to Seven Dials at all?" I

asked. "From what he tells me, Mr. Pickett was to meet him at the Curzon Street house last evening."

Stout's eyes flickered, but he answered readily enough. "To meet someone."

"Oh? Who?"

"What business is it of mine?" Stout scoffed. "I were below stairs when the visitor came, and below stairs when 'e went. You'll 'ave to ask 'im who 'e was."

I noted Stout didn't actually indicate whether he knew the name of Denis's evening caller, but I realized he'd never tell me even if he did.

It was interesting, though. That caller might have filched the knife from Denis's desk—or wherever he kept it—and returned in the morning to stab Mr. Pickett.

Who hadn't been expected. Why would a killer presume Pickett would be here?

Of course, the assailant could have been following Pickett about, seeking an opportunity to murder him for whatever reason he'd decided upon. Perhaps the killer knew Mr. Pickett had written to Denis for help and then wrangled an appointment with Denis to find out more about it. Had seen the knife and stolen it, then taken up his vigil on Mr. Pickett and killed him when the man had wandered into this back lane of Seven Dials.

I could not decide why anyone would go to all this trouble, or whether the coincidences that would have to happen were plausible, but this entire business was bewildering.

"My only wish is to ensure that Denis isn't wrongly accused," I told Stout. "If you remember anything that can help with that at all, please seek me out. A message left at Mrs. Beltan's bakeshop in Grimpen Lane, Covent Garden, will reach me."

"Not likely I will, is it?" Stout said. "Told you everything I know."

I was certain he hadn't, but I understood that arguing further would be futile.

"I thank you," I said, keeping my voice steady. "I will disturb you no further."

Stout blinked as though he'd expected me to snarl at him for not disgorging more information. He gave me a curt nod. "As ye say, guv."

Without a goodbye, Stout turned and tramped to the back stairs, where he wrenched open the door, scuttled inside, and banged the door closed behind him.

"Told you he were a hard bloke," Brewster said darkly.

"He is, but nonetheless, he did tell me a few things Denis did not reveal. That Denis had an appointment here late last night. That he stayed until morning with only Mr. Gibbons and Stout in attendance. Unusual, do you not think?"

Brewster gave me a reluctant nod. "Not His Nibs' way of doing things, no."

"I wonder if Gibbons will tell us who the meeting was with. Denis has given Stout a strange amount of trust. Gibbons has been with him for years and privy to most of Denis's business, but I wonder why Denis is suddenly letting a near stranger in on his secrets."

Brewster shrugged. "His Nibs keeps his own counsel. He might do a lot of peculiar things that don't seem natural to you and me, but he has his reasons."

He spoke with the calm acknowledgment of one who'd look the other way at almost anything as long as his pay packet continued to arrive.

"I am certain that is true," I said. "But this time, Denis's own counsel has landed him in Newgate. To get him out of there, I will have to pry into his affairs."

"He won't like that, I'm thinking."

"He has already told me so. But such considerations have never stopped me in the past," I said with confidence I did not feel. "If I thought Denis had committed this crime, I would agree with you and Stout about minding my own affairs, but I know he did not." I glanced up the steep staircase. "I'll have a look in Denis's office, if I may."

"None here to stop you," Brewster pointed out.

Stout had retreated, and the house appeared to be deserted. The downstairs rooms, which I'd seen earlier this morning, were empty of personal effects, likely used only for waiting visitors.

I mounted the stairs, a thick runner muffling my footsteps. There were four chambers off the landing on the first floor: three bedrooms and one study.

The most comfortable-looking bedroom must be the one used by Denis himself. The bed was an old-fashioned tester with tapestry hangings that could be pulled closed to keep out drafts. Downy pillows had been plumped against the headboard. The bed had been made, the room neat, though Denis must have slept here. No doubt Gibbons had tidied up.

A washbasin with thick towels stood in the corner, and a large wardrobe—empty now—reposed between the windows. A wing chair near the fireplace had a small table next to it, a place where a man could enjoy a book and a brandy.

Other than its pleasant furnishings, the bedchamber told me little. Denis must use it seldom because no personal items were here. Gibbons likely packed him a bag whenever Denis decided to spend the night and took everything back with them the next morning.

I left this room and entered the office. Here was a desk and chair similar to what Denis had in the Curzon Street house, the set drawn near the fireplace. The fire had been banked, dying off earlier today to judge from the new ash there.

The desk's top was bare—I rarely saw Denis peruse more than one letter at a time. Not for him the piles of dog-eared books and crumpled papers I'd observed on other men's desks, including my own. Denis was always painfully neat.

The drawers revealed clean sheets of foolscap, several full bottles of ink, and pens sharpened, ready for writing. I did find another letter opener, innocuous, if expensive-looking, and quite clean of blood. I wondered if Denis kept more than one here, or if Gibbons had already replaced the knife Spendlove had taken with a new one.

I sat down at the desk and laid the knife before me.

The blade was thin and sharp, which befitted something made to break wax seals and cut open the pages of new books.

Books were made by folding giant sheets of paper that were printed in a seemingly haphazard manner, but the placement of each block was in truth carefully calculated. When the large sheets were folded, each page came out in the correct order. A sergeant who'd worked for a bookbinder had explained the system to me in an idle hour.

The folds that occurred on the edges of the book needed to be cut open by the book's purchaser in order to read it. Denis could afford new tomes and must use a paperknife often.

I lifted the knife and studied the blade's edge. It must be new, because the metal was unscratched, with no nicks from repeated use.

While I recognized that the item was not cheap—the handle silver, the blade fine steel—I found no initials or inscription that made it unique. Not many men could afford such a utensil to cut open books, but hundreds must have been sold in this city.

Why was Denis—and the magistrate—so convinced the knife found in the wound belonged to him?

I put the knife back into the drawer, closed it, and left the chamber.

I descended to find Brewster emerging from the front drawing room, shutting its door behind him.

"Thought I'd have a look 'round meself," he said to my

inquiring glance. "Didn't find nothing to say who came and went here last night."

"Denis is too careful for that," I agreed. "I will tackle Gibbons about it, and if he won't tell me, I'll visit Denis and ask him point blank."

Brewster huffed a laugh. "Good luck to you."

If Denis didn't want me to know a fact, he'd never give up the information. This I understood, but I had to try.

"Where to now, guv?" Brewster asked.

"Back to Bow Street. I'd like to have a look at the body itself, if they'll let me."

CHAPTER 6

*B*rewster was not pleased with my idea. Though he did not refuse to accompany me the relatively short distance on foot toward Bow Street, he kept up a running muttered grumble about my plan as a means to pass the time.

Brewster turned away when we reached the corner where Bow Street intersected with Long Acre, saying he'd return to Mrs. Beltan's shop for more coffee. I sent him lumbering off and entered the magistrate's house, quieter now, once more.

Pomeroy was gone, I learned from a patroller who'd spied me enter. Spendlove, however, was there. He came at me from the shadows, an expert on how to keep a person unnerved.

"Captain Lacey." Spendlove's thin, reddish-blond hair was damp, showing he'd been out in the weather. His ruddy face bore the hint of a smug smile. "I told you I'd have him. With or without your help."

"It seems you were correct," I conceded. "Though I am of the mind that Mr. Denis was not the culprit in this instance."

Spendlove's smile didn't dim. "I know your loyalty to him. Be careful, Captain. Your wife's family protects you at the moment, but if information comes to light that implicates you in his criminal business, I will have you too."

I did not respond to his needling. "It is not loyalty, Mr. Spendlove, but simple facts. You are a witness to Mr. Denis standing over a body, but not to the actual stabbing itself. His story that he found the man and pulled out the knife is very likely true."

"Pah." Spendlove's spittle touched me, and I forced myself not to flinch. "My patrollers were all over that street the entire night, knowing Mr. Denis was in his burrow. They saw no one else but him with Mr. Pickett."

"Did they see Pickett enter the street?" I asked. "Was he searching for an address? Was he nervous? Excited? Or simply walking from one point in London to the next with no thought of visiting Mr. Denis at all?"

"Useless speculation," Spendlove said. "Give up, Captain. My quarry will go to trial swiftly, and just as swiftly hang."

"I'd like to have a look at Mr. Pickett's body, if I may," I said. "To satisfy my curiosity about a few points."

"Have some respect," Spendlove growled, though the corners of his mouth remained stubbornly tilted upward. "The man is dead. As I said, all this is useless speculation."

"If it useless, then what harm can I do?"

Spendlove managed to frown and maintain his infuriating grin at the same time. After a moment of silent deliberation, he pushed past me hard enough to nearly knock me down. "Very well. Come."

He marched along a side passage, not waiting to see if I kept up. I hobbled behind him, resisting the urge to strike him with my walking stick.

I'd entered the small building in the yard behind the Bow Street house once before, when a pathetic, small woman had been fished out of the Thames. I'd been sent for because they'd thought her Marianne Simmons, who had lived upstairs from me at the time.

The interior of the structure was as cold as it had been then, as tinged with the scent of death, and as sad.

Two bodies lay here today, each concealed by a long sheet. The table that Spendlove moved purposefully toward held the shape of a grown man, while the other hidden body was smaller and slighter. A woman, or a child. I shivered, and pity touched me.

Spendlove unceremoniously yanked back the cloth that covered Mr. Pickett and presented him with a flourish.

I looked down at a gentleman of middle years. He'd been on the slim side, neither handsome nor plain, his brown hair touched with gray. He was clean-shaven, bearing the smooth skin of a man who didn't have to scrape his face free of whiskers every day, as I did.

The man's shoulders were a bit spindly, his arms slender and without much definition. Not one who did much activity. An inspection of Pickett's hands would no doubt show me soft fingers and evenly trimmed nails, but I was distracted from further examination by the dark hole in the man's chest.

The wound was not large, a slit, though one wider than I'd have assumed. Thinking about the paperknife I'd found in Denis's desk, I agreed it would fit in the wound, but would have about a quarter of an inch to spare on either side. Then again, I hadn't seen the actual knife in question, which might correspond perfectly.

The man's chest was the same shade as the pale sheet that covered him, the few wisps of dark hair there stark against his skin. His back, from what I could see, held purpling bruising.

"How long did he lie in the street?" I asked.

"Not many minutes at all," Spendlove answered readily. "Denis had just stabbed the wretch."

"I meant before your men carted him here."

Spendlove shrugged. "Three quarters of an hour? Perhaps less. I was more interested in escorting Mr. Denis to the magistrate than as to how long Mr. Pickett reclined in the street."

I'd asked because a surgeon had once told me that he could tell how long a man had been dead by the amount of blood pooling in his back—or side, or whatever part of his body he'd come to rest on. The temperature of the body could indicate that as well.

"Was he warm?" I persisted. "When you touched him to ascertain he was dead?"

"I didn't touch him at all. It was obvious he was gone, wasn't it?"

Spendlove hadn't cared. He'd seen Denis with a knife and had pounced. Mr. Pickett hadn't been given much thought.

This morning had been cold and rainy, so Pickett's skin might already have been cool even if he'd been killed the instant before Spendlove rounded the corner to find Denis.

"What did the surgeon say who examined him?" I asked. "If one has been here yet."

"Said he was dead." Spendlove snapped the sheet over Pickett. "Stabbed through the heart. That's all the coroner needs to know."

I was no expert on bodies. I'd like to ask the surgeon who'd examined him or find someone to look over Mr. Pickett independently to tell me if anything was unusual. I did not fancy my odds on either of those things happening.

A coroner would have to view the evidence of the death and find that it was murder before Denis could be brought to trial for it. Not that there was much uncertainty about the cause of death in this case, but the process of the law had to be carried out.

Spendlove started to hustle me out, but I paused beside the other covered body. "Who is this?"

Spendlove cast an impatient glance at the table. "Woman

fished out of the Thames. A lightskirt, probably." His tone held no interest, and he strode out, clearly expecting me to follow.

I gingerly lifted the sheet. For some reason, I was taken with the notion that it might be the young lady who had sought me out in Grimpen Lane. Bundled against the rain, Mrs. Beltan had told me, with kind brown eyes.

The woman beneath the sheet had snarled, gray hair. She must have lain under the water a while, because her skin had an almost greenish cast, and fish had nibbled her flesh. Whatever clothes she'd worn had gone. She was not a young woman by any means, but she'd met a nasty end.

Had she fallen, inebriated, into the river? Or had someone pushed her there?

Dark bruises covered her torso, but it was difficult to tell whether those had come from her body knocking into things in the water or beatings she'd received beforehand. There were no obvious imprints of fingers on her arms, shoulders, or neck to show she'd been handled roughly, but again, it was difficult to see exactly.

Her belly held puckered scars, signs a woman had born a child. Did those children worry where she was? Or had she, as did many forced to eke out an existence on the streets, given them up to the parish to raise?

My heart was heavy as I replaced the sheet. So many had troubles in this world, far greater than Denis or myself. Could I solve them all? I knew I could not.

But it did not stop me from wishing to try.

I let out a breath and followed the impatient Spendlove back into the rain, leaving the dead to sleep.

————

I RETURNED TO GRIMPEN LANE AND MRS. BELTAN'S SHOP TO fetch Brewster. The woman was busy with ladies purchasing bread and pastries, so I could not quiz her further on the visitor who'd sought me.

"I should return home, I think," I told Brewster as we headed into Covent Garden. "Her ladyship will be rising soon and wonder at my absence."

"You're seeing sense at last," Brewster said. "The further ye stay from Bow Street Nick and Newgate the better, guv."

We reached a hackney stand, and Brewster hoisted me into a waiting carriage. He joined me inside, resting his bulk in the opposite seat.

"I must speak to Gibbons again today," I said as the hackney jolted down Southampton Street toward the Strand. I withdrew the note Denis had written to Gibbons and handed it to Brewster. "Can you arrange it?"

Brewster scowled as he skimmed the missive but nodded. "I'll make sure he lets you in."

I was silent for the rest of the ride. I couldn't explain that I needed the warmth in my wife's eyes and the comfort of both my daughters' smiles to erase the bleakness of rain-soaked Seven Dials and the unfortunates at Bow Street.

Donata, who kept very late nights during the Season, would have risen by now, as would my daughter. Gabriella tended to leave her bed a bit earlier than my wife, but because Donata had swept Gabriella into the social season with her, I begrudged neither of them their sleep.

Peter was absent because he'd gone off to school as soon as we'd arrived again in England. He'd borne up manfully when I'd ridden with him to the large house that held the school, not far from his grandfather's home in Oxfordshire. We'd shaken hands solemnly on our departure, but I'd watched him blink back tears. My eyes, in truth, had been moist as well. I knew the school would prepare Peter for Harrow, where he as a viscount would form connections that would benefit him in life, but I missed having the little fellow about.

My daughter, Anne, was with us, of course. She could toddle about now and say "Papa." I was ridiculously proud of her.

The hackney took us to my residence by way of Berkeley Square. Spring was coming even to London, the trees in the park budding out in fresh green. The carriage lurched around corners to South Audley Street and halted before the tall house leased by the viscounts Breckenridge, where Donata made her home in London.

Whatever the brutish Viscount Breckenridge had put Donata through during her marriage to him, he'd left her a lavish amount of money and the use of this house for her lifetime. Small compensation for her putting up with him, I knew, but I was grateful for it. While Lady Breckenridge had become, upon marriage to me, plain Mrs. Lacey, she held enough respect of the *ton* to remain a leading hostess. She'd not had to descend into obscure poverty with me.

I descended from the hackney, with Brewster's assistance, and paid the cabbie. Brewster started off toward Curzon Street, determined to hunt up Gibbons.

The footman stationed in the foyer opened the door for me, and I gladly entered our comfortable abode.

I admired the house as much now as I had when I'd first seen it. Donata had opted for the clean lines of a Robert Adam-style interior, with light colors, niches for statuary, and fine paintings. The main hall held little furniture apart from a few pseudo-Egyptian style chairs and a table with a vase of fresh flowers that were changed daily. The staircase wound gracefully upward from the main hall, adding to its elegance.

After divesting myself of my outdoor things, I thumped up the stairs I'd hurried down earlier this morning and tapped on the door of Donata's boudoir.

At her reply, I entered to find her at her correspondence, as she usually was first thing after rising.

"There you are, Gabriel." Donata turned to me from her

writing table, her relief apparent. "Barnstable told me you'd gone off with a ruffian he'd never seen before. I am pleased that you have returned, whole." She deliberately retained her composure, draping one arm languidly over the back of her chair. "An acquaintance of Mr. Brewster's, was it? Or a summons from Mr. Denis?"

I dropped a kiss to Donata's pleasantly scented hair. "It was Gibbons, Denis's butler. Denis is in Newgate, awaiting trial for murder."

I could not often surprise my wife, so it was gratifying to watch her lips part in astonishment. "I beg your pardon?"

I pulled the comfortable chair she kept for me next to her desk and sank down to relate the events of the morning.

"Good heavens," was all Donata could say when I finished. "You are convinced Mr. Denis did not kill this man?"

"He would never do anything so clumsy, nor would he let himself be caught." Which again brought up the question, *why had he?* "There is more to this than meets the eye."

"That is obvious." Donata had regained her equanimity and spoke briskly. "If he objects to you discovering the truth, perhaps this incident is part of a larger scheme."

"One he fears I will blunder into?"

"Mr. Denis is a strategist," Donata said. "He has proved that many times in the past, and he lets very few into his plans. As you say, he would never do anything so clumsy, so there must be a purpose in his actions."

"He meant himself to be found?" I asked, liking that I could put these questions to Donata's sharp mind. "A dangerous thing to do, considering Spendlove's obsession with landing Denis in the dock."

Donata turned her pen thoughtfully in her fingers. "Unless there is someone Mr. Denis wants to see in the dock even less."

"He is protecting the true killer, you mean?" My brows went

up. "The murderer would have to be a very special person indeed, for him to do that."

"You said Mr. Denis is confident he will walk away from this charge. So, if *he* is arrested, all will be well. He'll call in favors and go home. But perhaps this other person—one of those who works for him?—wouldn't be so lucky."

"In other words, he faces trial because he knows someone like Mr. Gibbons—I am only speculating it was Gibbons—would never survive it. Is Denis that self-sacrificing for the men he employs?"

"We do not know, do we?" Donata gestured with her pen, and a tiny drop of ink fell from its tip to the paper before her. "What about this Mr. Stout, whom Brewster is surprised has been employed. Perhaps he is more than a lackey impulsively hired? Denis had other people working for him in Rome but brought none of *them* home."

I recalled the large, hard-bitten man called Luigi, who'd terrified callers at Denis's leased house near the Palazzo Borghese. Luigi had been a Roman through and through and likely would not be happy in chilly London.

However, if Denis had thought any of his lackeys from the Papal States would be useful to him, he'd have ferried them back with him. He must have some compelling use for Stout to have paid his fare to England and trusted him in the Seven Dials house with only himself and Gibbons.

"Might be worth speaking to Stout again," I said slowly. "Not that he was pleased to talk to me the first time. Denis was in that house last night for a reason, and I wager Stout knows why, as much as he protests that he kept himself to himself."

Donata gazed at the painting above her desk, a misty country scene rendered by Mr. Constable. "What does Mr. Stout look like? How old is he, would you say?"

I described him, while Donata listened thoughtfully.

"Are you thinking he is related to Denis somehow?" I asked. "There is no resemblance that I could see."

Donata sent me a wry smile. "I admit, I fancied he might be Denis's long-lost son, or some such. But if Mr. Stout is the age you say, then no."

I could not stop my laughter. "A long-lost son? Denis isn't old enough to have a grown son, is he?"

"Mr. Denis is thirty-four." How Donata knew that precisely, I could not guess. "In my experience, gentlemen begin siring children at a young age. He could have a son or daughter of twenty if he was enjoying ladies when he was, say, fourteen or fifteen." She wrinkled her forehead in worry. "I do hope Peter proves to have more sense than that."

"Peter is eight years old," I scoffed. "He hardly notices young women at all, beyond familial affection for his sisters. I doubt that will change soon, especially after he is shut up in Harrow with beady-eyed tutors."

Donata fixed me with a steely gaze. "I imagine that at fifteen, there was hardly a barmaid in any village who didn't scheme for a night with you."

I flushed, because it was true I had been a lusty youth, though I was not quite so promiscuous as she was imagining. I had been more romantic, I liked to think, and less in thrall to a runaway appetite.

"I hope I conducted myself with some measure of honor," I said stiffly. "Even at that age."

"I am certain you did." Donata's answer was sincere. "Even so, my point is clear. Young men are not censured for their passions unless it carries their family into great scandal. But my speculation is for naught—Denis might have left by-blows in his life, but middle-aged Mr. Stout clearly isn't one of them. However, he might be an uncle, a cousin, an older brother ..."

"I don't believe he is any relation at all," I said, happy to change the direction of the conversation. "That is not to say he isn't important to Denis in some way. Familial ties for Denis are less that of blood and more of loyalty to his fellows."

Denis, as a child, had learned quickly who to trust and who to remove himself from. He'd been a clever lad, from what I gathered, earning the reputation as a good leader, but there was a reason he kept his emotions under such strict control.

"Certainly, speak to Mr. Stout again," Donata encouraged me. "You are good at ferreting out secrets before people mean to tell them. Mr. Gibbons as well—Denis has a longer history with him, presumably."

"Ferreting?" I attempted a frown. "Is that a reference to my long nose?" I tapped the appendage, hoping to make her smile.

Donata only rolled her eyes but leaned from her chair and kissed the tip of the nose in question. "You know full well when I am teasing you. Now, be off. I have a mountain of letters to write and cannot when you distract me with intriguing problems."

"At least I intrigue you." I rose, returned the kiss on her lips, then pressed her hand and left her to it.

Donata's industriousness brought to mind my own correspondence, to which I was woefully inattentive. Not that I had many letters to write—most of my close acquaintances in London lived within walking distance, and I preferred conversations to shutting myself in my study and laboriously scribbling sentences.

I did like to pen a note to Peter as often as I could, and I needed to answer a letter from my cousin Marcus in Norfolk about what he wanted to do with the farm this year. He had much more experience than I did on agrarian questions, but he sent inquiries to me as a courtesy.

Also, Mrs. Beltan had interested me with her tale of the woman who'd asked for me, whom she'd directed to write to me at South Audley Street. I didn't recall any such letter reaching me, but if I'd not recognized the hand, I might have pushed it aside and forgotten about it.

I requested coffee from Barnstable, who'd instantly appeared when I'd left Donata's chamber to assure himself I'd returned home without harm. I also asked him where Gabriella had gone —the house was too quiet to have her in it. Barnstable relayed that she was walking with Lady Aline Carrington, a robust lady who strode heartily though London's parks every day.

Happy Gabriella was in good hands, I accepted the coffee, shut myself in the study, and made myself attend to work.

Barnstable had already left any letters delivered today on the desk for me. One of them was in Marcus's hand, prompting me to answer his first missive, no doubt. He must be growing impatient with me. Another was a thin letter from Grenville, and a third was penned by a gentleman from whom I'd asked to borrow a tome on Bonaparte's discoveries in Egypt.

I set these aside and dug through my pile of unread correspondence. I was rewarded when I found a small letter folded into a neat rectangle and sealed with a tiny dab of wax. It was addressed to me in neat, feminine handwriting I did not know. The seal had no imprint—the sender had simply dribbled wax from a candle to keep the letter closed.

I opened it, finding a short missive written between the lines of a shopping list that had been crossed through.

A most humble greeting to you, Captain Lacey.

I make so bold to write to you, remembering the kindness you showed me and those I call my sisters, when you were inquiring into the whereabouts of another.

I wish to consult you now in a similar matter, though I hope in not so dire a circumstance. If you leave your answer as to whether you will or will not meet me with the proprietor of the bakeshop beneath your old rooms, I will call there to seek any response from you.

Mrs. Beltan indicated you had moved up in the world, making a fine marriage, for which I congratulate you.

I wait in hopes of your reply, but I fully understand if you affix no importance to my inquiry. It is a private matter of my own, and I thought to take a chance.

With my most sincere good wishes on your new circumstances, I remain, respectfully, a young woman you know only as

Lady.

CHAPTER 7

$\mathcal{M}$emories poured at me as I stared at the letter, dumbfounded.

Nearly four years ago, Marianne Simmons had taken me to a house in a lane off Holborn, where women who'd been made belly-full by their trade had their lyings-in.

At the time, I'd been searching for a young woman who'd been abducted and forced into this business. Marianne had told me of a genteel young lady who'd ended up there and had granted me an entrée to the house.

The woman I'd met had not been the one I sought, though she'd been distressed to hear of my quest. The others in the house had called her Lady, and she'd refused to give me any other name.

Lady confessed that she'd gone there to have a child and had decided to stay on after that and help the others. She'd been well-spoken, very likely gentry or even aristocratic in origin, but she'd declined to tell me her story. I'd expressed rage that an oaf of a man had inflicted his seed on her, and offered vengeance, but Lady had only smiled and said she'd made the choice and paid the consequence.

I still longed to find whoever that gentleman had been and remove his limbs from his body.

I'd sought her again when my daughter, Gabriella, had gone missing for a harrowing time. The few years between my visits had not changed Lady, who'd still lived in the house where she'd claimed to have found a purpose.

After that, I'd not heard from or about Lady. Now, she requested my assistance. Which, of course, I would give.

I took up my pen and wrote a reply, proposing that we meet at the bakeshop, whenever she was able, to discuss the matter. I'd take the note to Mrs. Beltan today or send Bartholomew if I couldn't manage the journey myself.

Once I'd folded and sealed this letter, more intrigued than I admitted, I made myself peruse the other letters. Marcus, indeed, had sent more thoughts about the farm, which I set aside to deal with later. The gentleman with the Egyptian book said he'd be happy to lend it to me and would send his man to deliver it later this week.

Grenville's short note declared he'd heard of Denis's arrest this morning. If I would be so good as to make my way to his home, he'd receive me to discuss it.

When I'd first met Grenville, his sardonic demand would have angered me. Now, I realized his perfunctoriness meant eager impatience to learn of this latest problem.

I summoned Bartholomew, my tall valet, and gave him the response to Lady to deliver to Mrs. Beltan's. I knew Donata would be hours at her correspondence, and Gabriella had not yet returned, so I took myself the short way to Grenville's elegant town house in Grosvenor Street.

Lucius Grenville, London's most famous dandy, had scandalized society last year by marrying an unknown actress who'd already been his mistress. Matrons who'd had high hopes that Grenville would wed one of their daughters were furious with him, and even his fellow dandies thought he'd gone too far.

Gradually, however, the more sensation-seeking of the *ton* grew too interested in his new arrangement to entirely condemn it. It was now becoming fashionable to have Grenville and his wife at soirees and suppers, provided there were no innocent debutantes there to be corrupted by them.

Marianne, who had risen to the role she now found herself in, was impressing her hostesses with her fine manners and natural grace. I'd come to realize she'd been a much better actress than her company had given her credit for, but I also had the feeling Marianne's origins were close to that which she now portrayed.

Like Lady, Marianne never mentioned her past. I knew she'd once upon a time taken up with a company of strolling players, which led to her employment at Drury Lane theater, but her instincts in what to say and do when in society were too well honed to be entirely feigned.

Grenville, I discovered once I entered his hallowed halls, was in his dressing room. When the footman ushered me inside this chamber, Grenville was standing in the center of it with his chin raised high. Gautier, his valet, busily tied a golden-colored cravat around Grenville's neck into a complicated knot.

"A new style," Grenville said, his voice muffled. "Gautier is a genius at cravats. I tell him the knots should be named after him, but he demurs."

Gautier ignored this quip while he finished his artistry and tucked the ends of the cloth inside Grenville's silk brocade waistcoat.

"Your cravat is yellow," I observed in mock amazement.

Pure white linen had been de rigueur for a very long time. A black cravat or stock might be worn during the day and for riding, but white was the gentleman's choice for evening wear.

"Butternut," Grenville corrected me. "I thought it time Brummell's strictures were relaxed a bit. He's been gone from us five years now, poor fellow."

Grenville, who'd easily stepped into George Brummell's place once that man had exiled himself to France to avoid his creditors, dictated without words what the society gentlemen should be wearing. In the next few weeks, I'd no doubt see a number of dark yellow cravats around the necks of the upper classes.

"As to this business with Denis," Grenville said as Gautier eased a black cashmere frock coat over his shoulders. "You're already in the thick of it. Tell me all."

I did not need to ask how he knew so quickly about my involvement in the incident. Any number of Donata's servants would have passed word to Grenville's that I'd been whisked away by Gibbons this morning. News of the sensational murder had likely already flown around London.

I seated myself on a straight-backed chair and regaled him with my tale, my valet's brother, Matthias, entering to quietly furnish me with coffee.

"It is a devil of a thing," Grenville said once I'd finished. "I wrote to you after I read the sordid details in the latest broadsheet, and Matthias announced you were already investigating. I knew Mr. Pickett, you see. Or at least, something of him."

"Did you?" I exclaimed. Grenville's eyes gleamed with gratification as I rose to his bait with proper astonishment. "You might have said so at once."

"I wanted to hear what you knew, first." Grenville stuck his arms out straight from his sides while Gautier, unbothered by our revelations, began to brush down his coat. "I met Mr. Pickett not long ago. He was introduced to me at Tattersalls, by Langley, an old school friend. Pickett struck me as a rather excitable man, worried about many things. He feared he was up to his neck with the so-called Cato Street conspirators, though neither Langley nor I could fathom why. It seemed unlikely."

We had all been following as the Cato Street plot unfolded in the newspapers. The gentlemen, who called themselves the

Spencean Philanthropists, had been planning the murder of the entire cabinet, Lord Liverpool with them. More details about the conspiracy had been revealed almost every day since the arrests weeks ago, including the informants who'd been planted in the group. I'd never seen the name Pickett mentioned.

"Up to his neck?" I asked in bafflement.

"So he said, but I could not decide if the fellow was sincere or not. If he was convinced he was about to be arrested at any moment, why announce the fact to us?" Grenville shrugged, causing Gautier to cluck in disapproval. "I tried to assure Pickett that the whole thing was nothing to do with him, but he persisted. Although, who knows? Perhaps one of the conspirators managed to escape the net and silenced Pickett before he could name him."

"Now we are entering the realm of the fantastic," I said. "The journalists have listed all the conspirators and their backgrounds with painstaking thoroughness. Spendlove was at the raid—as was Pomeroy. Spendlove would have told me with triumph if Pickett had been one of them."

"Then why was Pickett so certain?" Grenville asked. "There must be something in it."

I was aware of people who persuaded themselves that if anything exciting or dangerous happened—the more notorious, the better—it had something to do with them. Pickett could be such a man.

However, I had to admit that the Runners had arrested only those actually inside the Cato Street house that night. It stood to reason that some of the group might have managed to lie low and avoid capture.

In that case, though, why had Pickett freely offered this information to Grenville? Had Pickett meant he was one of the plotters who'd escaped or that he'd been associated with the conspirators in a more obscure way? And was this connection why he'd contacted Denis?

"I hope he was exaggerating and had nothing at all to do with the Cato Street men," I said. "If Denis agreed to help Pickett escape to the Continent, Denis might face a treason charge. Spendlove would be in transports of joy if this proved true."

"I'm not certain I believed him," Grenville said. "As I mentioned, Pickett was an excitable fellow. Would he not worry that we'd rush to fetch a Runner to arrest him?"

"Perhaps he knew you'd not credit him if he burst out with it in the way he did," I suggested. "Or, perhaps he knew of your associations with Denis and hoped you would encourage Denis to help him."

"Well, we can stand in my dressing room speculating all we like, but it will not bring us to the truth. *Someone* must know whether Pickett was involved and what he wanted of Denis."

"I was on my way to Curzon Street to read the letter Pickett sent to Denis." I idly twirled the head of my walking stick. "But I was preempted by a summons to Grosvenor Street to watch Gautier tie your new cravat."

It spoke of our long and comfortable friendship that Grenville endured this gentle chide without offense.

"You know I cannot venture from my house unless I am properly attired," Grenville said. "Can I, Gautier?"

"No, indeed, monsieur," Gautier answered calmly.

"The very edifice of society might crumble if I were to be seen with one of the buttons at my ankle undone or my waistcoat an iota out of place. Think of the distress I'd cause."

"Very amusing." I took a final sip of the very good coffee, thanked Matthias, and rose. "When you can tear yourself away, perhaps you will accompany me to Denis's to read his correspondence?"

"I'd be honored, old chap." Grenville nodded at his valet. "Gautier, prepare me for an afternoon's walk to Curzon Street."

ONCE GAUTIER HAD FINISHED, GRENVILLE DONNED A PAIR OF sturdy boots, and we tramped through Mayfair to Denis's house. Brewster stepped out its front door as we approached.

"Better come in, guv," he said. "Gibbons agreed to let you have a butcher's, but he's not best pleased about it."

"Denis instructed him to," I said in surprise.

"Aye, but Gibbons is a protective sod. Do anything for His Nibs, would Gibbons."

Brewster ushered us through the foyer to an echoing hall empty of the usual horde of Denis's men. Many of the watchers I was used to seeing here must be with Denis, guarding him against the perils of Newgate.

"He has the letter upstairs." Brewster jabbed his thumb upward. "In the usual place."

He made no move to follow me as Grenville and I mounted the staircase, unworried that danger could befall me here.

The house was eerily hushed, as though holding its breath, awaiting its master's return. Grenville and I did not speak as we ascended past the serene painting of the woman pouring out a jug of cream, fearing to break the odd silence.

I assumed that by *the usual place* Brewster meant Denis's study. I approached the closed door, wondering if it would be locked and I'd need to hunt down Gibbons for a key.

Gibbons himself wrenched open the study's door from the inside the moment before I reached it. He scowled at me in greeting.

"Mr. Pickett's correspondence is on the desk."

I nodded as I stepped past him, Grenville beginning to follow me.

Gibbons half closed the door, blocking Grenville's path. "Only Captain Lacey has Mr. Denis's permission."

I frowned in annoyance. "Mr. Grenville is hardly here to make off with the silver—"

"It is quite all right," Grenville interposed quickly. "Mr. Denis had no notion I'd be accompanying you, and I'd hope my employees would do the same if someone came to my home in my absence. I will await you downstairs, Lacey."

Grenville gave Gibbons a gracious nod, which did not soften Gibbons the slightest bit, and turned away. Gibbons closed the door behind him with a solid *thunk.*

Gibbons remained in the room, not about to let me sit and read the correspondence on my own. It was equally obvious that I would not be allowed to take it away with me.

Gibbons positioned himself near the door and kept his yellowing eyes on me, like a gargoyle who'd guard the place for the next century.

I hid a sigh, seated myself at the desk, and pulled two very short missives that lay there toward me.

The first was formal, an introduction.

Sir,

I am Bernard Pickett, a man who has recently risen to good fortune, at least so I believed. I have come into some trouble lately and have been assured by Lord Eccleshal, Sir Humphrey Godden, and Mr. Jones-Graves that you are the man to turn to in such times. I have been informed that your fees are quite high, but I am prepared to pay anything for your assistance. What I ask is nothing that will put you in danger, nor is it of an immoral or obscene nature. A simple matter, but one I cannot undertake myself.

I remain, in hope of your understanding,

Bernard Pickett

The second paper held Denis's terse reply.

I will meet with you to discuss the matter. Number 45 Curzon Street, 7 pm, Monday, March the 20th. I will send a coach if you require it.

Denis

As usual, Denis had used a large blank sheet for the three short sentences. Mr. Pickett had written back on the lower half of it.

Sir: I cannot tell you the relief I have had at receiving your reply. Thank you for your kind offer of the carriage, but I will not need it. The address is close enough for me to seek you on foot. I look forward to the meeting on Monday next, where I will explain what a wretched man I am.

Written in haste in sincere gratitude,

Bernard Pickett

I turned both letters over, but there was only one direction on them, that to Denis himself. Nothing addressed in return to Pickett. The first letter had also not come here to Curzon Street but had been directed to James Denis at an address in Jermyn Street. Denis had recently purchased a business on that road, a gaming hell known as the Nines. He must use an office there to filter his correspondence.

I examined the reply Denis had written, but no direction was on it either to or from Denis. "How did he get his response *to* Pickett?" I asked in bafflement.

"Mr. Denis has his replies hand-carried back to the Nines," Gibbons intoned. "The gents what contact him know to look for their answers there."

"Pity." I laid the letters down in defeat. "I hoped I'd discover where Pickett lived. Close enough to walk, he writes. Even if he was not robust, that leaves many streets and houses in a wide radius." I doubted Spendlove would reveal Pickett's address whenever he found it out. Pomeroy might not either.

"I can tell you where the bloke was staying," Gibbons surprised me by stating. "When he came to the Nines for Mr. Denis's reply, I followed him."

CHAPTER 8

"Good Lord." I blinked at Gibbons, who stared lugubriously back at me. "You saw no reason to mention this before?"

"Ye only asked to see the letters," Gibbons said. "Ye didn't say why."

I curbed my temper with effort. I suspected that shouting at Gibbons would only silence him. "Very well, where did Mr. Pickett go once he'd received Mr. Denis's answer?"

"Park Place," Gibbons answered without hesitation. "Round the corner from St. James's Street. There's a club there at number 7, with flats for gents."

I wasn't familiar with all the clubs in St. James's, but Grenville would be.

"This hints that he's a bachelor," I mused. "A wife or children would need a house or a hotel."

"Many a gent stays at clubs or in rooms in Town," Gibbons said. "With family left in the country."

"Possibly, though I'd think Pickett's appeal to Denis would mention the dear wife and children who'd be devastated if something happened to him." I lifted Pickett's first letter. "He writes more like a man worried about his own skin, not one concerned for another's sake."

Gibbons' pinched expression told me he was not much bothered about what Pickett wrote, and I didn't argue further.

I read through each letter again, trying to memorize the sentences to repeat to Grenville. I wondered if Lord Eccleshal, Mr. Jones-Graves, or Sir Humphrey Godden would have any further knowledge of Pickett. So might Grenville's friend Langley, who'd introduced Pickett to Grenville at Tattersalls. I did not know any of the gentlemen Pickett mentioned personally, but through Grenville, Donata, or Lady Aline, I might find a way to speak to them.

I wondered what Pickett had meant when he'd assured Denis that his problems were not *immoral* or *obscene*. Surely conspiracy to commit murder and overthrow the government would fall under acts that were immoral. Or perhaps he was trying to distance himself from them.

In the second letter Mr. Pickett described himself as *wretched*, and the tone was one of both relief and urgency.

Pickett had fully intended to meet Denis in the house I now sat in at seven o'clock yesterday evening. When he'd missed the appointment, Denis had carried on with his business, unworried.

"Why did Denis go to Seven Dials?" I asked abruptly. Stout had told me he'd gone to meet someone, but I wanted to hear what Gibbons would reply. "I assume he departed here after it was clear Pickett wouldn't be coming?"

"Mr. Denis had his supper," Gibbons said coldly. "At half past eleven, he announced we'd go to the Seven Dials house and spend the night there. I gathered the belongings he'd need, and we went."

"What did he do there? And why stay the night?"

Unlike Stout, Gibbons didn't state bluntly that Denis's business was his own. He simply did not answer.

"It might be important," I said in a hard voice. "Whoever Denis met in the Seven Dials house might have stolen his knife and killed Pickett with it."

"They did not."

Gibbons abruptly scowled as though he realized he'd just admitted Denis had invited someone into the house. Had he used the word *they* to indicate more than one person or to hide the gender of the guest?

"How can you be certain they didn't take the knife?" I asked.

"Would have noticed." Gibbons spoke in the tone of a man who'd have stopped a thief making off with Denis's things, no matter how trivial the item.

"It would be very helpful to know who Denis was speaking to," I persisted. "Whoever it was might have been the killer. If we find *him*, Denis will go free."

"It's nothing to do with Mr. Pickett getting himself stabbed," Gibbons snapped. "Mr. Denis don't want you mucking about in his affairs. He told me to show you the letters, nothing more."

"Did *you* see who killed Pickett?" I asked him.

Gibbons shook his head. "I didn't." He sounded genuinely regretful. "I were downstairs in the kitchen, cooking Mr. Denis's breakfast. I didn't know anything was wrong until Stout ran in, shouting at me."

"Could Stout have witnessed the murder?"

"No," Gibbons said firmly. "He'd have said right away. We don't grass to the beaks, but he'd have told *me*. Whoever fit up Mr. Denis for this murder had better watch out." The fury in his eyes could have chilled even the most battle-hardened soldier.

"You trust Stout quite a lot," I observed. "So does Denis. Could not Stout have killed Pickett?"

"No," Gibbons said at once. "Stout's not a murderer."

"You are certain of this?"

Gibbons turned his full anger on me. "Reformers think like you do, that in the criminal classes, as they call them, every man runs about robbing, killing, looting, maybe setting buildings on fire and ravishing women if they have the time. It ain't like that. A man who steals for a living might still go to chapel and be high-minded about never taking a human life. It's the same in soldiering, innit? There are some who know their way around cannons, some who can shoot a rifle, and some who can ride a horse and swing a pretty sword. Ye have your task you're good at, and ye do it. Stout knows about moving goods from one place to another without anyone being the wiser. He don't need to stab any man in his way, because he knows how not to be caught."

More information than I'd obtained from Gibbons since I'd met him. "There is a difference between your lot and soldiering," I observed quietly. "All of *us* are trained to kill."

Gibbons' eyes narrowed. "Ye killed many men in your day, Captain?"

The stench and sounds of the battlefield poured to me from the place I'd buried them, along with the smell of smoke from cannons and carbines, and the acrid odor of blood, horses, death. The screaming of men and animals, the roar of guns, our bellowing cries as we charged.

I forced myself back to the present, where the tick of the case clock in the hall resounded in the silence.

"Quite a number," I said quietly. "To be sure, they were doing their best to murder me at the time. Very fierce, were Bonaparte's soldiers, unquestioningly loyal to him. If I'd stopped to apologize to any for what I was commanded to do, I'd have been dead and buried long ago."

"Hmph." Gibbons' gaze held a modicum more respect. "But ye had your own way of soldiering, didn't ye? Didn't try to do any sapping or tell the generals how to run the battles."

"I did want to do the last bit." I gave him a slight smile, the sharpness of the memories receding. "In this I was deterred. But I take your point. Pomeroy was good at rallying his men into doing their jobs, and I was good at charging wantonly at the enemy, swinging a pretty sword, as you say. Stout is expert at moving goods. Brewster is a thief who knows fisticuffs. Robbie, I suppose, is also good with his fists."

"He is," Gibbons said. "None of them are murderers."

I noted that Gibbons did not volunteer what his speciality was. I could imagine him sliding a knife through a man's ribs without a qualm. I'd met men as cold as he was in my army life, and they had been used as assassins.

"We are back to wondering who did kill Mr. Pickett and why," I said. "Did the murderer mean to stitch up Denis for it? Or was it coincidence that Pickett met his end in the street outside Denis's house?"

"Don't know, do I?" Gibbons growled.

"Neither do I, unfortunately." I rose from the desk, leaving the letters where they were. "Why did Pickett miss his appointment, and why journey to Seven Dials? To find Denis? Or to meet someone else?"

Gibbons had resumed being close-mouthed and only stared coolly at my questions.

I hadn't really expected him to answer. "Thank you for your help, Gibbons." I made my way past him to the door. "If you remember anything else about last night or this morning that might be helpful, please send word."

Gibbons stood like a stone while I exited the room. I turned back to find him ramrod stiff in the middle of the chamber, watching me with an iciness that cut.

He did not move to close the door, and I didn't bother. I tramped to the stairs and down, saying my good-byes to the painted milkmaid in her vivid blues and yellows along the way.

———

Grenville and I left the house, Brewster joining us. The wind through the streets had turned blustery. Clouds scuttled overhead, the rain gone, but cold had taken its place. We bent our heads as we trudged up South Audley Street, the sharp breeze making conversation all but impossible.

We'd nearly reached Grosvenor Chapel when a shout of "Captain!" behind us made me turn. I beheld a small and wiry man jogging after us, his stride hampered by a slight limp.

I recognized him as Lewis Downie, who worked for Denis. He'd once been a lightweight pugilist, until a broken hand turned him into a groomsman for Denis's horses. He did other jobs as well, often sent by Denis as a messenger on various errands.

We waited for Downie to catch up. He gave us a nod and continued around the corner of Grosvenor Chapel, taking the narrow lane that led to the burial ground. The long brick church with its rows of arched windows loomed beside us as we followed him, the wall cutting the wind.

When we reached the gate that separated the churchyard from the lane, Downie stopped and faced us, hunkering into his coat.

"Heard some of the questions you were asking Gibbons," he said. "He weren't exactly straight with ye."

I was not surprised by this. "What did he leave out?"

"If you're thinking Gibbons lied because he landed Mr. Denis in the nick, you're wrong," Downie said. "He's a cold fish, is Gibbons, but he'd lay down his life for Mr. Denis. He keeps mum from habit, which is usually a good one. But I don't see why it hurts for you to know. Mr. Denis needs out of that place, don't he?"

Brewster rumbled with impatience. "Just tell him what ye came to say."

"I know who Denis went to Seven Dials to meet last night." Downie glanced about as though worried he'd be overhead, but we were the only ones standing in the narrow street. "It were a toff, weren't it? One what didn't want to be seen rolling up to Mr. Denis's Mayfair home in a carriage with his crest on the door. So, Mr. Denis goes off to Seven Dials to meet him."

"Do you know the name of this toff?" Grenville asked eagerly.

"I do. Not because His Nibs told me, you understand, but because he's done the arrangement before. Last time it was me who went with Gibbons to man the place while they met in secret. This time he took Stout." If Downie resented the substitution, he didn't show it. "The man in question is the Honorable Mr. Enoch Haywood. A big mouthful for such a small cove."

"Haywood?" Grenville started.

Downie nodded. "He always wants to meet in the dead of night in some out-of-the-way place, insisting Mr. Denis brings only one or two trusted guards who keep from sight. I don't know what Mr. Denis did for him, but His Honorableness has been twitchy about it ever since. He should be in transports, shouldn't he, thinking Mr. Denis is about to be hanged?" Downie trailed off morosely. "We can't let that happen, Captain. I'm too old to seek a new man to work for, and I'd never find another place as soft."

"I understand, Mr. Downie," I said.

"You don't, and that's a fact. Life is precarious for gents like me. But never mind. You find out what happened, and I won't have to worry."

I imagined it was indeed difficult for a pugilist who was past his prime and couldn't fight anymore to put bread on his table. Whoever stepped into the hole Denis left might not be interested in employing Downie or any other of Denis's faithful lackeys.

"Thank you for the information, Mr. Downie," I said sincerely. "Very helpful. I will put it to good use."

"Doubt the toff did in the Pickett bloke," Downie said. "The Honorable Mr. Haywood is very prissy. Probably never lifted a knife in all his days."

"Even so, it is a step forward," I assured him.

"Gibbons trusts no one, not that I blame him. He's had a hell of a life." Downie rubbed his gloved hands together against the cold. "I'll be getting back indoors before he misses me."

Touching his forehead in a half-salute, he trotted along the chapel's high wall back to South Audley Street and disappeared around the corner.

"Enie Haywood." Grenville shook his head in disbelief. "Who'd have thought it? I concur with Mr. Downie, that Haywood is more likely to hide behind a tree than attack a man with a knife. He isn't feeble—he's a good rider and competent at shooting defenseless waterfowl—but he's very careful with himself. He'd be more worried about getting his gloves stained than ridding the world of Mr. Pickett."

"I would be interested in what he has to say about it," I said grimly.

"We can certainly speak to him. He might not reveal why he wanted to meet with Denis, but perhaps he could tell us whether he saw anyone near the house when he came and went. His coachman might prove useful as well."

I did want to interview them both, and I'd be grateful for Grenville's help. At the moment, however, I wished to find Pickett's lodgings and look over what he'd left behind.

I took the opportunity in the relative shelter of the chapel to tell Grenville and Brewster what I'd learned from Gibbons and the letters. After some debate, we decided it best to visit Pickett's rooms right away.

We left the chapel for South Audley Street, where Grenville procured a hackney to take us to St. James's. The hackney was stuffy and rather odorous but as the conveyance spared my knee more soreness, I did not complain too much.

The coach turned down St. James's Street from Piccadilly and then lurched around a corner after we passed Brooks's club and entered the narrow lane called Park Place.

CHAPTER 9

*W*e halted before a building that rose four floors from the street, with rectangular windows and a fanlight over the black door. The building next to it, of similar architecture and size, must hold the gentlemen's lodgings.

Grenville had told us during the ride that he recognized the club Gibbons had described.

"The lads at White's call this the Pretenders' Club," Grenville said as he opened the carriage door. "Its members, you see, are gentlemen, but not connected to any families considered important. Those at White's condescendingly say there's nothing wrong with them, salt of the earth, yes, but one doesn't take them into one's circle." He shook his head. "The fools don't realize what power such men have."

"Was Pickett a powerful man?" I asked. "Wouldn't I have heard of him, if so?"

"Not necessarily." Grenville leapt lightly from the coach and stood by to assist me if need be. I appreciated that he didn't simply reach for me as though I were a feeble elderly uncle. "Such things aren't talked of. But the future is in the upstarts who actually hold all the money these days, even if they're not invited into White's, or to Brooks's, that bastion of radicalism."

I managed to gain the street without falling or seizing Grenville's arm for support. "Brooks's is a bastion of radicalism?" I asked in amusement.

"To those in White's, yes," Grenville answered with a straight face.

"The question is, did Pickett have money?" I asked. "Enough to make him enemies? His letter to Denis said he'd recently come into good fortune, but not what that fortune was. The house he'd inherited in Bedfordshire? Though Pomeroy said it was small."

"Perhaps we'll learn of it here." Grenville stepped to the front door of the club and rapped on it.

Brewster, who'd hopped off the back of the hackney, announced he'd keep watch. He regarded the buildings with suspicion, suspecting he wouldn't be welcome, even below stairs. He leaned against the hackney's wheel, folding his arms, resembling a boulder too sturdy to notice a few wind gusts.

A footman opened the door, but we were prevented entering by a thin man who hurried out of a vestibule. He wore the bland but polite expression of one ready to turn us away, then shock came over his face when he recognized Grenville.

"Sir." He bowed with exaggerated respect. "What brings you to our humble club, Mr. Grenville?"

"My friend, Captain Lacey." Grenville indicated me with a wave of his gloved hand. "We have bad news, I am afraid, Mr. ... er ..."

"Hawes," the man supplied. "Gilbert Hawes. I am the manager here. What is this bad news?" He gazed at us with the trepidation of a man expecting his entire world to crumble.

"Mr. Bernard Pickett," I said. "He has rooms here."

"Mr. Pickett, yes." His worry fled, his expression puzzled.

"I must explain that Mr. Pickett is deceased," I said as gently as I could. "He was killed this morning."

Mr. Hawes flushed, then his face drained of color. "Deceased? But he's ... He needs to ... He cannot be dead, sir."

"I am sorry, but it is true." I sent him a sympathetic nod. "I saw his body."

Mr. Hawes stared at us, then his legs abruptly gave way, and he clutched at the coat stand against the wall. Grenville and I both caught him by the elbows and lowered him onto a nearby bench. The footman gaped at us but with far less distress and no real anguish.

"Needs to what, Mr. Hawes?" Grenville took a seat next to the man, planting his walking stick between his knees. "You said Mr. Pickett needed to do... something?"

"What?" Hawes gulped. I took pity on him and handed him the brandy flask I carried in my coat pocket. Hawes drank deeply then let out a long breath and passed the flask back to me. "Thank you, sir. This is very sudden. Er ..." Hawes gathered his thoughts. "I meant Mr. Pickett had an appointment this evening, to dine with his friend, Mr. Cudgeon."

"Cudgeon?" Grenville asked in surprise. "Adam Cudgeon?"

"Oh, yes, they are great friends." Hawes flushed anew. "Were, I suppose I should say. They dined together here or met at a pub in Piccadilly. Cudgeon wasn't a member, you understand. Only a guest. He is in trade."

Hawes intoned this last as though assuring us that the Arlington was very careful with its membership.

"Would you let us see Pickett's lodgings?" Grenville asked. "It might be helpful."

He did not explain how it would be helpful or volunteer that I was acquainted with any Runners. A manager's loyalty was to the club members, not to the watchmen or the magistrates, and Hawes might refuse us entry if he believed we'd immediately rush to Bow Street once we were finished here.

"Of course," Hawes agreed without argument.

He then fell silent as he stared straight at Grenville. I wondered at his sudden wordlessness, then realized Hawes was making an odd hand signal, bringing his smallest and ring finger around to touch his thumb.

I was puzzled, but Grenville nodded at him and tapped the side of his nose.

Hawes thawed. He jumped up from the seat, no longer feeble, and rushed into his vestibule, returning with a ring of keys. "If you will follow me, sir." He spoke to Grenville alone, ignoring me entirely.

The footman seemed as baffled by Hawes's change in behavior as I was but opened the door to let us out without a word.

We left the club for the house next to it, whose door Hawes opened with one of the largest keys.

Inside was a quiet hall paneled in white-painted wood, the only furnishing a single tapered-legged table in the niche formed by the turn of the staircase. The table's top was bare, suggesting a place a gentleman might set his valise or hat while he removed his coat. A row of greatcoats hung on the back wall of this hallway beside a rear door, which probably led to a small yard.

Hawes ascended the rather steep staircase, which was carpeted with a blue-and-gold runner. I held on to the polished banister as we went up, and up, and up, finally emerging to the low-ceilinged third floor.

Pickett could not be that wealthy or powerful, Pickett's own words notwithstanding, if his rooms were so high in the house. The first-floor flats would be the most costly, the prices decreasing as we climbed.

Hawes opened a door just off the landing and ushered us inside. The rooms we entered faced the rear of the house, another reduction in rent.

At first glance, all was tidy, the front room containing little furniture or personal possessions that I could see. A closed door across the room presumably led to the bedchamber.

"I thank you, Mr. Hawes." Grenville turned to him. "We will be very careful, I promise."

His words were dismissing, Grenville more or less blocking Hawes from following us in. Hawes took the hint, winked, backed out of the room, and shut the door. He took the keys with him but did not lock us in.

Grenville waited until we heard his footsteps retreat down the stairs before speaking.

"How interesting." He laid his hat and stick on the table next to the door. "Now we know that Hawes, at least, is a member of a secret society."

I regarded him in bewilderment. "How do you conclude that? Is that why you and he were winking and blinking at each other?"

Grenville opened a cupboard that stood between two small windows and ran his fingers across the coats hung on pegs inside it.

"In a way," Grenville said as he studied the coats. "Hawes made a signal with his fingers, as members of such societies do for one another, and I thought it best I acknowledge it. Therefore, Hawes believes I am a fellow member, but you, unfortunately, are not."

"Which is why he suddenly behaved as though I no longer existed." There were no other cupboards or tables with drawers in the front room, so I moved to the door to the bedchamber. "What secret society is this? Are you truly a member, and if so, why haven't you seen Hawes there?"

"My dear Lacey, every gentleman in London is a member of some secret society or other." Grenville sounded amused. "I have no idea which ones Hawes attends. I didn't know what signal to make in return, so I only nodded and pretended I knew what he meant but was being discreet."

I'd opened the bedchamber door—which fortunately wasn't locked—but turned back in amazement.

"Every gentleman in London is a member of a secret society?" I demanded. "What the devil are you talking about?"

Grenville slid past me into the bedchamber, as though we were speaking about nothing more remarkable than the weather. "It is fashionable for anyone who calls himself a gentleman to be in a secret society—the Freemasons, for instance. The men who led the War of Independence in the Americas were Freemasons, many with ties to gentlemen in the same body here. General Arnold, whom my American friends call their most famous traitor, was a prominent Mason. But it's more than that. When our new Majesty, King George, was Prince of Wales, he was a member of several societies meant to oppose the policies of his father. He's left all that behind now, of course."

I listened to this with my mouth open so long it was beginning to dry out. I snapped it closed. "Are you a member of all these societies?"

"Quite a number of them, yes." Grenville moved to the wardrobe in this room, which held more garments. "I was hotheaded in my youth, ready to announce my views on reform to any who would listen. In fact, many of the guests who grace the door of your wife's soirees were in them with me. Mostly, we wasted a lot of breath and consumed buckets of port without changing a thing. But from many of these societies come the seeds for policies made in Westminster."

"I thought that happened in the clubs." I understood that the rulers of Britain drew allies to their positions over bowls of punch at White's or Brooks's. Parliament formalized those backroom agreements, with the king more or less an afterthought.

"It does." Grenville turned from the wardrobe to a tall bureau. "But by the time discussions reach the clubs, we have already narrowed down the arguments. In the secret meetings—which I doubt are very secret at all—we can air our opinions and disagree openly. The gentlemen are sworn not to repeat what we discuss with outsiders, and a good thing too. A hundred years ago, we'd have been arrested and carted off to hang simply for blustering about the Corn Laws."

Grenville opened a drawer in the bureau, gently moving the garments inside.

"Grenville," I said.

He looked up in inquiry. "Yes?"

"*Yes?*" I repeated. "Is that all you have to say? You've just told me that you, and Hawes, and apparently every man in London except me, are in secret political societies ready to overturn the government. And you behave as though it is nothing of consequence."

Grenville's brows rose. "You were never in such an organization in the Army? Not even the Masons?"

"I knew officers who were Freemasons, but I never paid much attention. If lordlings want to wear strange clothes and communicate with ridiculous finger movements, I wish them well. I thought these groups were dedicated to philanthropy, not murdering cabinet ministers."

"Many are," Grenville said, still untroubled. "It was a la mode years ago to be a bit revolutionary, especially when things were stirring in France against the Ancien Regime. Not that we meant events to turn bloodthirsty here, but we were fired up with the spirit of liberty for all. Young Prince George spoke loudly about being free of monarchs—this was long before he became one, of course. Bonaparte's rise changed our praise of him to worry he'd overrun us, but some societies continued to believe that Bonaparte had the right of it. He was a great reformer, after all, ridding the Continent of fairly archaic and rather backward systems."

I grew steadily cooler as I listened to Grenville's speech. "I spent my entire youth sweating in faraway lands or freezing in closer ones while Napoleon's soldiers did their best to cut me down," I stated. "His reforms meant nothing to me while artillery balls were flying past my face."

The amused tone with which Grenville had given me his explanation fled. "Oh, I do beg your pardon, my dear chap. I realize it's much different to theorize over sweet wine in warm drawing rooms than to return to your tent every night thanking God you are still alive. All my friends' pontificating didn't drive Bonaparte out of Spain and Belgium. You did."

"Do not assign too much divine power to ordinary soldiers," I said in annoyance. "We obeyed orders to fight where we were pointed. Our commanders didn't want Bonaparte stomping his boots all over England, plus Boney threatened the very supply of port you drank in your meetings."

"I take your point, my friend." Grenville lifted his hands, conceding. "I should not speak of such things so cavalierly. What I meant to convey is that secret societies abound in London and the rest of England. They did in the past and they do now. Most of them are harmless, with no more power than a broom and a dustbin."

"The Cato Street one was not," I pointed out. "Pickett told you he feared he was involved with them. A curious way to put it. He'd know, wouldn't he, whether he was or not?"

"One would think so." Grenville returned to his examination of the bureau drawer. "Perhaps he attended one meeting, realized what they were about, and decided against returning to another. Then when they were all arrested, he panicked."

"Telling everyone who would hear him that he might be entangled with the conspirators?"

"He might have been so upset he didn't know what to do," Grenville suggested. "Hoping Langley and I would reassure him or suggest a way out of his dilemma. I'm afraid we were only bewildered and suggested nothing."

"Which was most likely why he wrote to Denis," I said. "Perhaps to ask assistance in covering up whatever he'd been doing, or for help in fleeing to the Continent. The second request is more likely. Denis has done such things for others in the past."

"We'll never know, will we?" Grenville said with a sigh. "Someone made certain Mr. Pickett never reached Denis at all." He closed the drawer and opened another. "Not much in here. Linens and unmentionables, which are clean and well-made though not extravagant. A man of decent means but not lavish ones."

I sat on the edge of the bed, both because my knee was aching and because I wanted to search the bedside table. Its only drawer revealed something more promising—letters and a leather-bound journal.

I drew out the journal and flipped through pages. Pickett hadn't written much, only dates and initials, probably of his appointments. In the final entries I found one that indicated an appointment with a bootmaker yesterday afternoon. The next one read *J.D. 45 Curzon Street, 7 pm.* I gathered this indicated his meeting with Denis at seven o'clock last night.

The only entry for today was *A.C., Fox Run, 8 pm.*

Fox Run was the name of a tavern in Piccadilly, an ordinary place. "A.C.," I said to Grenville. "Hawes mentioned Pickett was to have dined with a man called Cudgeon tonight. Could he be the *A.C.* here?" I held up the page to show Grenville. "They're meeting at the Fox Run."

Grenville shut the drawer. "I wager he is."

"You knew the man's name," I said. "It surprised you."

"Because I have had dealings with Mr. Cudgeon myself, as has many a gentleman. His Christian name is Adam, so yes, he must be A.C." Grenville faced me. "Mr. Cudgeon, you see, is a manufacturer and seller of guns. Some of the finest shooters in the country, in fact."

CHAPTER 10

"Guns." My misgivings rose. "Mr. Pickett is becoming more and more in the thick of things, isn't he?"

"Cudgeon makes hunting weapons," Grenville said. "Fowling pieces, mostly, though some pistols and rifles too. Like Purdey, though he's not as famous. Very well-crafted shooters, I must say. I own several."

I laid the diary on the bed and stood, my misgivings becoming dark uneasiness. "Pickett believed his name might be connected with the Cato Street men, and he had dealings with a gunmaker. I do not like this at all."

"I've never heard that Cudgeon sympathized with radicals," Grenville said. "He's an artist with his fowling pieces and charges a hefty price for them, but he sells to gentlemen to shoot at game birds. Also dueling pistols, so we can shoot at each other from time to time. Hardly the same sort of weapons an army would use."

"According to you, London is rife with secret societies," I reminded him. "Perhaps Cudgeon truly is supplying such weapons, or the promise of them, to revolutionaries. He is in position to make them on demand, isn't he?"

"We could ask him," Grenville said. "If he's not aware that Pickett is dead, he might arrive at the meeting. At the Fox Run, you said?"

"It seems so."

"Then I propose we go there this evening and discover what we can from Mr. Cudgeon. If he comes, that is."

While I'd be escorting Donata and Gabriella out tonight, Donata rarely left the house before ten. I could meet with Cudgeon at the tavern and have plenty of time afterward for whatever entertainment I'd be attending.

"I think that an excellent plan," I agreed. "Let us dine at the Fox Run."

Grenville looked thoughtful. "I say, Lacey, surely we've solved it. Pickett at some time joined a political society that shared his views, whatever they were. Unbeknownst to him, he hobnobs with fellows from the Spencean Philanthropists. He purchases a cache of guns from Cudgeon and gives one as a gift to a member of the Spenceans—or perhaps a few of them commissioned Pickett to buy them, as Cudgeon is particular to who he sells to. Pickett believes they'll use them for hunting, and thinks no more of it. When the Cato Street men are arrested, Pickett sees the name of his chap on the list of those jailed. He's all in a lather, which is when he burst out with that information to Langley and me."

"It is plausible, I suppose," I said when he paused for my reaction.

"Pickett, in a panic, contacts Denis to spirit him out of the kingdom," Grenville continued. "Maybe there *are* more conspirators who did not get caught in the Runners' nets, and they worry about Pickett telling all in his fear. They begin to follow him, watch who he speaks to. Pickett misses his meeting with Denis in Curzon Street—for reasons unknown—but manages to procure Denis's address in Seven Dials. The followers corner Pickett moments before he reaches Denis's door, kill him, and flee. Denis walking outside and finding the body was simply his ill luck."

I nodded slowly. "I'd agree with you, except for one thing. How was Pickett killed with Denis's paperknife?"

"Ah." Grenville deflated. "I'd forgotten that point. Well, perhaps my theory is all a wash, and Denis murdered him after all."

I gathered my thoughts. "I don't believe so. When I visited Denis in Newgate, he seemed amazed at the turn of events— amazed for Denis, that is. He'd never met Pickett, had no idea what Pickett meant to ask from him, and had no concern when the man didn't arrive at his appointed time. Also, I cannot envision Denis assisting the Cato Street conspirators, in case you form the notion they'd hired him to kill Pickett. I doubt Denis would benefit by overturning the government or even be interested in doing such a thing."

"Mm." Grenville's enthusiasm dimmed. "Then, we must return to who could have entered Denis's house and stolen his knife. Or—here's a thought. The theft of the knife and the murder have nothing to do with each other. One of Denis's lackeys takes the knife, which he believes Denis will never miss, but drops it in the street when he leaves the house. When Pickett is cornered, one of the murderers spies it, scoops it up, and uses it to do the deed. The weapon will never be traced back to them."

"A rather unlikely coincidence," I said. "Though it would be a convenient solution."

"I am grasping at straws, I know. But it must be one or the other, Lacey. Either conspirators killed Pickett to keep him from giving the magistrates further information, or Denis did it for reasons of his own."

"Or Gibbons or Stout, who were both in the house at the time, committed the deed," I said. "Whether they meant to land Denis in it or not, I can't say."

I returned to the four letters I'd found with the diary. All were notices from merchants asking for payment. One, a furniture maker, had dunned him twice. Aristocrats and high-placed gentlemen like Grenville didn't receive requests to pay their accounts, but those in Pickett's rank did.

I tucked the letters inside the diary and slid everything into my pocket. "We can speculate all we like, but we need evidence if I am to clear Denis of this charge. Spendlove will be collecting proof like mad. He wants this conviction—it will be the pinnacle of his career."

"Mr. Spendlove is rather like a dog after a bone," Grenville agreed. "Let us hie to the Fox Run at eight and lie in wait for Mr. Cudgeon. He will recognize me, but I will act amazed at the chance meeting. I shall engage him in conversation about shooters and try to bring things around to Pickett."

"If he even turns up," I said. "He must have read of Pickett's death by now. You saw it in a broadsheet only hours after the occurrence." I imagined journalists had been quite excited by both a gruesome murder and the name of James Denis connected to it.

"A chance we must take," Grenville said.

There was nothing more to find in Mr. Pickett's lodgings. His clothes, as Grenville indicated, were those expected from a man with modest means and not extravagant ones. I found no evidence of whatever good fortune Pickett had mentioned in his letter to Denis, the house in Bedfordshire notwithstanding. Apart from the dunning notices and the journal in the bedside table, there were no more personal papers.

We made certain we'd left the chambers neat, went back downstairs to the club to thank Mr. Hawes, who again gave all his attention to Grenville, and departed.

———

I directed the hackney to South Audley Street, where I'd descend before Grenville continued home. We agreed to meet at half past seven at the Fox Run tavern and wait for Cudgeon to show himself at eight.

Grenville also promised he'd arrange for me to speak to the Honorable Mr. Haywood, Denis's guest in Seven Dials last night, as well as to Langley, his friend who'd brought Pickett to Tattersalls.

As the hackney rattled away toward Grosvenor Square, Brewster descended the outside stairs to the kitchen, and I entered the house that was now my home. It was past five in the afternoon, and I wanted to see my family for some of the day at least.

Therefore, I was very pleased to see Gabriella gliding down the stairs to me as I divested myself of hat and coat. I nearly smothered her in an embrace when she came off the stairs, and she laughed.

"Are you all right, Father?" she asked. "Bartholomew said you hied off somewhere with Mr. Grenville."

"Bartholomew was correct." I drew Gabriella to sit with me on a padded bench in the lower hall. Above us hung a painting of a clear carafe of water and a plate of lemons so bright I could taste them. "I will be off again with Grenville in a few hours. But I will happily escort you later this evening to … wherever we are going."

Gabriella, the child whose absence had left a hole in my life for many years, laughed again, warming me through. I hadn't quite forgiven her mother yet for taking her away from me.

"The opera first, then a ball at the assembly rooms in Duke Street," Gabriella told me. "Lady Aline says those rooms are much more entertaining than Almack's, with far better libations."

I smiled, hearing Lady Aline's voicing this opinion in her decided tones. "Then we will enjoy the rooms in Duke Street, where you will no doubt dance. But only with young gentlemen who are respectful to you," I finished with fatherly severity.

"I will not dance at all, not without Emile here." Gabriella's confidence of Emile's commitment to her sent a small ache through my heart.

There was nothing actually wrong with Emile Devere, Gabriella's intended, I repeatedly told myself. He'd been uncomfortable speaking to me alone when he'd visited us in Grenville's villa outside Rome, but I granted this was mostly because he was not very fluent in English. I spoke passable French, though I was unfamiliar with his dialect. Gabriella sometimes had to translate between us, which meant I could not ask Emile pointed questions I did not want Gabriella to hear.

Young Emile currently worked for his father in the family's metal works in Lyon, which he would eventually inherit. The factory was small and turned out such things as a village black-smith might—nails, horseshoes, carriage and wagon parts—though on a larger scale.

It sounded interesting to me, truth to tell, and I hoped to see the ironworks when I found myself in Lyon.

Emile was deferential to me and blatantly fond of Gabriella, but I chafed against the day he'd take her away from me entirely.

Gabriella declared they'd visit us often, or I could travel to them. However, I knew that once Gabriella became Madame Devere, running her own household and raising her children, she'd have increasingly less time for her old father living far away in England. Her mother and stepfather would be there to watch every minute of her life, while I would have only snippets in letters and brief visits.

I could not help but wish she'd have chosen one of the young men Donata and Lady Aline had picked out for her before she'd announced her preference for Emile. Then she'd live in one of the large houses nearby, and I could see her every day if she liked.

This was selfish of me, because Gabriella should be allowed her happiness. If she'd grown up with me, if I'd had as much time with her as I'd liked, I might more graciously let her go. Or so I believed.

I was saved from my dismal thoughts by a screech high above—our house was never quiet for long. My youngest daughter had begun to cry, and her wails quickly escalated to screams. Doors slammed on an upper floor as maids hurried to calm her.

Gabriella and I both rose, making our way in mutual agreement for the stairs.

"Anne is awake, it seems," I said lightly as I led the way up.

"Indeed," Gabriella answered with good humor.

"I suppose you believe we spoil her rotten. Perhaps *I* do, but Donata does not hold with such things. Unfortunately, Anne has the Lacey temperament and vigorous constitution."

"Not unfortunate," Gabriella said. "I have younger brothers and a sister, remember. They have always been quite loud, and when we were young, poor Mama had no idea what to do with them."

Mama was Carlotta, my erstwhile wife. After Carlotta had left me, she'd borne the French officer she'd run away with three more children. Gabriella always spoke of her siblings— and her stepfather, Major Auberge—with great fondness. Whatever mistakes her collective parents had made in their lives, Gabriella had no bitterness toward any of us.

We continued the climb to the top of the house and entered the nursery. Though the day outside was gloomy, this room glowed with light and warmth. The nanny, Mrs. McGowan, had lifted Anne from her cot, instructing her to please be quiet before she shattered the windows.

Anne caught sight of me. "Papa!" she shouted.

"There's my girl." As I reached for her, Anne squirmed mightily in Mrs. McGowan's grip and launched herself at me.

I caught her without mishap, and Anne began a loud, babbled conversation in unintelligible words.

"Is that so?" I asked her, my eyes wide. "How remarkable."

"She needs to be dressed, Captain," Mrs. McGowan said with disapproval.

Anne wore a nightgown covered by a warm wrapper with a woolly cap to keep the cold from her downy head. At Mrs. McGowan's pronouncement, she bellowed another word she'd recently learned. "No!"

"I'm dressed." Gabriella spun once to show Anne her muslin gown in soft yellow. "Let us find you a frock like mine."

"Yes!" Anne agreed at the top of her voice. She abandoned me, now lunging for her beloved sister. "Gabba."

Gabriella took her without dismay and carried her into the nursery's dressing room, Anne continuing her wordless observations.

"She will be a handful," Mrs. McGowan warned.

She already was, but I preferred for Anne to remain strong-willed and knowing her own mind, so she'd not be cowed by whoever tried to control her later in her life.

Gabriella had Anne quieted now, so I thanked Mrs. McGowan and descended the stairs. I heard Donata's tones floating from her own dressing room, where she instructed her lady's maid and assistants which gown to bring out, and no, not those slippers with that shawl.

I continued past without interrupting these dangerous tasks and took myself downstairs to the library. There, I opened Pickett's diary and went through his appointments, paying particular attention to the previous month.

Grenville might have the right of it, that someone in one of these damnable societies had feared Pickett would tell the wrong person the wrong thing, and so silenced him forever.

Perhaps more gentlemen in Pickett's group had been involved with the Cato Street men and wanted no further attention drawn to them.

I took out a small notebook I'd purchased to jot my notes in and listed the possibilities Grenville and I had pondered.

The door opened deferentially, and Bartholomew's fair head poked around it.

"Captain?" He sounded hesitant, as though fearing he'd interrupt something of great importance.

"Come in, Bartholomew. I am hardly penning a masterpiece of world literature."

Bartholomew grinned. He approached the desk with his usual briskness, holding a small, folded letter between his fingertips.

"Thought you'd like to know, sir. I took the letter to Mrs. Beltan's as you asked. There's been a reply."

CHAPTER 11

"So soon?" I asked to hide my eagerness—I'd only sent him off a few hours ago. "Did you wait there for it?"

"No, sir. I told Mrs. Beltan to forward any response to the house and came on home. The lad she hires for errands brought it to the kitchen door just now. I thought you'd want to see it right away."

I did. "An excellent thought. Thank you, Bartholomew." I took the letter from him, pretending I wasn't impatient to read it.

"No trouble, Captain. I'd been missing Mrs. Beltan's scones." Bartholomew sighed in nostalgia for the nights he'd spent in the cold attic at the top of that house. "She gave me a dozen. Only charged me for six."

"Kind of her." I noted that the practical-minded Mrs. Beltan had not given him all twelve for nothing. "I too miss her baking. She has a good heart and talented hands."

"As you say, though Lady B's cook is a fine one too. I've gained a stone since we moved here, I think."

Bartholomew patted his firm and youthfully slim belly, bade

me a cheerful good evening, and departed to go about his duties.

I quickly broke the plain seal on the letter and opened it to find that Lady had written her response beneath my note to her.

I was pleased to receive your very kind reply, Captain, and happy that you remember me. If you can speak with me tomorrow at Mrs. Beltan's shop, I will make my way there at two o'clock. I realize you must be a very busy man these days, so there is no need to reply to this letter. I will await you there tomorrow, and at two o'clock all days after that for a week. If you discover you cannot find the time, then I will cease bothering you.

I remain, as always, in respect,

Lady

I set aside the letter and made a note in my book—*two o'clock, Mrs. Beltan's bakeshop.* I was quite curious to learn what Lady had to say and would make certain I arrived at the appointed time.

I noticed in Lady's letters her full knowledge that I'd married into a prominent family who'd dragged me into their whirl. I also heard the undercurrent of humor that had underlain her tone whenever she'd spoken to me at the lying-in house.

Again, I wondered who the blackguard was who'd brought her to that sad place. Courageous of her to lay the blame on herself, but if I ever found the man who'd ruined her, I'd take him apart.

———

AT HALF PAST SEVEN GRENVILLE AND I, ACCOMPANIED BY Brewster, seated ourselves in the Fox Run tavern and accepted pints of mediocre ale from the proprietor.

Brewster took a noisy sip, made a face, and placed his tankard on the table. He wiped his mouth but said nothing, keeping an eye on who came and went through the door.

Busy Piccadilly arced between Hyde Park Corner to Haymarket, skirting Mayfair and St. James's. This tavern, almost exactly in the middle of the arc, attracted gentlemen who took rooms nearby as well as those who worked for such gentlemen. About half the patrons were men in coachman's livery or servants taking their day out, the other half well-dressed gents seeking a meal or a drink.

Most of the conversations I could hear were of sport, mostly racing and boxing, and the money to be made—or lost—betting in each. One gentleman moaned he'd wagered a monkey on a steed who'd sauntered in dead last on a point-to-point.

"All but sat down and quit at the final hedge," he said, to the amusement of his friends. "Rider should have put barbs under his tail or at least sharpened his spurs. Finally, the beast decided to hop over and trot in, looking delighted he'd lost me my little all."

His unsympathetic friends roared with laughter, slapped him on the back, and ordered more ale.

"Sharpen his spurs," I repeated in disgust. "Barbs under the tail. If he tries any of that on a horse, I'll demonstrate exactly how it feels."

"He is speaking figuratively, I'm certain," Grenville said soothingly. "A man upset he lost his cash."

I took another sip of lukewarm ale to contain myself. I was here to find out more about Mr. Pickett and why he should be murdered, not explain the compassionate care of horses to idiots.

The time ticked past, Grenville checking his pocket watch more often than need be. The racing lovers trailed off into general discussion, and I made myself cease listening to them.

Eight o'clock came and went. I began pulling out my watch as often as Grenville. Brewster sat like a stone, as though prepared to wait all night.

"Well," Grenville said at half past eight. "I suppose this was a wasted errand. I thought it better to meet Mr. Cudgeon as if by chance, but I can always make an appointment with him and pretend I need a new fowling piece. My huntsman usually takes care of that, however, and Cudgeon knows it."

"I could make the appointment," I suggested. "With you to recommend me."

"You have a huntsman yourself," Brewster interrupted to inform me. "In his young lordship's big house in Hampshire."

I had known that, but I didn't consider Peter's properties under my command.

"But I am a boorish lout, and wish to purchase a shooter of my own," I appended.

Grenville grinned at me, then he quickly set down the ale he'd raised to his lips. "Hang on. I believe this is our man."

A large fellow had pushed his way inside, his round belly proceeding him into the room. He had a fringe of lank gray hair under a fashionably tall hat, which covered a large bare spot, I saw when he removed his headgear. A well-tailored greatcoat flowed from broad shoulders to breeches and top boots.

The man had a round face, a bulbous nose, and a wide mouth that stretched into a smile as he loudly greeted the proprietor. The proprietor, seemingly used to him, waved him to a table, a pint of ale already in his hands.

Grenville rose, and as though he had no intention at all of encountering Mr. Cudgeon, sauntered between the close-packed tables. His gait conveyed he might mean to speak to the pretty barmaid or perhaps engage someone he'd spotted in conversation.

As Brewster and I watched, Grenville artfully bumped against Mr. Cudgeon's broad back.

"I do beg your pardon, sir," Grenville exclaimed. "Why, good heavens, aren't you Cudgeon, the gunsmith?"

Cudgeon, who'd turned abruptly when Grenville had run

into him, softened into an expression of delight. "Mr. Grenville. What an honor to see you."

"Hardly an honor to be barreled into by me," Grenville said with a light laugh. "Terribly sorry, old chap. I always have a hundred things on my mind." He delivered the apology in the languid tones of one who did as little as possible all day.

"Not at all, not at all." Cudgeon gave Grenville a small bow. "Please join me, sir. Let me stand you an ale. It would be my pleasure."

"How kind." Grenville gave him a gracious nod. "I'm with a friend, however. I couldn't possibly impose on you."

"No imposition in the least. Is this the captain I have heard so much about?"

I had risen when I heard the direction of the conversation. Brewster, whom Cudgeon assumed was a servant, remained where he was, watchful.

Grenville indicated me with a leisurely gesture as I approached. "Captain Gabriel Lacey. Lacey, this is Mr. Cudgeon, who makes the finest shooters in all of England."

Cudgeon flushed and made a gesture of protest, but I could see he thought the epithet his due.

"Well met, Captain Lacey." Cudgeon stuck out a hand. I shook it, finding his grip firm. "Let us sit."

Cudgeon indicated a table in the front of the room, where all would be certain to see us. It wouldn't do Cudgeon's business any harm for the story that he'd drunk ale with Lucius Grenville to be repeated about Town.

We sat. The proprietor brought more ale, and we sipped companionably. Before I could decide how to bring the conversation around to Mr. Pickett, Cudgeon wiped a dribble of foam from his mouth and saved me the trouble.

"Was to have met a chap here tonight, a client. But the poor fellow was murdered, can you believe it? Stabbed as he walked along a London street. What sad pass have we come to?"

Grenville leaned forward, exuding sympathy and shock. "Oh, dear. How awful. Was he a good friend?"

"Eh? No, no, I barely knew the man. We spoke together, of course, while I was filling his orders. From a village in Bedfordshire, I believe—Something-on-the-Something-or-Other. Stayed in St. James's, I believe, when he was in town."

"Do you know, I believe I read of that today," Grenville said with a guileless air. "Cut down in Seven Dials, I understand. But you know what that district is like. A Mr. … Pickett, his name was? Good Lord. And he was a client of yours. How fortunate you weren't with him at the time."

"Would I had been, Mr. Grenville." Cudgeon shook his head sadly. "Would I had been. I'd have gone at those chaps with a stout stick. I daresay you would have as well, eh, Captain?"

"Indeed." I patted my walking stick. "I keep a blade at my side at all times. London is sometimes more dangerous than the battlefield."

Grenville sent me a glance that told me I was laying it on thick, and I lifted my tankard, finished with my speech.

"Ill luck for you too." Grenville oozed solicitude. "Terrible thing for *him*, but now you've lost a client. Never good for a businessman."

Cudgeon lifted his large shoulders. "He'd recently given me a down payment for an order—six new birding guns and three pistols. He said the shooting in his area was good, and he was hosting friends to take a brace of pigeons or grouse in the autumn."

"I suppose you were meeting him here tonight to deliver the weapons?" I asked.

Cudgeon tried and failed to conceal that he thought me a simpleton. "I'd hardly deliver them in a tavern." He eased the words with an indulgent smile. "Pickett was going to bring me the final payment this evening, then I'd have the guns delivered to his house in Bedfordshire."

I watched Cudgeon carefully, but he seemed to have nothing more on his mind than sorrow that a man had been killed and regret that the he'd not receive the last payment for an order beforehand. He betrayed little worry about why Pickett had wanted so many weapons.

On the other hand, Cudgeon was good at not letting me look into his eyes. Such a thing *could* mean he was guilty of providing weapons to a band of conspirators. Or, it could mean he'd learned through years of selling to the aristocracy how to be courteous but remain at arm's length.

Grenville commiserated with Cudgeon for a bit, both of them appalled at how dangerous it was for a man to simply walk home of an evening.

"But he wasn't walking home," I pointed out. "He was in Seven Dials, and he lodges in St. James's. Why did he go to that part of London, I wonder?"

Cudgeon shrugged. "He might have had another appointment."

"Why in Seven Dials?" I persisted. "A terribly dangerous area, I've heard. He must have known no good could come of that. Though if he wasn't a London man, I imagine he simply lost his way."

Cudgeon 's conviction that I was an empty-headed oaf increased. "Possibly. But where a man walks in London is his business, isn't it? Or ought to be." His tone said I should keep further speculation to myself.

"Exactly." I nodded, as though I thought Cudgeon wise. "He should go where he likes and not be stabbed to death for it."

Cudgeon lifted his brows. "Quite."

I subsided. Cudgeon and Grenville left off speaking about Pickett and began a discussion of firearms. Grenville proved he knew much more about weapons and shooting than I had previously been aware. He'd told me that his hunting master was in charge of acquiring his fowling pieces, but apparently,

Grenville could take them apart and put them back together himself when he had a mind to.

I realized Grenville had expertise filed away that he didn't boast of. He brought out these skills when necessary and kept silent when they were not. Very likely another reason so many people admired him.

Cudgeon settled in to enjoy his conversation with Grenville, happy with the company. At half past nine, Grenville, seeing that Cudgeon could likely talk all night, rose with every show of reluctance, and explained that we had more engagements that evening.

"Indeed." Cudgeon launched himself to his feet with surprising speed. "An important gent such as yourself must have a dozen invitations to answer. So kind of you to share a pint with me, Mr. Grenville."

"Not at all," Grenville said. "Perhaps our paths will cross here again one evening."

"I'd be gratified if they did." Cudgeon pumped Grenville's hand in an enthusiastic handshake, then belatedly realized he should shake mine as well. He released me much more quickly than he had Grenville and saluted us with his empty glass.

Grenville and I then exited the Fox Run, Brewster draining the last of his ale before slipping out behind us.

"Well, Lacey, do we believe Cudgeon's our murderer?" Grenville asked once we were in a hackney, heading back to South Audley Street. "He betrayed little concern about what Pickett intended for the weapons and took his story of wanting them for the grouse season at face value. Likewise, he showed no fear that the man's death was any way connected to him."

"Is Cudgeon a good liar?" I mused. "Or simply a businessman shocked at Pickett's death? What happens to Pickett's down payment, I wonder? Does Cudgeon return it to the family, or will he consider it his because he fulfilled the order, even if it wasn't delivered. Is it enough money to kill a man for?"

"Who knows?" Grenville shook his head. "I'm afraid this is a tricky one, Lacey. Pickett's murder *must* have been done by a footpad and is nothing more complex. Perhaps this footpad broke into Denis's house and managed to steal only the knife before he heard someone coming and fled. Pickett, on his way to visit Denis, sees the burglar, they tussle, and Pickett is stabbed. Knife left in the wound in the footpad's haste to get away."

"It's as possible as any other solution," I said tiredly. "Except I saw Pickett's body. He did not struggle. He was killed swiftly, was probably dead before he even realized it."

"That would be a mercy for him. I didn't know the chap well, but I feel sorry for him. Pickett stepped into something he didn't intend to and was killed for his pains."

Grenville's description of Pickett evoked pathos. Then again, Pickett had conducted himself recklessly, in my opinion, which had done nothing more than get himself killed and send Denis straight into Spendlove's clutches.

"What do you propose now?" Grenville asked. "I suppose we could go to whatever village Pickett was from in Bedfordshire and find out more about him."

"I think we can discover things closer to home." I leaned my hands on my walking stick. "I believe it is time, my friend, that you introduced me to one of your secret societies."

CHAPTER 12

*G*renville regarded me in vast surprise. "My dear fellow, have you run mad?"

"What better way to discover whether Pickett was truly involved in some sort of conspiracy?" I asked in a reasonable manner. "Let us suppose for a moment that someone did not want him talking about the guns and who he'd purchased them for. Was it the Cato Street men? Or a person connected to them? I must begin *somewhere*."

Grenville conceded this. "As I told you, most people belong to several. We will have to attend meetings until we find a group that contains gentlemen who knew Pickett." He did not seem delighted at the prospect.

"Is it so dangerous?" I grimaced when the hackney hit a solid bump. "The way you describe these societies, they sound rather benign. Perhaps Pickett simply met gentlemen in his who were more serious."

"Not so much dangerous as tedious," Grenville said. "You will soon tire of the discussion and be none the wiser about Pickett's connections."

"It is worth a try. Spendlove will have Denis for this, and I refuse to let him go down for something he didn't do." I lifted a hand. "Before you remind me how willing I was in the past to see the man arrested, Denis has saved my life, yours, and my wife's on numerous occasions. Besides, I know in my bones he did not commit this crime. Denis fears I will get in the way if I investigate—rightly so, I imagine—but I can't leave it to chance and Spendlove."

"I do agree with you, my dear fellow," Grenville said as soon as he could break in. "If any meetings are still going, I'll take you to them, never worry."

"Forgive me." I realized I'd slid to the edge of the seat in my agitation, and made myself relax. "This problem is confounding me."

"I do not blame you for your frustration. It is true that Denis has done us both good turns, more than once, and I also do not wish to see him sent down for this murder." Grenville huffed a short laugh. "Even if his butler is rude to me."

"Gibbons is not known for his courtesy," I agreed, and we shared a moment of amusement.

The conversation ended when the hackney stopped in front of my front door in South Audley Street. Grenville had his own social schedule with Marianne this evening, so he let me off by myself. I bade him a good night, and the hackney rolled away.

Rain had returned, and with it, fog. Nowhere in this fog did I see Brewster, and I hadn't noticed him climb down from the hackney.

I was not left to puzzle long. Brewster appeared on foot from the direction of Grosvenor Chapel, his form breaking through the mists.

"Thought I'd stay and keep an eye on the Cudgeon gent," Brewster said by way of explanation.

"Good thinking." I signaled to the footman who was about to open the front door to keep it closed for a moment. "Did he do anything interesting?"

Brewster shrugged. "Drank a bit of ale, then got up and walked over to another table of gents, merchant class like himself. He joined them, but they didn't do much. Talking and laughing like friends, no one very serious."

"No meeting with fellow conspirators then," I said.

"Boasting to each other, from what I could hear, about how much money they've been making in their various trades. Cudgeon gave himself airs because Mr. Grenville joined him for an ale." Cudgeon would milk the connection as much as he could, I knew.

A gust of wind swirled the mists, and we turned to the door, ready for warmth and shelter.

Footsteps burst along the cobbles as a man dodged around a carriage and came straight at me, a blade gleaming in his hand.

Brewster shoved me unceremoniously out of the way. I tripped on the step to my own house and grabbed at the railing, but fell like a sack of logs in front of the door. Brewster grappled with the assailant, twisting the man's arm until his knife clattered to the pavement.

The man writhed like a demon, quickly breaking Brewster's hold. He didn't lunge for the knife but sprang out of Brewster's reach.

"Keep yourself home and out of this business," the stranger snarled at me before he fled into the fog.

Brewster was after him before the words died away, bootsteps loud on the cobblestones.

The door had opened behind me, and the footman and Bartholomew hurried out to help me stand.

"Who the devil was that, sir?" Bartholomew demanded in indignation. "Want me to go after him, Captain?"

"No need." I steadied myself once I was on my feet and reached down to scoop up the knife. It was plain, with a leather-wrapped handle. I slid it into my pocket. "Brewster will know how to deal with him."

Bartholomew and the footman got me inside, and the footman shut the door. The light and comfort of Donata's home embraced me, and I let out a breath of relief.

I worried a bit for Brewster but reasoned he knew how to look after himself. I could only wait for his return.

The upper floors of the house were a flurry of activity, as maids and footmen prepared for the ladies of the house to leave for the evening. I ducked into my chamber to stay out of their way and let Bartholomew help me from my muddy coat and trousers. The assailant had torn my coat sleeve, which Bartholomew tutted over.

On went another suit, this one more formal. Bartholomew brushed my boots while I strove to regain my equilibrium.

"Grenville has decided colored cravats will be the next fashion," I told him, groping for a lighthearted topic. "At least, they will be once London sees him in one tonight. Do *not* rush out and purchase me colored linen," I said as Bartholomew drew an eager breath. "It is merely an observation. I will continue with white."

"Of course, sir," Bartholomew said, pretending not to be disappointed.

Brewster had returned, thankfully, by the time I descended the stairs to meet my wife and daughter, who waited at the front door. He came up from the backstairs, and I headed to him while Donata and Gabriella watched me in curiosity.

Brewster shook his head as I approached. "He got away from me. Didn't recognize him. Sorry, guv."

"Funnily enough, I'd rather you *didn't* catch a man ready to cut into us," I said admonishingly. "He might have had another knife." I pulled the one I'd found in the street from my coat pocket, where I'd transferred it when I'd changed. "Do you recognize that?"

By Brewster's stillness, I decided he did. "Not this one in particular," he said. "But let me keep it."

He'd pried the knife so firmly from my hand I hadn't much choice but to relinquish it to him.

I left him to join the ladies, waving them out to the carriage that had reached the doorstep.

Donata had covered herself from the rain with a long dark cloak and voluminous hood. Two footmen held a canopy over her head, so that not one drop of water touched her ladyship from doorstep to carriage. Gabriella followed under the same canopy, her cloak almost as encompassing. I ducked after them.

I took the rear-facing seat once I was assisted inside, gazing across at Donata and Gabriella. The coach jerked forward as soon as the footman slammed its door, carrying us into the night.

"I vow, no gentleman is escorting two more beautiful ladies than I am this evening," I told them. I meant it—I was quite proud of my elegant wife, and Gabriella had become so pretty it was heartbreaking.

Neither of them appeared to be impressed by my observation. "Well, Gabriel?" Donata asked crisply. "What were you whispering about with Mr. Brewster?"

"And who nearly stabbed you at the front door?" Gabriella burst out. "Bartholomew told me all about it, so you needn't pretend nothing happened."

Other gentlemen might protect their ladies from sordid tales of their adventures, but I knew it was fruitless to keep silent. I described the incident in the street then continued with the story of meeting Mr. Cudgeon with Grenville. I included all Cudgeon had said—or didn't say.

"Mr. Brewster recognized the knife?" Donata asked.

"Thought he did," I amended.

"Mr. Brewster is perceptive." Donata gave me a decided nod. "It means he has some idea who the culprit is. Mr. Pickett's killer, perhaps?"

"Not very likely," Gabriella broke in before I could answer.

"The man who killed Mr. Pickett followed him to a quiet and dangerous area. He didn't try to stab him on a crowded road in Mayfair."

I listened in consternation. "You two are an alarming pair. Have you been discussing murder as you dressed for the opera?"

"We are naturally interested, Father," Gabriella said. "I am not an insipid miss who needs to be sheltered from the world."

She did need shelter, but I agreed that she was no fool. "I believe you have the right of it," I said. "I doubt he was Pickett's killer. He meant to warn me off, but he had to know Brewster would never let him near me."

"A friend of the murderer's then?" Gabriella suggested.

"I will reserve judgment until I hear what Brewster discovers," I said. "Now, may we speak of more pleasant things? How was your day with Lady Aline, Gabriella?"

Gabriella knew when she was being checked, but her eyes shone with enthusiasm as she described the apothecaries' gardens she and Lady Aline had visited in Chelsea, which contained healing plants from the world over. That led to talk of travel in general, Gabriella recalling how much she'd enjoyed Rome. She hoped we could make another such journey, and I absorbed the joy that she spoke easily of traveling with me again.

I was so enjoying our discussion that I was sorry when we reached Covent Garden. The two ladies eagerly descended, I more reluctantly, then I escorted them upstairs to Donata's box.

"I have a matter to discuss with you," I whispered to Donata as I seated her. Gabriella had moved to the front row, and we were relatively alone for the moment. "But later."

Donata sent me a steely gaze. "You do like to tease, Gabriel."

"It is nothing very dreadful, I assure you." At least, I hoped it would not be.

Donata could say nothing more, as the opera had already begun and her friends were storming in to speak with her. I made my way to Gabriella in the first row of chairs and we both focused on the performers.

Lady Aline soon arrived in a bulk of rustling silks and waving feathers. Gabriella, who'd become very fond of Lady Aline, jumped up to meet her and guided her to a chair near mine.

"Thank you, dear girl. You are a credit to your papa." Lady Aline huffed as she settled herself. "Lacey, my boy, I heard you were seen running in and out of Newgate prison this morning. I vowed to all it could not have been you." She pinned me with a hard blue gaze, willing me to tell her she was right.

"Unfortunately, it is true," I said with a bow of humility. "A friend was arrested for a crime he did not commit, and I am trying to help him."

Aline's stare sharpened with interest. "Good for you. You are certain of his innocence?"

"I am. Though I seem to be one of the few who believes him." Even Gibbons had seemed annoyed he hadn't witnessed the murder and so couldn't be certain.

"You were the only one who thought your Colonel Brandon innocent of stabbing a man," Aline reminded me. "You were proved correct."

I could have had Brandon released sooner during that incident if he hadn't been such a fathead. I wondered why Denis was behaving similarly, in his own way.

As the opera wound on, I decided to seize the opportunity of mining Aline's knowledge of London society.

"Who is the Honorable Enoch Haywood?" I named the man who'd had an appointment with Denis in Seven Dials the night before the murder. "I've never met him, have I?"

"Almost certainly not." Aline lifted her fan from her lap, snapped it open, and moved it languidly in front of her face. "His brother, the Earl of Shawbury, is a bit of a recluse, only coming to Town when he must. Haywood is the ambitious one, hobnobbing like mad with those he believes will advance his political career. Grenville steers clear of him, as does Donata. So, no, you likely have not met him." Her eyes twinkled with sudden impishness. "Would you like to?"

"I should speak to him, yes," I said, trying not to sound too eager.

"Then you are in luck. He is here tonight." Aline turned to the rail of the box and vigorously waved a gloved hand. "Halloo, Haywood," she shouted across the crowd. "Come here and speak to me, lad. At once."

CHAPTER 13

a small man in a box opposite us snapped his head up at Aline's call. A look of dismay came over his face, which he quickly masked.

"It isn't necessary to bring him on the moment," I protested, but in truth, I minded not at all. I couldn't predict how long it would take Grenville to hunt down Mr. Haywood and persuade him to speak with me.

Such was Aline's power that the gentleman rose, bowed to his companions, and made his way out of his box.

Not long later, the footman who attended Donata admitted a slim man who halted, nonplussed, when he beheld the seats full of duchesses and marchionesses. The ladies turned to stare at him, a few lorgnettes rising.

I watched Haywood's annoyed bewilderment rapidly become smooth cordiality. "Good evening," he said to the assembled company. He bowed to Donata. "Mrs. Lacey."

Haywood was no doubt priding himself on giving Donata the correct form of address. Many stumbled over *Lady Brecken-ridge*, her former title, often settling on *Lady Donata*, acknowledging her as an earl's daughter. But technically, once married to me, she'd become plain Mrs. Lacey. I couldn't decide if Haywood was deriding her on her comedown or showing off his knowledge of protocol.

"Over here, Haywood." Aline motioned imperiously to him.

I'd risen when the man entered. Haywood reached out a hand when Aline introduced me to him as though he didn't mind me towering over him.

His hand was small, like his stature, but his grip was firm. Though Grenville and Downie both agreed Haywood was more likely to flee than to murder anyone, he stared at me with the determination of one who'd fought to prove his worth his entire life.

Haywood was in his mid-forties, I judged, with dark hair just thinning on top, a sharp face, and a sharper nose. He was dressed in a black frock coat, a watered silk waistcoat, and a voluminous cravat, which was glaringly white. I noted that though his clothes likely had been tailored for him last week, he avoided the excesses of some fops. His cravat was neatly tied, his collar points low, his hair combed simply. No garish cravat pins or long watch fobs marred the lines of his suit.

"Captain Lacey." Brown eyes glittered up at me in frank assessment. "Pleasant to meet you, sir."

I expected him to remark that I was Grenville's friend or make some reference to the highborn company I kept these days, but he said nothing at all. He'd known full well who I was before he'd come in here, as though he kept a dossier in his head of every person in London.

Perhaps he did. Unlike his earl older brother, who was born to his position, the Honorable Mr. Haywood had to strive to make his own living. His children would carry no courtesy title, and if the earl had plenty of offspring, Haywood's sons would move further and further from inheriting the peerage. *Shirt-sleeves to shirtsleeves in three generations* was the saying, the consequence of primogeniture.

The fact that Haywood didn't fawn over meeting a friend of the great Grenville increased my respect for him. That he'd obeyed Lady Aline's summons without hesitation did as well.

Then again, perhaps he'd learned how to say the right things to the right people at the right time, like many other successful MPs.

I gestured for him to sit, and he took the chair I'd vacated beside Lady Aline. I moved down one to sit next to him. Haywood and Aline and made polite remarks about the weather, her family and his, and what they most wished to do when they returned to the country in the summer.

Haywood behaved as though he wanted to do nothing more in the world than sit and converse with Lady Aline, but he twitched. Because of the closeness of the chairs, I felt when his heel jumped up and down, the man impatient to finish this ordeal.

"Captain Lacey wished to become acquainted with you," Aline said when the inane chatter ran out. "I will leave you to it."

She heaved herself up, obliging Haywood and me to spring to our feet once more. Gabriella began to rise to assist, but Aline waved her down. She snatched up her lorgnette and reticule and swayed past the other ladies into the small sitting room beyond the box. On stage, the soprano burst into a beautiful run of notes, tugging at the heart and pulling even the most jaded spectator's attention.

"Captain?" Haywood addressed me warily as we resumed our seats.

I bent closer to him so our words would not reach the ladies behind us. "You had an appointment with James Denis last night, I believe."

Haywood's brows snapped together. "You have appalling manners, Captain Lacey. I am not the only one who says so."

I gave him a conceding nod. "I am aware that most of London wonders why Grenville has bothered with me."

I was also aware of a flicker of fear in Haywood's eyes. His anger at my abrupt question was meant to hide it.

"My business with Mr. Denis is my own," Haywood stated.

"He was arrested this morning."

"Yes, I know. Why this is a concern of yours, I cannot imagine. Good night, sir."

Haywood began to rise, but I put a strong hand on his arm and forced him back down. "Mr. Denis is something of a friend of mine. I do not want to see him tried when I know he did not kill Mr. Pickett."

Haywood's pointed face flushed. "None of that has anything to do with me."

"I know that you met with Denis in an out-of-the-way house in the middle of the night, right before a man was killed on his doorstep."

"I met with him there because Mr. Denis understands the need for discretion. Something *you* need to learn, it seems."

"If I did not intend to be discreet, I would have simply shouted at you in the lobby," I said. "I am trying to piece together what happened. It would be in your interest to do the same, do you not think?"

"Of course it would be. I am not a fool, and I know the Runners could accuse me if they knew I'd been there. But neither do you need to interfere in a business that does not concern you."

"It concerns me when the man has done me good turns in the past."

"He has done good turns for many." Haywood's mouth hardened. "But he does not give out his favors freely—he expects something in exchange. Quite a lot of something, in fact."

Such was the manner by which Denis kept himself living well and free from pursuit. Many a prominent man in England —and likely beyond it—was indebted to him.

"Perhaps he has done you a favor you cannot pay back," I suggested. "If he dies, then you no longer owe him for it."

Sweat beaded on Haywood's upper lip. "It is never that simple."

"I agree. I imagine his death would be a disaster for many."

"I am pleased you are following along, Captain."

I bit back exasperation with his obliqueness. "At least tell me something that will help him. What did you see or hear when you were in Seven Dials? Anything might be useful."

"Nothing," Haywood growled. "I spoke with Mr. Denis in his drawing room, and our conversation was quite focused. I did not watch who passed in the street, in case a ruffian was lying in wait for the buffoon who managed to get himself killed. The murder happened early this morning anyway, long after I departed."

"True, but was there a hint of anything worrisome? Perhaps Mr. Pickett tried to approach the house while you were there. I have learned he had an appointment with Denis earlier that evening and missed it. Was he searching the street for Mr. Denis's abode, perhaps?"

"If there was a hint of anything at all, I did not note it," Haywood said impatiently. "I was more worried about my own errand—and no, I will not tell you the nature of it—than about what went on in and around Mr. Denis's home." He paused to catch his breath. "The butler is a cold fish, but I've met him several times before. Loyal to the death, I'd say. The other fellow …" He broke off. "I did not know what to make of him. Wouldn't trust him very far, I think. I hadn't seen him there before."

Stout, he meant. I thought about my encounter with that man and again wondered why Denis had not only hired him but brought Stout deeply into his confidence.

"You saw nothing outside?" I asked.

Haywood turned a sneer on me. "First, it was quite dark

when I arrived, and Mr. Denis's dour butler drew the curtains as we sat down. When I departed, it was still dark and had started to rain. Between the front door and the door to my carriage, I saw nothing. I wanted to leave that place as soon as I could."

"I am surprised your coachman would enter Seven Dials after dark," I observed.

"He was reluctant, that is true. He left me at the door and disappeared, turning up again in an hour, as I'd instructed. I imagine he found a safer place to wait the time."

"Perhaps I could speak to your coachman," I said.

Haywood's belligerence rose anew. "What the devil for?"

"He might have noted someone lurking when he drove into and out of the street. It is worth asking, anyway."

"He will have seen nothing." Haywood sprang to his feet, anger pushing aside courtesy. "I have heard that you are a stubborn lout and won't let a thing go once you have your teeth in it. The description is apt, I find."

I rose beside him. "Which is how I've helped my Runner friends arrest the correct murderers and saved those wrongly accused."

"Good God, you think much of yourself." Haywood checked his tone as the ladies, including Donata, turned heads our way. "Forgive me, sir. This whole business has upset me. I mean no insult."

His half apology was his way of preventing me from calling him out. If he'd heard that I was a stubborn lout, he'd have also heard I was a dead shot.

"Not at all," I assured him. "I am certain it has been unsettling. If you assist me, we can restore our mutual friend home, and you will have nothing more to worry you."

Haywood shot me a dark look. Denis likely had a stranglehold on this man, which neither Denis's freedom nor his death would loosen.

"Very well," Haywood said ungraciously. "I will tell my coachman to expect an army officer to interview him."

"At a convenient time for you, of course." I gave him a bow. "Send word to me at South Audley Street when he is free."

"I will do so. Good night, Captain. Mrs. Lacey." He turned to the ladies and gave them a collective bow, bidding them all farewell.

I followed Haywood from the box to the sitting room beyond, where Lady Aline reposed, sipping a glass of sherry. Haywood bowed to her with practiced deference and departed.

"Well?" Aline asked me once the footman who manned the door had shut it firmly. "Did you discover what you needed?"

I sank into the chair beside her, not ready to face any more opera at the moment. "Not really, but it was somewhat helpful. Thank you."

"Mmm." Aline took another sip of sherry. She might appear to be languid and sleepy but her gaze on me was keen. "You will tell me all later, won't you, dear boy?"

I had to assure her that, indeed, I would.

————

I STAYED WITH LADY ALINE FOR A TIME, BUT MY ENCOUNTER WITH Haywood had rendered me restless, and I soon excused myself. I left the room, winding my way downstairs and out of the opera house to the cold air on the portico outside. I often did such a thing, so no one would remark upon my absence.

Brewster materialized out of the shadows as I leaned against one of the portico's massive pillars, drawing a long breath. Covent Garden market beyond the opera house was quieter now, but plenty of people moved about the large square between me and the pleasingly simple church on the other side.

Before Brewster could say a word to me, a carriage drew close to my pillar. Several large men climbed down from its top, but Brewster so swiftly stepped in front of me that I could not see who they were.

"Go back inside, guv," Brewster ordered. "Now."

"'E just wants to talk, mate," one of the men said—to Brewster, not to me.

"Who does?" I demanded. Brewster's advice was likely sound, but my irritation at the interruption, not to mention my curiosity, kept me in place.

The carriage door opened, and a man in a wool greatcoat, calfskin breeches, boots, and a low-crowned hat stepped from it. The shade of his hair was lost in the darkness, as were the color of his eyes. Those eyes held strength, however, far more than Mr. Haywood's had.

I'd never seen him before.

"I do," the man said. "Well met, Captain Lacey." His tone was friendly, his accent that of someone who'd practiced smooth speech all his life rather than being raised to it.

"Sir." I gave him a polite nod around Brewster, who would not budge. I instinctively didn't trust this fellow with his ruffians, but I'd learned not to disdain any source of information. "Why did you wish to speak to me?"

"Name's Arthur, William Arthur." Mr. Arthur seemed unsurprised when I betrayed no recognition. "I've come to give you a bit of advice."

"You may give it," I said. "It will be up to me whether I follow it."

The man chuckled. If I'd met him in a pub, I'd think him congenial, but in the darkness of Covent Garden at midnight, surrounded by his bullies, it was a different matter.

"Let Jimmy Denis hang," Mr. Arthur said, his manner still companionable. "He's overreached himself, and he's finished. Cease trying to prove his innocence and offer him your good-byes. I promise I won't forget whatever you do in the days to come."

CHAPTER 14

I stared at the man in perplexity and growing anger. "You won't forget it?" I repeated. "Why should this inspire me to do as you ask?"

Brewster answered me before Mr. Arthur could. "Because he wants to take over. Now that Creasey is dust, once His Nibs is gone, there's none to stop Arthur."

I understood. Mr. Creasey had been one of Denis's greatest rivals, until Denis had rid the world of him very effectively. Mr. Arthur must have stepped into the void left by Creasey's removal and now wanted to continue with whatever plans he had, undeterred.

"I am pleased you believe my power to discover the true killer so formidable, Mr. Arthur," I said coolly.

Arthur never lost his friendly tone. "You have quite a reputation, Captain. Jimmy uses you often, and he is an excellent judge of character."

"But are you?" I asked.

Arthur chuckled. "I am, indeed. Which is why I warn you. If you succeed in freeing our Jimmy, I might become angry with you."

"I am not interested in your threats." I took a step forward, despite Brewster trying to prevent me. "And if you think in any way to harm my family or friends to ensure my compliance, I will make certain you regret it for the rest of your life."

Arthur's eyes widened, but the grin never left his face. "Who is making the threats now? But never you worry, Captain. My grievance is with you alone. Your wife and daughter and your gentry-cove friends have never done me a bad turn—why should I take my pique out on them? I believe in dealing directly with the person who has angered me, no one else."

This speech did not reassure me. "Your insistence makes me wonder if you didn't kill Mr. Pickett yourself, in order to incriminate Denis. Or had one of your toughs do it for you."

Another chuckle, a warm sound in the cold night. "I might have if I'd thought of it. But luck shone my way instead." Arthur touched his hat. "Well, I've said my piece. Your choice, as you say, whether you heed me. Good night, Captain."

I did not reply. In a chance beam from an open door behind me I saw that Mr. Arthur's face held the hardness of one who'd ground through a difficult life, with eyes as gray as a cloudy dawn. Behind the steady voice and agreeable manner lay a man as cold as Denis ever was. Arthur might promise he'd keep my family out of this game, but if he ever changed his mind, they'd be in dire peril.

The door shut, and the brief insight into Arthur's true nature vanished.

He nodded to me before swinging himself into the carriage once more. It rumbled away, his ruffians swarming back to the top as it went.

"Bloody hell." I released the words with fervor. "If *he* is what will follow Denis, then I will run to Newgate and drag Denis out of there at once. Or else lock myself and those I love in with him."

"He's not a good man, no," Brewster rumbled, his ire still high. "Many like him, though. Find him amiable."

"He has cultivated his guise well," I agreed. "If I'd met him in another circumstance and had no idea what sort of man he was, I might think him amiable myself. *Jimmy,* he called him. I'm certain Denis is pleased with *that.*"

Brewster unbent enough to laugh. "Arthur gives him that moniker because they was on the streets together as lads. Though Arthur is a little bit older than His Nibs."

Older, but Denis had managed to outwit Arthur in the game of power. Was the diminutive name Arthur's attempt to keep Denis in his place?

"Damnation," I said feelingly. "Now I must look over my shoulder for *him.* Exactly what Arthur is counting on, blast the man."

"You could do what he says and stay out of it," Brewster said without much optimism. "Send your wife and Miss Gabriella away to Oxfordshire."

I did want Gabriella and Donata far away from London, though I knew what answer Donata would give me.

"And let that man take over?" I demanded with a touch of incredulity. "I think not."

With this pronouncement, I marched back into the opera house, having not the least idea how I would go about relieving Denis of his predicament.

MY VISIT FROM MR. ARTHUR PUT ME OUT OF TEMPER. I COULD not sit still and watch the opera, so I paced outside of the Breckenridge box until the interval. At that point, the box emptied, Donata seeking me to escort her downstairs. We'd be going from here to the subscription ball in Duke Street.

Though I hardly was in the mood for more festivities, I did

not want to rush churlishly off home and leave my wife and daughter to the dangers of men like Mr. Arthur. My mood was not assuaged by the fact that Donata's friends piled into our carriage, though I was not unhappy to ride to the event with Lady Aline and Gabriella.

Listening to my daughter chatter about the lovely singing in the opera soothed me somewhat, and by the time we arrived in Duke Street, my temper, as well as my determination to not let Mr. Arthur intimidate me, was restored.

The assembly rooms were full, the affair lively. I tried to divert myself by speaking with those I'd come to know through Grenville and Donata, but even the topics of horseflesh or army campaigns did not engage me as usual.

Grenville arrived, though without Marianne. Our hostess, a tall duchess with much rouge on her lined face, displayed disappointment that he'd not brought his scandalous wife.

After he'd greeted all those who hurried to toady to him, Grenville presented to me a gentleman about his own age, with a mop of dark brown hair and pleasant blue eyes.

"Lacey, this is Rudolph Langley," Grenville said.

"Ah." I offered my hand to Langley, who shook it with a firm grip. "Mr. Pickett's friend."

"Mr. Pickett's acquaintance, rather," Langley corrected me. "I did not know him well, but I am so very sorry to hear of his death. He was a decent sort."

"You're one of the few I've met who knew him at all," I said. "Forgive me if I ask too many pointed questions, but I have so little information."

Langley looked surprised at my declaration, but he nodded affably. "Fire away."

"How did you meet Mr. Pickett?"

"At the races," Langley said without hesitation. "He liked a flutter, as do I. Any race meeting within a day's drive was likely to find the both of us there. We'd strike up conversation when we saw each other. We frequent Tattersall's as well—did anyway." He broke off awkwardly.

"Do you know if Mr. Pickett has any family?" I asked. "They'd need to be informed of his passing."

Langley shook his head. "From what I gathered, he was very much alone in the world, though this did not seem to weigh on him very heavily. A distant cousin of his passed away earlier this year—I think he said it was a cousin, but to be honest, I didn't pay as much attention to his ramblings as I ought. He inherited a house in Bedfordshire. Not a grand estate, he was quick to point out, but a small home. There was a mere hundred and fifty pounds to go with it, I believe, which he already spent furnishing the place. He jested about becoming lord of the manor, only a very small manor." Langley's smile wavered.

Perhaps this inheritance truly was the good fortune Pickett had declared he'd come into in his letter to Denis. For a man who lived in two small rooms to suddenly have a house at his disposal and the money for new furniture must have seemed like a windfall.

It also might explain his order of shooters from Cudgeon. The lord of the manor needed fowling pieces. However, it did not tell me why so many, and where he'd obtained the money for a deposit if he'd spent his legacy on furnishings. I recalled that two of the dunning notices I'd found in Pickett's rooms had been from a furniture maker. Had he overspent on new chairs and tables? How then, had he expected to pay Cudgeon?

"Did he have many friends?" None had come forward, but Langley might be able to confirm whether Pickett did or not.

"Not that I knew of," Langley answered. "He did tell me he'd become acquainted with a few gentlemen when he went to inspect the house in Bedfordshire. Gentlemen of the area who'd known his cousin, I believe. He was keen to impress them, poor chap."

"I told Lacey about Mr. Pickett's bizarre statement that he

was linked to the Cato Street conspirators," Grenville broke in. "Do you think there was anything in that?"

Langley's laugh was tinged with pity. "I do not see how. Perhaps he met one of them in passing one day, and then became convinced, after the arrests, that the Runners would come looking for him. If you'd met Pickett, you'd understand, Captain. He was full of grandiose statements. Always certain the next race would win him a vast sum, but it never did. He could only wager a pound here, a shilling there, nothing that would do him any good."

"Did he ever win?" I asked.

"No." Another laugh. "Well, once or twice he managed to turn his one guinea into two, and he was very pleased. I never win either." Langley gave me a wry smile. "It was one thing we had in common."

There was little more Langley could tell us about Pickett. When they'd conversed, the topic had been mostly horses and racing, or which bookmakers were trustworthy and which were to be avoided.

Our conversation then turned to riding, as all three of us were mad for it. Langley was interested in my cavalry experience, and we made a tentative agreement to meet so I could give him some instruction.

When Langley was ready to move to other guests, I thanked him, and Grenville drifted away with me.

The rooms were too crowded for a proper discussion about what I'd learned from Haywood at the opera, but I did tell Grenville I'd spoken to him.

"I am glad," Grenville said with an air of relief. "Saves me the bother of seeking him out. A rude thing to say, but Enie Haywood has one interest—himself. His coachman, on the other hand, might be the perfect source for who went into and out of Seven Dials that night."

"I hope so." I scanned the room, finding Donata in a knot of ladies, all of them speaking at once, it seemed. Langley had become engaged in conversation with several other gentlemen, his gestures subdued, as though he was unhappy about Pickett's death but determined to show nothing of it. "Langley's all right, is he?" I asked.

Grenville's brows went up. "I've known the fellow since I was a lad. We dodged bullies together at school. If you are asking if he could have killed Pickett, I suppose he is physically capable of it, but the question would be why. Langley is not hot-tempered, and he has no enmity toward anyone. Apart from our school bullies—he still doesn't like them."

"You joke, but I am open to all possibilities. Could Langley have worried about Pickett's claim of being involved with the Cato Street men?"

"Highly doubtful. Langley is refreshingly uninterested in secret societies and politics, beyond voting for his local candidate."

I nodded absently. I couldn't see amiable Mr. Langley meeting in back rooms, plotting the murder of cabinet ministers, but he might be an expert dissembler.

I could not monopolize Grenville's attention at so well-attended a gathering, and he soon was waylaid by gentlemen keen for his conversation. I noted with amusement their attention on his new cravat.

Lady Aline sought me out, declaring she was tired of the overheated venue and asked that Gabriella accompany her home. I decided to depart with them, leaving word with Jacinthe, Donata's lady's maid, that I'd gone. Donata would be well protected by Jacinthe, her coachman, and the burly footman who always tagged along to carry things for her.

We rode in Lady Aline's carriage to Berkeley Square, where I said good night to both of them—Gabriella would remain at Lady Aline's, as she often did. That lady's hours of sleeping and waking suited Gabriella more than Donata's did.

Aline directed her coach to take me home, and I swallowed my pride and accepted the offer. Though it was a short way to South Audley Street, and Brewster had ridden on the back of the coach from Manchester Square, I did not fancy meeting Mr. Arthur or his toughs in the dark rain.

I told Brewster good night when I reached the house and mounted the stairs to the upper floors. Bartholomew undressed me and helped me slide into a thick banyan, in which I settled down to wait for Donata in her dressing room. I knew she'd be quite late, and I didn't want to be fast asleep in bed when she arrived.

I did nod off in the armchair, my early morning and full day taking its toll. When Donata sailed in, I jumped awake, snorting inelegantly.

"Gabriel," my wife greeted me, dropping a kiss to the top of my head on her way to sit before her dressing table. Jacinthe immediately removed the necklace of thick diamonds from Donata's bosom and laid it carefully into a case.

Jacinthe, ignoring me as usual, assisted Donata out of her gown and into a peignoir, then unpinned and brushed out her hair. Observing the two was like watching a dance. They'd performed this ritual for so many years that they moved in perfect coordination, each playing her part, their gestures elegant.

Or, perhaps I'd dozed off again as I watched. When my vision cleared, Donata stood over me, and we were alone.

"I am pleased you arrived home without being set upon by another man with a knife," she said. "I will have to thank Mr. Brewster for that." Her voice softened as she took my hands. "I am happy you waited for me."

Donata's touch stirred warmth inside me, but I'd lingered here for a different reason. "I have things to tell you," I said.

"Ah, yes. The matter you declared you wished to discuss, and then left me hanging without a hint as to what it was. Let us find a comfortable sofa to repose on, and you can regale me with it."

She released me and moved into her bedchamber, and I heaved myself from the chair and followed.

Donata sank onto a long settee replete with pillows that faced the fireplace and waited for me to join her. I did so with pleasure, stretching my feet toward the fire's warmth.

"I had a letter today," I told her after we'd settled in. "From Lady."

I'd long ago told Donata the tale of my search for Miss Thornton and those I'd met along the way. She'd puzzled about Lady's identity with me, but neither of us had drawn any conclusions.

"Did you indeed?" she asked, her brows climbing.

"She wants to meet with me." I explained about the cryptic letter Lady had written and my reply to it. "I will speak to her tomorrow afternoon at the bakeshop and discover what she wants to tell me." I hesitated. "Would you care to accompany me?"

Donata sat back, clearly surprised by my request. Emotions warred behind her eyes before she shook her head.

"Best I do not," she said in resignation. "If this young woman is gently born, as you speculate, she might worry about me recognizing her. Even if that is not a concern for her, I am certain she will not speak freely to you if I am there." Her disappointment was obvious.

I studied the yellow heart of the flames before me. "You are likely right, but I had no intention of keeping a rendezvous with a young lady from your knowledge. I am interested in who she might be and why she's seeking my help. No other reasons."

"You do not need to reassure me, Gabriel," Donata said in a light tone. "I am not a jealous harridan."

However, she *did* grow uneasy whenever I spoke to a lady

she perceived as a threat to our happy marriage. I chose not to remark upon this.

I could not become angry at Donata's distrust, because many gentlemen in her circle took mistresses. Her own husband had most blatantly done so. It was an unusual man, in her experience, who remained faithful to his wife.

Donata slipped her hand into the crook of my arm and rested her head on my shoulder. "Go to your rendezvous with my blessing," she said. Her grip tightened. "But upon your return, you must tell me *everything*."

———

I SLEPT LATER THAN USUAL THE NEXT DAY, WHICH WAS HEAVILY overcast, clouds plus smoke from London's many chimneys blotting out the sunlight. It was difficult to haul myself from the nest of Donata's bed, leaving warmth and comfort for cold grayness.

I took my morning ride, though I was inclined not to, knowing the exercise kept my bad knee from becoming unbearably stiff. After that, I had time to consume a light midday meal —Barnstable insisted—and hire a hackney to Covent Garden for my appointment with Lady.

Donata and I had debated her coming along with me in her coach and waiting upstairs in my rooms in Grimpen Lane for the meeting to conclude. Donata had at last decided against it, stating that Lady would hardly fail to notice the Breckenridge carriage lodged in Russel Street. Besides, she concluded, she'd not be able to stop herself peering out my sitting room windows.

Hence, I found a hackney on Mount Street, and Brewster and I made our way through the gloomy afternoon to Grimpen Lane.

Brewster had not, in fact, returned home the previous night.

He did not like the idea of Arthur's ruffians lurking about and had wanted to ensure they left us well alone. None had approached the house, he'd reported, which was welcome news.

We descended together in Covent Garden and continued to the bakeshop on foot. I had arrived early, not wanting Lady to be concerned that I might not appear.

I did not glimpse her through the shop's window and decided to step upstairs to my rooms for a moment. If Lady needed a private place to speak to me, I'd bring her there, and I wanted to be certain all was tidy.

Brewster clomped upstairs ahead of me. I followed, remembering the many times I'd hauled my tired body up this staircase.

I noticed that Mrs. Beltan had made a start at replacing the faded wallpaper. Instead of shepherds and shepherdesses gazing at one another in old-fashioned garb, I looked upon a blue-green toile pattern of dizzying curlicues. I wasn't certain it was an improvement.

Brewster swung open the door to my rooms on the first landing and froze. Worried Mr. Arthur had appeared to send me another warning, I quickened my pace.

I reached the top of the stairs and peered around Brewster's bulk. "*Bloody* hell."

James Denis sat comfortably in the armchair before my flickering fireplace, an open book in his hands. At my exclamation, he looked up from his reading and gave me a nod. "Captain."

CHAPTER 15

"*D*o the jailors in Newgate know you are gone?" was the first coherent sentence that came out of my mouth.

Denis calmly marked his place in the book with a strip of paper, closed it, and set the book on the table beside him.

"They do. I was released this morning at an early hour."

"This morning?" I repeated, dumbfounded. "Could you not have sent word?"

"It was too early, even for you," Denis said. "I meant to dispatch a message through your landlady for you to meet me in these very rooms, but Mrs. Beltan indicated you had an appointment here anyway, so I decided to wait for you."

"Why here?" I demanded. Brewster still would not move, though Robbie stood guard at the window. I knew no enemy was within—that is, no enemy of Denis. "Do you fear to return home?"

Irritation flickered across Denis's face. "I have been home. For a much-needed repast and rest. I came back here to intercept you after your appointment had concluded."

Brewster finally stepped aside to allow me fully into the

room. "I am all a-flummoxed," I said. "How did you convince them of your innocence?"

"I did not. However, my barrister spoke to a High Court judge who decided there was not enough evidence to hold me in Newgate for the murder, at least for the moment. I had to give my oath I would not leave the metropolis, but otherwise I can go about my business."

"What about the inquest?" A coroner's jury might very well have decided Denis had plenty of opportunity and should be tried for the crime.

"I was not required to give evidence. The verdict returned was murder by person or persons unknown."

Meaning he had people behind the scenes to manipulate events. Any of us mere mortals would have faced a coroner's jury who were in complete agreement we should be kept imprisoned until our trial at the Old Bailey.

The coroner's verdict, however, didn't acquit Denis. The investigation would continue, and he could be arrested anew if all evidence led back to him.

"Spendlove will not like this," I said decidedly.

"Which is why I wished to speak to you. I would like you to continue looking into the matter and discover who truly killed the man."

"Do you?" My temper rose. "When I visited you in your rather comfortable quarters in Newgate, you told me plainly to leave it alone."

"I did then, yes." Denis touched his fingertips together. "It was necessary for you to keep clear until I could be released. Things were in motion I did not wish you to interrupt."

"Do I understand this aright? You already had a scheme worked out to get yourself released, and now that that this plan has come off, you expect *me* to find the correct culprit for the Runners?"

Denis nodded. "You put it bluntly, but essentially, you are correct."

"And you could not tell me this—" I ceased my rant as a woman in a large bonnet and swirling coat passed sedately in the lane below. Lady had arrived for our appointment. "You will have to excuse me, I am afraid," I said stiffly. "I have a previous engagement."

Part of me was pleased to see Denis's eyes widen with surprise. Without further word, I turned on my heel and stalked out of the room.

Brewster followed me down. I heard Denis come after him, his steps light, and then Robbie's more heavy tread. The four of us emerged, one by one, into the dank air of Grimpen Lane, where a light rain had begun to fall.

Lady had disappeared into the bakeshop. I signaled to Mrs. Beltan, who'd poked her head out, to let her know I'd be there in a moment.

"Come to Curzon Street when you are finished," Denis told me with his usual air of cool command. "I would be interested to hear what conclusions you have drawn on this problem."

I eyed him coldly. "Why do you suppose I have drawn any conclusions? You told me plainly to leave the matter alone."

"Because I understand you rather well, Captain," Denis said. "I shall—"

He broke off as his gaze became arrested by something behind me. I turned to see Lady walking toward us from the bakeshop, the brisk wind fluttering the gray ribbons of her bonnet. She halted between one step and the next, her half boot neatly avoiding a puddle on the cobblestones.

"I do beg your pardon, Captain Lacey," she said in her smooth voice. "I had thought you finished with your conversation." Lady gathered her skirts, ready to turn away. "I shall await you inside."

"It is no bother," I answered. "I will escort you."

Denis was somehow in front of me. He lifted his hand to tip his hat and then removed the hat altogether, giving her a neat bow.

"Allow me, madam." Denis offered his arm in the elegant cashmere of his greatcoat.

Lady regarded him, mystified. After one hesitant moment, she slid her fingers into the crook of his elbow.

Denis walked with her the few steps to the doorway of the bakeshop, opened its door, bowed to her again, and withdrew, settling his hat back on his head.

He turned to find the three of us—Brewster, Robbie, and myself—staring at him. Denis's brow creased the slightest bit before he walked past us in silence, heading for the mouth of the lane. Robbie jumped and lumbered after him.

Brewster dove into the bakeshop ahead of me. He accepted a steaming mug of coffee from Mrs. Beltan's assistant, thanking her graciously, before he stepped out into the lane again.

"I'll just be here, guv." He took a noisy slurp of the coffee. "Keeping an eye out."

"Thank you, Brewster. Come inside if it's too cold."

"Be fine. You watch yourself."

With that admonishment, Brewster turned away to eye the street, and I continued into the warm, baked-bread-scented shop.

Mrs. Beltan had settled Lady in the corner by the front window, her best table in the small space. A teapot, cups, and a jug of cream already reposed there. Mrs. Beltan fussed around Lady, recognizing gentility when she encountered it.

"Give me a shout if you need anything, dear," Mrs. Beltan said to her as I approached. Before she retreated, she shot me a look that said I'd answer to her if I upset Lady in any way.

Lady had untied and removed her bonnet, setting it on an

empty chair as I settled myself opposite her. "It is not the thing to remove one's headgear in a public place, I know." She poured a fragrant cup of tea, dolloping in a smidgen of cream, and pushed it to me. "But while this bonnet keeps the rain off beautifully, it is rather hard to see around, let alone drink tea in."

She handed me the cup on its saucer and then offered the plate of petit fours Mrs. Beltan had provided. "Cake, Captain Lacey?"

"Perhaps later," I said, politely demurring. "Though, I assure you, Mrs. Beltan's pastries are excellent." Her tea was not, unfortunately, but I would bear it for the sake of hearing what Lady had to say.

"The treats are enticing, I agree." Lady set down the plate and took a sip of tea, making no comment on its quality. "Now, Captain, you must be wondering what I wish to ask of you. As I said in my letter it is nothing as dire as what you have spoken of with me before—at least I hope not—but is as important to me."

I paused in the act of lifting the delicate cup, nearly lost in my hand. "Is everything all right?" I asked with concern. "Is someone threatening you?"

"Nothing like that." Lady sounded amused. "*I* am perfectly well. I remain in the house where you met me and I am, as I have indicated before, happy there. The situation quite suits me, though you do not believe it. What I am consulting you on is a more personal matter." She leaned toward me, her eyes taking on sudden and deep sadness. "I would like you to help me find my daughter."

I sat back, barely stopping myself from blurting out, *Your daughter?* in great surprise.

But of course, she'd gone to the lying-in house for the same reason the game girls did—to bear a child she'd conceived out of wedlock. The father had declined to acknowledge his deed, and her own family had either turned her out or refused to help her raise the child. A woman with no money, no family behind her, no friends, and no support could only give up her child and hope for the best.

Lady studied me with the warm brown eyes I recalled, which held shrewdness behind their softness. I set down my teacup and pitched my voice so Mrs. Beltan and her helpers in the kitchen would not hear.

"If you will forgive me asking a painful question—who took the child when you bore her?"

Lady's answer was calm—she'd mastered her emotions well. Only someone studying her closely would see her deep anguish. "I had spoken to a minister of the parish. I did not want my daughter sent to the Foundling Hospital. He agreed to find a family to foster her, and from there, he would look for someone to adopt her. He was a kindly man, and only lectured me on my sinful ways for a quarter of an hour. I was careful from whom I asked help."

Because somehow, after she was compromised, this very young woman had cultivated an astuteness that kept her from relying on the wrong people.

"Did the minister do as he'd promised?"

"He did," Lady said with approval. "Vicky went to a foster family who were a large, boisterous lot, but very caring. My daughter lived with them until she was three, then was adopted by a family in trade—they had a business importing carpets. The wife was no longer able to bear children herself, and she longed for a little girl. That was four years ago. Then recently, the husband died, quite unexpectedly, and the family has disappeared." Lady's hands tightened around her cup. "I wish to know what has become of Vicky. Not to interfere, you understand, not to try and take her back, only to know if she is well …"

She trailed off as her wretchedness finally broke through her serenity.

I took a sip of the too-bitter tea, giving her a moment to compose herself. "The name of the family?" I asked quietly.

Lady flashed me gratitude for going directly to practical matters instead of oozing unwelcome pity. "Redding. They had a shop in the Tottenham Court Road and a warehouse at the London Docks. Now the shop has other tenants, and the warehouse is deserted."

"You've learned much about the family," I said. "It was my understanding that when a woman gives up her child, she knows nothing more about them."

"That is often true." Lady resumed sipping tea, as though we discussed nothing more emotional than a library book, but her gloved fingers shook. "However, some mothers who leave their sons or daughters with the Foundling Hospital have every intention of returning for them. She'll put a memento in with the baby, such as a comb or a locket—something special to her. The theory is that this will help her recognize her child when she comes back to fetch her, or him. Unfortunately, many mothers can never return. They barely have the funds to keep themselves, let alone a child, or they realize their children are much safer under that roof. The Foundling Hospital is a grim place, but the children are fed, clothed, and taught rather than being left to starve on the streets."

Yet, she'd striven to make certain her child did not end up there. From what I understood, the orphans were trained to go into service, becoming maids and boot boys for large houses in London. I'd had occasion to pass the hospital whose gates faced Upper Guildford Street near Russell Square and agreed that the edifice was grim.

"You kept a closer eye on her than most would," I said.

Lady gave me a calm nod. "I also help those who regret their choice and wish their children returned. I have learned how to go about it, but now I am defeated." She stilled for a long moment, her gaze fixed on the spray of red roses dancing across the porcelain teapot. "It was a wrench to let her go, Captain. I knew it was for the best—at least, I convinced myself this was so. I am unable to explain what having to make the decision was like."

"My daughter was two years old when her mother deserted me and disappeared, taking Gabriella with her," I said, my tone as unemotional as she'd tried to make hers. I swallowed the profound pain of that day and continued. "I did not see Gabriella again until she was nearly eighteen. In all the time in between, I had no idea whether she was dead or alive."

"Oh, dear, I am sorry." Lady set down her cup, her unhappiness instantly turning into sympathy for me. "You told me once of your daughter, but I did not know her entire history. Then you *can* understand. Others might say it is different for men, but in my opinion, that rather depends on the man."

The bleakness from my past kicked at me. "I was devastated. But then I found her again." With effort, I shook off the memories of my fears and forlorn hopes. Denis had, in fact, discovered Gabriella's whereabouts for me and had brought her to London. Hence my determination to solve his current problem, as much as he infuriated me. "We will do the same for your daughter."

Lady flashed me a sudden smile. "Your optimism is why I sought you out, Captain Lacey. I remembered your determination and kindness when we met. I've followed your adventures with much interest in the newspapers. The journalists give Mr. Grenville a great deal of credit for bringing criminals to justice, but I know it is mostly your doing."

"Grenville's name sells more newspapers," I said without rancor. "I solve a problem because it interests me, or it aids someone who needs assistance. The newspapermen can print whatever they want."

"Exactly." Lady looked me fully in the eyes. "So, you will help me?"

"Of course." I'd decided that the instant I'd read her letter, before even knowing what the trouble was. I swallowed another sip of tea, then decided it best to set the cup aside. "What about the minister who first took your daughter? Vicky. Did you name her that?"

Another smile. "I did. Victoria, the goddess of victory. I hoped this would keep her safe in the world. The minister, to his credit, retained the name, though she was given Redding as a surname when she was adopted. The minister himself has retired from the rough streets of London to a peaceful country village in Essex."

He likely wouldn't be keeping a close eye on a child he'd adopted out years ago.

"I will start by hunting down the Redding family and see what I can learn," I stated.

"I have no intention of interfering with their raising of her," Lady said quickly. "I only want to know that she is well."

"I understand." I spoke the words reassuringly, but if I discovered that Vicky Redding was in any way unhappy, I'd take her out of the situation. Perhaps I could find some way for her and her mother to live together in comfort.

As Lady bathed me in her gratitude, I saw anew what a beautiful woman she was. Hardship, abandonment, and poverty had not destroyed her. I admired her resilience.

"I must confess something," I said, flushing. "When I first encountered you, I wanted more than anything to remove you from your situation. At the time, I had not been free to marry, but if I had been, I would have proposed it."

Lady laughed, a silvery sound. "You are gallant indeed, Captain Lacey. I think you *would* have offered, out of kindness and pity." She took a sip of tea, her cheerfulness restored. "But you love your wife, my dear friend. I see it in every line of you."

I warmed. "I do."

"Very unfashionable, but it makes me like you more. Lady

Donata Pembroke is a fine woman. She has a sharp tongue and sharper opinions, but a good heart."

"You know much about her," I said in surprise.

"I observe from the shadows." Lady sent me a glance that held a hint of mysteriousness. "I wager she is far happier with you than she was with her former husband. He was a wretch."

"That is true. I knocked him to the ground once."

Lady's laughter rang out again. "How delightful. I would have turned you down, however, if you had offered your hand. I am very proud, you see."

"And we would have starved together," I said. "I had a half-pay packet, a moldy house in Norfolk, and nothing else to my name."

"Then it is fortunate we went our separate ways."

Lady might also have refused my proposal, had I made one, because she did not wish to come out into the light. If she'd married me, there would be awkward questions about her origins, and her family might have appeared on the horizon to object, mayhap to drag her back to a home she could do better without.

Lady's gaze drifted to the window and the lane now empty of all but the pacing Brewster. "What a curious gentleman," she said thoughtfully. "The one who opened the door for me, I mean. Who is he?" She asked it with nothing but neutral interest.

I pondered what to tell her, though I had the feeling that if Lady truly wanted to know Denis's identity, she'd find a way to discover it. "His name is James Denis. He is an … acquaintance … of mine."

"Not gently born, I think. Though he has learned impeccable manners."

I halted her musings before she became too intrigued by him. "Denis is a very dangerous man, I must warn you. He was recently arrested for murder but managed to get himself released from Newgate, likely by nefarious means."

"I assumed the danger from the presence of the large man who attended him. Though I wasn't certain if *he* was in peril or caused such things himself. Did he commit the murder he was accused of?"

"I certainly wouldn't have allowed him anywhere near you if I thought he had."

Lady regarded me in quiet amusement. "You have very decided opinions of your fellow man, Captain. You are perceptive, from what I have observed, but those opinions can also blind you, I think." She set aside her teacup and lifted the plate of petit fours. "Now, shall we enjoy these cakes?"

———

DENIS WAS LONG GONE BY THE TIME WE DEPARTED THE BAKESHOP. I escorted Lady, laden now with bread and pastries courtesy of Mrs. Beltan, to Russell Street and a hackney stand. She insisted she could walk back to Holborn, but I worried that Mr. Arthur might decide she was a person to leverage me into good behavior, despite his declaration he'd leave those close to me alone. I felt better when she was rolling away in the carriage to be lost in the crush of Covent Garden.

Brewster and I returned home. Denis had requested I attend him right away, but I'd promised Donata to return to her after I met with Lady, and she would always take precedence over Denis.

I rode in the hackney in silence, lost in thought, while Brewster, who sat inside with me, kept a sharp eye on the streets around us.

Donata was not only up but dressed and waiting for me when I returned. I'd planned to seek her out in her chambers, but she pattered down the stairs to me as I began to ascend them. She forestalled any greeting, seized my arm, and marched me to the library, bidding Barnstable to fetch coffee along the way.

Once in the library, she nearly shoved me into a chair in front of the fireplace before taking the one next to me.

"Do not laugh," Donata commanded, when I had to chuckle at her eagerness. "I have been waiting an age."

It had been only a few hours, but my wife was not the most patient of women.

"Very well," I said, and launched straight into Lady's tale.

Donata listened with gratifying attentiveness, letting me relate all without interruption. Her face softened as I spoke, her wariness changing to compassion.

"The poor woman," she said feelingly when I'd finished. "Yes, you must discover what has become of the little girl. I will help any way I can."

I warmed to her instant solicitude. "I wonder if any of your charitable organizations aided the widow of Mr. Redding or her children. There are records of that sort of thing, aren't there?" I had only a vague notion of such details.

"The money we raise from our subscription balls and garden parties goes into a collective pot," Donata explained. "We use a man of business to keep account of it all and record what monies are paid out. I would be happy to consult him. Aline could inquire about her charities as well. If Mrs. Redding sold her husband's business, there should also be a record of that."

"I would love to suppose Mrs. Redding sold up and retired in wealth to the seaside, where Lady's daughter will live out her young years in idyllic bliss." I shook my head. "What I fear is Mrs. Redding's husband died a pauper, and the wife and children were forced into a workhouse."

"There would be records of that too," Donata said with a practical air. "We will locate Mrs. Redding and discover what has become of young Vicky, never you fear."

I clasped her hand and lifted it to my lips. "You always astonish me, my dear."

Donata looked pleased but tried to shrug it off. "You needn't be astonished that we ladies can cut to the heart of a matter. Nor that we are happy to chivvy others to our cause."

Before I could reply with another compliment, a discreet tap sounded on the door. This was followed by Barnstable entering with a parcel, along with a maid bearing a tray, the savory odor of the promised coffee wafting to me.

"A package has come for you, Captain," Barnstable announced. He removed the bulky parcel from under his arm and placed it on the desk.

Donata rose briskly, and I swiftly stood up beside her. "I will leave you to it, Gabriel. Set the coffee there, Joan. That will be all, thank you."

Joan calmly laid the tray on a table near the windows and arranged mug, coffee pot, sugar, sugar tongs, and small plate of sweet biscuits neatly on it before gliding away. Barnstable also faded out the door, leaving it open for Donata.

"I must dash." Donata stood on tiptoe to kiss my cheek. "One can be late for morning calls, but not *too* late. I will confer with Aline, and we will form a plan of attack."

She patted my chest and swept through the door, off to rally her troops. An amazing and resourceful lady.

I poured myself a cup of the rich coffee Donata's talented cook had brewed and turned to the package Barnstable had left on my desk. My name and address had been printed in block capitals on a card tied to the brown-paper parcel, which enclosed something soft.

I cut the string with my knife and tugged open the paper. Carefully. Incendiary devices had been delivered to this house before.

Inside, I found a bundle of clothes—a man's coat, trousers,

waistcoat, shirt, cravat, and even his small clothes. Pomeroy, true to his word, had sent me Mr. Pickett's things to look over.

I thanked him silently as I pulled out the items and spread them across the desk. I smoothed out the coat, and then paused, frowning. I ran my hands over it again, and then sat back, my heart beating faster.

"Good Lord," I whispered to myself.

CHAPTER 16

"What is it, Lacey?" Grenville demanded of me as he pushed into my library an hour later. "I received your summons and rushed over as soon as I could."

He might claim to have rushed, but he was as flawlessly garbed as ever, with an intricately tied cravat, today's a soft peach color. Now he dropped into the chair I'd reposed in when I'd told Donata of my meeting with Lady and regarded me with eager curiosity.

"The clothes are too dry," I stated, gesturing to the coat and trousers draped across my desk.

Grenville waited for me to elaborate on that grand statement, then sat up straight when nothing more was forthcoming.

"Whose clothes, for heaven's sake? And why do you believe them to be too dry?"

"I beg your pardon. They are Pickett's. Pomeroy sent them to me this afternoon. I asked if he'd mind if you had a look at them, to see if they could tell us anything about the man. That was before we went through the garments at his flat, of course." I touched the coat's fabric. Like the ones at Pickett's lodgings, it was wool of a decent weave, not the quality Grenville wore, but neither was it the coat of a working-class man.

"Ah." Grenville rose and came to the desk, his pique vanishing. He laid a hand on the coat then lifted one trouser leg and studied its hem. "I agree with you. These are remarkably dry."

"Do you see my point?" I asked, trying to stem my excitement. "Yesterday morning, it was pelting down rain. Pickett would have been soaked if he'd walked across the city to Seven Dials, or even descended from a hackney and stood before Denis's door a few minutes. After he was killed, he lay in a puddle in the street before the patrollers trundled his body off to Bow Street. You can see the marks of the puddle." I traced the discoloration around the coat's shoulders and where it would have lain across Pickett's hips. "And it is damp there. But the rest of the coat and trousers are nearly bone-dry."

"Could they not have dried out at Bow Street?" Grenville asked.

"No indeed. It is dank and cold in that house. I doubt anything would dry there in a week. These things should at least be very damp. My coat from yesterday still is from all the rain, and Barnstable has hung it by a fire in a warm house. Why isn't Pickett's?"

"Because he didn't walk in the rain." Grenville's eyes began to sparkle. "Nor took a hired coach, you believe? Didn't simply manage to stay out of the wet until he alighted in Seven Dials?"

"I think it is simpler than that." I rested my hands on the desk. "I think Pickett never left his rooms—or wherever he was at the time of his death. I think he was killed somewhere else and *then* his body was taken to Seven Dials and left on Denis's doorstep for him to find."

Grenville ran his hands over the coat once more. "You might be right, Lacey. Which would mean he was killed before the rains began. Which was when?"

"It was a fair day on Monday. I remarked upon it when I went riding that morning. It began to cloud up Monday afternoon."

"And the rains started later that evening," Grenville confirmed. "I remember because I wore a new coat, and Gautier fussed like a hen that it would become ruined. So—Pickett had gone indoors by eight o'clock on Monday night. Someone killed him and then transported him to Seven Dials, by carriage or enclosed cart presumably, so that he never got wet. This should put Denis in the clear, should it not?"

"Unless Pickett went to Curzon Street before the rain started, was murdered there by Denis, and taken to the Seven Dials house afterward. Spendlove might say that. Why Denis would do such a thing will not be taken into consideration. Therefore, we must decide exactly where Pickett was on *Monday*, not early Tuesday morning."

"Excellent." Grenville rubbed his hands together. "Let us begin."

I curbed my ebullience. "I might be wrong, of course. Pickett could have hired a watertight carriage and taken great care not to become wet between his flat and Seven Dials."

"But, as you say, he'd have been rained on rather heavily when he descended," Grenville reminded me. "I was awakened by the pounding rain far too blasted early Tuesday morning for my liking. My house has thick windows, and my chamber is nowhere near the roof, which means it was coming down hard. As there was no hackney in sight when Denis walked out of his house, that means Pickett would have been standing there for a time, waiting for whatever he'd come for. Plucking up courage to knock on the door? Or meeting someone else in the street? Either way, he'd have received a soaking. No, I believe your first conclusion is the right one. His body was carried there and arranged in front of Denis's house."

"By whom and for what purpose?" I asked in frustration. "It is a maddening question. Was it by Spendlove himself? The man is ready to do anything to bring Denis to trial."

"I am not certain Mr. Spendlove could be secretive enough," Grenville said. "He might have hired thugs to carry out the deed for him, it is true, but I imagine we could easily discover this, if so."

"Pomeroy would bully it out of any accomplice," I agreed. "And while I do not like Spendlove, he does have a fondness for the law. I do not truly think he'd go as far as murder, even if he felt it justified—for example, if Mr. Pickett *was* involved with the Cato Street Conspiracy and a traitor, Spendlove would be more likely to drag Pickett by the collar to the magistrates and wait for his reward than kill Pickett himself."

"Mmm. I am not as generous in my belief of Spendlove's character as you are but let us hold him in reserve. Do we return to Pickett's rooms?"

I seated myself behind the desk, opened the top right drawer, and pulled out Pickett's diary that I'd brought home. I flipped the pages until I reached his entries for Monday. I'd scanned them before but hadn't given any appointments before his scheduled one with Denis much thought.

"At two o'clock, he visited his bootmaker," I read. "In Finsbury Square."

Grenville lifted his brows. "I've not heard of any bootmakers in Finsbury Square. Libraries and betting shops, yes."

"Hang about—his handwriting is difficult to decipher. This might say *bookmaker*." I raised my brows. "That puts a different spin on things."

"Indeed it does, as we know Pickett liked to wager on horses. We shall have to see what this bookmaker says. Anything else?"

I closed the diary. "I return to the valuable insight we might gain in one of your secret societies."

"Yes, I meant to tell you before I was distracted by the intriguing question of Mr. Pickett's clothing. I arranged an invitation to a meeting rather late tonight. I warn you not to expect too much. These things are more often an excuse to drink excessively than to plot to overthrow kingdoms."

"But one of the members might have joined Pickett in a society a little more dangerous than yours."

Grenville made a conceding gesture. "Will you tell Spendlove your new idea? About Pickett being murdered elsewhere, I mean."

"I want to be more certain first. Again, Spendlove might simply conclude Denis himself killed Pickett elsewhere, though why Denis should have the man dumped in front of another house owned by him, I do not know." I scrubbed a hand through my hair. "This is confounding me. Now that Denis is a free man —for now—he expects me to solve the crime immediately."

"Free man?" Grenville stared at me. "What do you mean, a free man?"

I had not included this detail in my hastily scribbled note summoning Grenville here. "He managed to be released from Newgate, somehow. I only just learned this myself a few hours ago."

"Good Lord," Grenville said feelingly. "I actually pitied him, shut up in that insalubrious prison and certain to hang."

"He bade me come to him in Curzon Street as soon as I reached home, but I had a more pressing appointment. With my wife," I added as Grenville sent me a quizzical glance. "I wanted to report to her. She is the regimental sergeant-major, after all."

My lightness of tone made Grenville smile and cease his questions, which is what I'd intended.

I did not wish to reveal Lady's request for me to help find her daughter—I doubted she would want someone as well-known as Grenville in her business. Not because Grenville could not be discreet, but because journalists remarked upon his every move. Hence, his name was blazoned from pages about our investigations. He might not be able to keep Lady's business private as much as he wished to. Everyone in London knew exactly what Lucius Grenville was up to every day.

"Let us adjourn to Curzon Street," I suggested. "I will try to pry any information I can from Denis, then we will attend your meeting tonight and bring the conversation around to Pickett."

"I am willing to wager none have ever heard of Mr. Pickett," Grenville said. "Why don't you visit Denis on your own? I have plenty to do, and I refuse to kick my heels in his downstairs hall because his butler will not let me up to speak to his highness."

This disappointed me—Grenville often asked astute questions, and his presence had a calming effect on my impatience. However, I took his point. He had no reason to sit idly and wait for me.

"Very well, I will tell you what I learn later this evening. I have forgotten what outings I'll be attending tonight with my ladies, but I imagine I will see you at one of them."

"You will be at Lady Radcliffe's soiree," Grenville said. "Which I will not attend—she made a point of not inviting my wife." His tone said he'd not forgive this slight easily. "However, I will await you at Drury Lane theatre afterward."

I marveled that Grenville knew my social schedule better than I did, but he and Donata, whenever they met, nattered like the old friends they were. "Done," I said.

"You've given me much to consider." Grenville took up the walking stick he'd dropped beside the chair in his hurry. "I will pop into Brooks's for a while this afternoon. The three gentlemen Pickett mentioned in his letter attend there, and perhaps I can strike up a conversation if any of them are about."

"As well as display your new cravat?"

Grenville knew I teased him, but his nod was solemn. "I

must reveal it at some point, and those at Brooks's will be flattered I chose to do it there. Good day, Lacey. Be careful what you say to Denis. Your lady wife will want you safely home."

"Donata will march over and extract me herself if there is any trouble," I said with conviction. "Until this evening, then."

"*Au revoir.*" Grenville departed, managing to move with both haste and elegance, a trait I knew I'd never master.

I went over Pickett's clothing once more after Grenville had gone, hoping to come upon secret messages sewn into a hem or a lining, but I discovered nothing. This did not surprise me. Pomeroy, who was thorough, would have found and removed anything interesting before he sent the bundle.

I folded the garments, finished my now-cold coffee, and departed to visit Denis at home.

———

GIBBONS OPENED THE DOOR AT NUMBER 45 AND SHOWED ME upstairs at once. He said not a word, but his apparent satisfaction when he saw no one with me but Brewster told me Grenville had been right not to come.

Denis sat at his desk going over letters, with no indication that he'd spent a day and a night in notorious Newgate prison.

Gibbons pointedly waited until I'd seated myself in front of the desk before he plunked a glass of brandy on the small table next to me. He withdrew, the room warming a bit once his chilly presence had gone.

Robbie, in his position by one of the windows, gave me a nod, in a more friendly manner than he'd shown in the past. He betrayed relief his master was home and hope that he'd remain here.

The usual procedure was for me to sit quietly until Denis was finished with whatever papers absorbed his attention and deigned to notice my presence. Today, my ill-humor would not let me remain still.

"If I am to help you, I need *all* information you have about Pickett," I stated into the silence. "I want to know about the men who referred Pickett to you as well as exactly why you were at the Seven Dials house. Also, why the devil you decided to let Spendlove catch you over a body with a knife in your hand."

Denis's fingers twitched at my impertinence, but other than that, he did not acknowledge my outburst. He made a few more notes, signed a page, blotted it, and neatly set the papers aside.

"The young woman," he began. "What did she wish to consult you about?"

I blinked a moment, my thoughts in disarray, then I realized to whom he was referring. "It is a private matter," I said stiffly.

"That I perceived. What was this private matter?" Denis regarded me with quiet obstinacy. "If you believe I will rush to her family and reveal her whereabouts and whatever she discussed with you, you have learned nothing of me over the years."

"Her family want nothing to do with her," I said tightly.

"I suspected that. In my experience, genteel young women do not meet with gentlemen, even for business, without a companion or chaperone to guard their virtue. From this, I conclude that the lady is living independently, and either has no family, or no wish for her family to intrude upon her life."

"Your conclusions are correct," I had to admit. "Before you press me for her name, I do not know it. She will not tell me. She calls herself Lady."

Denis's brows rose a fraction. "An apt moniker. Is she seeking information about someone? Her own child, perhaps?"

I stopped myself from demanding how the devil he knew that. It was not difficult to conclude how a young woman came to be alone in an insalubrious part of London, instead of residing with a protective family.

"I suppose it does no harm for you to know." No one of my acquaintance was more discreet than Denis or had more resources at his disposal. "Perhaps you could help *me* in return for keeping you away from the Old Bailey. Yes, her daughter. The girl was adopted by a family called Redding, but Mr. Redding is deceased, and Lady has lost track of them."

Denis lifted his pen and made a note on a clean sheet of paper. I gave him a few more details about Redding's business Lady had imparted to me as we'd enjoyed the cakes, and about the parish minister who had assisted in having young Vicky adopted. Donata had said she and Aline would help, but Denis could obtain information most of us could not.

Denis laid his pen down once I'd finished. "I will make a few inquiries."

"Thank you," I said sincerely. "Will you now condescend to tell me how your barrister managed to procure your release? I'm surprised Spendlove isn't battering down the door with his army of patrollers."

"Because a certain gentleman helped my barrister with his arguments to the judge. This gentleman has much pull with the Lord Chancellor as well as the Home Department. He is an ambitious sort, and there are plenty who want to be seen doing him favors."

"I imagine High Court judges aren't fond of Spendlove either," I said.

"I have no idea about that, though you are likely correct. Judges also have ambitions, as do barristers. A favor for a gentleman who is likely to one day be a powerful cabinet minister might help a man on his way to becoming an attorney general. Or even Lord Chief Justice, with a peerage created for him. Wheels need plenty of grease."

"And you can grease them."

"Favors beget favors. Those in Chancery have a ruthlessness you would never find in the most hardened criminal."

I believed him. The way of politics was fraught with peril, which is why I avoided it.

"Who was this gentleman with much pull who had you released?" I prompted. "It was The Honorable Mr. Haywood, wasn't it?"

CHAPTER 17

*J*f I expected Denis to fall back to his chair, press a hand to his heart, and exclaim that he had no idea how I'd guessed the truth, I'd have been disappointed.

"I agreed to keep the matter confidential," Denis replied without expression.

His way of telling me *yes*.

"I buttonholed Haywood at Covent Garden last night," I explained. "He, too strongly, told me to leave the matter of your arrest alone and not to interfere, which was almost exactly what you'd said to me." I reached for the brandy and took a large sip. "By which, I concluded he was assisting you. He must owe you a tremendous favor."

"No longer. That debt is discharged."

I noted Denis did not ask how I knew that Haywood had come anywhere near him. He must conclude that one of his lackeys had spilled that information. I would not impart that I heard it from Downie, to spare him Denis's wrath.

I raised my brows. "You let Haywood out of your net? I was not aware any of us were allowed to go."

"You paid your debt to me a long time ago, Captain," Denis

said calmly. "Mr. Haywood was becoming desperate to slide away from his, so much so that I decided it was of more benefit to be rid of him. I tell you this so you that do not pursue him in order to pry the truth from him. He would be a dangerous foe. I advise you to leave him alone."

I tucked away the fact that Denis had just said I owed him nothing. "You and Haywood did not concoct between yourselves to murder Mr. Pickett, did you?" I asked as though such a thought did not horrify me. "To provide Haywood with an opportunity to pay off his favor?"

"Nothing so dramatic." Denis moved a paper on his desk a fraction of an inch. "I told you, I never met or saw Mr. Pickett. I did not kill him, or even conceive of killing him. Why he came to Seven Dials is a mystery to me. However ..." Denis moved the paper again. "Haywood *might* have. When I stumbled over Mr. Pickett's body, I assumed he had."

"That is why you let yourself be arrested," I said in sudden understanding. "You thought Haywood was presenting you with a way to pay off his debt, and you took it. Why the devil were you outside, anyway? Alone?"

Denis shrugged. "Restless. I'm used to odd hours, but I was ready to return home. Gibbons insisted on cooking breakfast for me, and I went out for some air while I waited. Haywood and his arrogance had tainted the atmosphere inside. Alone, because I knew none would come near me so close to my own house. My arrogance, you can say."

Or great confidence in his power. "No one stole that knife from your desk, did they?"

"I had it in my pocket," Denis said. "I'd brought that knife with me, as I prefer it, and I wanted to carry it back home. There was no weapon in Pickett's chest or anywhere near him. I briefly slid my knife into the wound and out again, so I'd be caught with Pickett's blood on the blade."

"Dear God, you took a serious risk. If Spendlove had seen

you put it in, you'd even now be swinging from the gallows. Haywood could do precious little about it."

A minute smile crossed Denis's lips. "Spendlove's patrollers are not as efficient as they might be. I had to wait a bit before one came around the corner and saw me. I nearly gave it up and went back inside."

I sat up straight, setting the brandy aside. "How long did you wait?"

"A matter of minutes. I wouldn't have minded so much, except it was raining quite hard."

"Exactly. Was Pickett very wet?"

Denis paused, eyes flickering as he thought back. "I would not say so."

"Then I might very well be right," I said in triumph. "I believe Pickett was killed elsewhere and brought to your doorstep."

Another pause. "Which would *not* negate my theory that Haywood murdered him or had someone do it for him. Strengthens the idea, in fact."

"Proving it will be a devil of a thing, though. Especially if Haywood is as powerful as you claim—or has as much pull with powerful people."

Denis leaned slightly toward me. "I have told you about Haywood in confidence, Captain, a confidence that I expect you to keep. Meaning even Mr. Grenville must remain in the dark."

"Grenville is more trustworthy than you or your men give him credit for," I said with a touch of indignation.

"That may be, but the fewer who know a fact, the easier it is to keep from others. I know you tell everything to your wife, which I believe is unusual in a marriage, but I have faith in Lady Breckenridge's discretion."

I sat back in my chair, taking up the brandy again. "You wanted me to stay out of the way so Haywood could have a word with the right people to have you released. I am annoyed you didn't simply explain, but I suppose there was no way for you to tell me privately. I wager even Gibbons did not know."

Denis shook his head ever so slightly. "No one."

Except Robbie, presumably, who stood by the window as usual.

"Very well, we will proceed from here," I said. "Is there *anything* you can tell me about Pickett, or about Haywood, that will help me prove you did not commit murder?"

Denis frowned as he mused. "There was nothing in Haywood's manner during his appointment to indicate he would murder a man to relieve his debt. He was desperate to have it erased, he told me, and I do not like dealing with desperate men. I told him to go away and let me think about a deed that would recompense me for the bother I'd gone to for him, and he went. When I sent for him the next day, he was delighted to work for my release."

"Did he say anything to confirm your theory that he'd killed Pickett?"

"Unfortunately, no." Denis's frown deepened. "I could be entirely wrong about him—perhaps *he* believes *I* killed Pickett in order to give him the opportunity to aid me."

"That will not help." I drummed my fingertips on the table. "If neither of you killed the man, we are back to anyone in London being able to."

"Not necessarily," Denis said with an assuredness I did not share. "Search among Pickett's connections, trace his movements, irritate people into confessing to you. I am confident you will accomplish your task in the end."

"I am touched by your faith in my abilities." I took another sip of brandy and changed the direction of the conversation. "What can you tell me about William Arthur? He accosted me outside the opera last night to demand I let you rot."

Denis was not surprised by this revelation either. Doubtless his lackeys who kept an eye on things had told him of the encounter. "You need not concern yourself about Mr. Arthur. He will stay in his territory, and I in mine."

My voice hardened. "The last time I was caught between you and a rival, he kidnapped my son."

The tension in the room increased. I knew Denis had been unhappy at that turn of events, and it was the most likely reason he claimed my debt to him had been paid. "Mr. Creasey wildly overstepped himself, and he was a fool. Arthur is much more canny and understands how powerful your wife's family is. There will be no repeat of what happened with Creasey. Arthur will not use others to get to you."

"Excellent. He will come at me directly, then."

Denis shook his head. "He will leave you alone now that I am home. It is another reason I was in a hurry to be released—there are those who highly desire to take my place. I advise you to be guarded while you are out, as usual, but do not let Arthur concern you."

"My life was much safer before I came involved with you," I observed. "My own fault, I know."

"It was not safer." Denis pulled the pages toward him, a signal he wished the interview to end. "You are simply now more aware of the perils of living away from the Army."

I rose as Denis returned his concentration to his papers. "I laugh to remember that I thought coming to London would give me a modicum of peace." I took one last drink of the brandy, which was too good to waste, and made for the door.

At the last moment, I turned back. "You were quite intrigued by Lady," I remarked. "You took off your hat."

Denis's gaze turned ice-cold. "I can manage to be polite when it suits me," he said coolly. "Good day, Captain."

How I would keep the information about Haywood freeing Denis from Grenville, I did not know, I reflected as I walked home, Brewster accompanying me in silence. If we found the true killer soon, the issue of Haywood would become irrelevant, but I was beginning to despair of solving this puzzle.

Anyone from a footpad to Haywood's brother, the Earl of Shawbury, for whatever reason, could have murdered Pickett and left him in Seven Dials.

Additionally, my speculations about Pickett's dry clothing might be entirely wrong. Pickett could very well have taken himself to Seven Dials and met his death there, keeping himself out of the rain as much as possible in the process.

When I reached home, I only had time to jot a few notes about what Denis and I had discussed before dressing for the evening. I wasn't certain what a gentleman wore to a midnight meeting of a secret society but decided my suit for the soiree would have to do.

I escorted Donata alone that evening, as Gabriella had spent the afternoon with Lady Aline, and she and Aline would meet us at the gathering.

I would encourage Gabriella to stay with Aline again tonight. In spite of Denis's assurances that Mr. Arthur would fade back into the shadows, I felt Gabriella would be safer in Aline's home. Her servants guarded the place better than sentries looking after the Crown Jewels. If Donata's family was powerful, Aline's was even more so.

I related my conversation with Denis regarding Lady as Donata and I rode the short distance to Grosvenor Square.

"I am glad he agreed to help," Donata said as the carriage creaked along the line of coaches to our host's front door. "He will have connections that we do not."

"You seem happier with Denis now," I observed. "Have you thawed to him at last?" When Mr. Creasey had put Peter in danger, Donata had squarely blamed Denis. She'd frozen him out as only Donata could.

"Not at all." The feathers on Donata's turban trembled. "I can acknowledge that Mr. Denis is helpful when he wishes to be without speaking to him or greeting him."

"You would give him the cut direct, in other words."

"Indeed."

"I do hope you never have cause to give *me* the cut direct," I said lightly. "I can see it would be quite painful."

Donata smiled, which softened her eyes, and she touched my cheek. "So far, you have done nothing to warrant it. But we are both fairly young, so who knows what may happen in the future?"

The carriage halted abruptly at the door of the lit-up mansion, and a footman opened the door, ending our unnerving conversation.

The soiree was crowded, and I quickly lost sight of my wife, who was swept into a group of ladies who closed around her with glee. Nor was I able to get near Gabriella and Aline when they arrived.

I spent my time in the card room full of gentlemen and smoke, where I played cautiously. I won a few guineas and lost them again, but as long as I was in balance when I finished, I was content.

At eleven, many of the soiree guests moved on to the theatre in Drury Lane. I was up another guinea at cards, so I took my small winnings and bade my fellow players good night.

I escorted Donata to Drury Lane Theatre and Lady Aline's box, then returned to meet Grenville in the theatre's foyer. Grenville's coachman, Jackson, waited with his carriage, and we rode in some luxury to Piccadilly and our meeting.

Once we left the coach, Grenville led me to a warm room upstairs from a coffee house very close to the Fox Run tavern. A few tables dotted the small space, with enough chairs pulled in so everyone could sit.

I recognized many of the gentlemen there, having met them in various places—Tattersall's, Grenville's gatherings, assembly rooms, the theatre or opera. About a quarter of those attending were strangers to me, but the rest nodded in greeting as Grenville ushered me in.

He'd been correct to warn me that the "meeting" would be little more than consuming large quantities of drink and airing petty grievances. A vast bowl of punch sat in the middle of a table, most of it port from its fragrance, with slices of orange floating in it.

A servant ladled a cup out for me. I sipped politely but someone had decided to ruin this port with a large amount of sugar, and I soon put it aside.

The discussion tonight was about the usual things— domestic tariffs that kept the prices of luxuries high and foreign tariffs, which made exporting wool expensive and discouraged buyers in other countries. What was the point of pouring money into sheep rearing when one couldn't expect a decent return? Running the flocks on plantations in Scotland helped, but then there were all those Scots angry about losing their farmlands. Not that the Scots were good at farming anyway, a few scoffed. Meager crops were all that could be expected from that terrain. I wondered if there were any Scotsmen in the gathering and if they were fuming.

Others were unhappy with the newly installed King George. He'd been a compatriot when he was Regent, promising all sorts of things to his loyal coterie. All forgotten now. The man was a pig to his wife, who wasn't a bad sort, was she? Her misfortune getting stuck with the boor, poor thing.

Most agreed that reforms needed to be made and George should behave better, but no solutions were presented.

Grenville sent me a surreptitious glance, and I kept my expression neutral.

No one mentioned Mr. Pickett, Mr. Cudgeon the gunsmith, the Cato Street Conspiracy, or anything about assassinating the cabinet or overthrowing the king. There was general grumbling and much slurping of punch, and then the conversation turned to the latest pugilist bouts.

Grenville and I excused ourselves after a few hours of this. Some of the gentlemen had already begun to drift away, and we decided to drift with them.

Grenville went down the stairs ahead of me, saying he'd fetch Jackson. As I started to follow, a heavy hand landed on my shoulder, and a voice whispered in my ear.

"If you want to attend a true meeting, Captain, and find out about our Mr. Pickett, tell Mr. Grenville to go home without you." A man who'd been quiet during the gathering now spoke to me in gravelly tones. "Come back here. I'll wait."

CHAPTER 18

*W*hen I stepped outside, I announced to Grenville I was ready to go home, and that Brewster and I would walk there. I disliked misleading Grenville, but I did not want the man who'd whispered to me to harm Grenville for knowing things he shouldn't.

I'd already determined that Brewster would accompany me back to the meeting. I was not so rash as to go alone, and I noted that these men spoke openly in front of their servants. Brewster could wait outside if they refused to admit him.

"No need to walk," Grenville said in response. "The night is turning beastly." Rain had begun again, and the wind was cold. "Jackson will drop you at home."

I could not argue without betraying myself, so I followed Grenville to the carriage. I knew full well the man who'd drawn me aside could be an enemy, but I did not think so. He'd sat through the meeting, sipping punch and watching the others in some derision.

I would not throw away an opportunity to learn something of relevance by being overcautious. It could be that the man could tell me nothing, and it would be a wasted errand. But such was the perils of investigating a crime.

Grenville planned to join Marianne at the theatre, but he saw no oddity in me going home while Donata remained out. This had become my habit, leaving my wife to enjoy herself to the small hours of the morning while I sought my bed. In any case, she was safer with Lady Aline and her legions of devoted servants than she would be with me at present.

Grenville bid me a cheery good night as I stepped down at South Audley Street. Brewster hopped off the back of the coach and joined me. I waited until Jackson had turned the corner into Mount Street before settling my coat more closely about me and heading for Piccadilly once more.

"Bloke who came at you on your own doorstep last night was one of His Nibs'," Brewster announced as he fell into step with me.

"Was he?" I asked in surprise. "I didn't recognize him."

"One of the hangers-on who does odd jobs for him. His Nibs gives out those knives as a reward to those he's pleased with. They're good blades—cost a fair bit."

"I will guess the man was taking Denis's admonition for me to stay away from his business as leave to attack me." With Denis now bidding me to aid him, I supposed I'd no longer have to worry about that assailant.

Brewster gave me a curt nod. "I had a word with him and explained why it hadn't been a good idea."

I was certain I knew what Brewster "having a word" involved. "There was no need for that."

"There was need," he grunted. "It's me job, guv, to make sure coves know to leave you alone."

I swung my walking stick, letting the sword rattle inside. "I believe, Brewster, that there are coves following us even as we speak."

"I pegged 'em." Brewster nodded without looking around.

"Not sent by His Nibs this time. We could step into His Nibs' house here until they grow tired of ye." We'd reached Curzon Street, and Denis's house was not far off our route.

"I don't want to miss speaking with those who might know something useful," I said. "Let us hope our followers are only curious about where we are going."

"Chance would be a fine thing." Brewster growled.

We continued walking, though I now regretted not seeking a hackney. I heard no footsteps behind us—our followers were too skilled—but I knew they were there from flickers in the shadows.

I chose Clarges Street to take us to Piccadilly. All routes there were narrow, prime places for an ambush. I picked Clarges Street because it had a number of large houses on it—Grenville had leased one here for Marianne before they'd married. As I'd suspected, this lane was tight with carriages taking ladies and gentlemen to and from outings, and one house was hosting a gathering of some kind.

Brewster and I slipped among the coaches and their passengers. Servants and coachmen would be on the lookout for pickpockets and other thieves, so our pursuers would have to lie low or find another way around.

We reached Piccadilly without further mishap, hopefully losing our followers in the crush behind us.

I feared the gentleman who'd taken me aside would be long gone, but no, he lingered in the street near the Fox Run. Frowning with impatience, he led us into a narrow lane not far from Burlington House and its new Arcade and through a battered wooden door.

Brewster and I went up a rickety flight of stairs and entered a smoky room, with a fire in a tiny fireplace feebly trying to warm it.

A glance around at the faces watching me enter—many of them indulging in pipes, hence the miasma—showed only a few from the meeting I'd recently left. I also recognized Mr. Cudgeon.

Cudgeon laid aside his pipe and creaked to his feet as we entered. "This is Captain Lacey," he announced in the same cheerful tone with which he'd spoken to Grenville and me the night before. "He is trying to find out who did for Mr. Pickett."

The inhabitants of the room nodded at me, as though this was a perfectly sound introduction.

"Good evening, Mr. Cudgeon," I said, bowing to him. "From our conversation, I thought you indifferent to Mr. Pickett's fate."

"The Fox Run was not the place to discuss it," Cudgeon said. "I am quite unhappy about his death for various reasons."

The man who'd brought us here spoke. "Pickett was a good man. When Mr. Cudgeon told us you were asking about him, I thought we should speak to you. We need to know what happened to him."

"We do indeed, Mr. Dunwood." Cudgeon waved me to a polished wooden tavern chair. "Sit down, Captain. Tell us what you've discovered."

The furnishings here were mismatched as well as battered, as though tables and chairs had been taken from taverns as they discarded them. I sat, the seat creaking beneath my weight, while Brewster faded into a corner.

A servant thunked a dented pewter tankard on the table before me, lifted a keg, popped its cork, and streamed pale, foaming liquid into the vessel.

I took a swallow once the servant had gone and found the same weak ale that the Fox Run served. Possibly these fellows had procured it for their meetings. "My first thought was that one of you lot had done it."

My light comment brought a chuckle from some, but Mr. Dunwood eyed me severely. "That could be. They had better hope not."

A few men shuffled feet, uneasy, but I could not tell if their discomfiture came from guilt or fear of Mr. Dunwood's temper.

"Why *did* Pickett buy the guns from you, Mr. Cudgeon?" I asked.

Cudgeon regarded me without worry. "I don't know any more than what I've already told you. He said for fowling in Bedfordshire. Seemed reasonable to me."

I scanned the room. There were a dozen in attendance, ranging from well-dressed gentlemen in tailored suits to working men in homespun coats and thick boots. I hadn't met a one of them, apart from Cudgeon, before tonight.

"Did Pickett order them for any of you?" I asked the others.

All shook their heads. I noted that Cudgeon and Dunwood watched their reactions closely.

"He said he'd joined a gentleman's hunting club in Bedford-shire," a man in the very back of the room said. "Wanted to impress them with Cudgeon's shooters."

"Eh?" Cudgeon sat up straight. "You never let on about a hunting club, Mr. Saxton."

Mr. Saxton, who was as large and rough-looking as Brewster, shrugged broad shoulders. "No one asked."

"Did he mention the names of the gentlemen in this hunting club?" I asked, trying to be patient.

"Not to me," Saxton answered. "He was proud to know such gents. Said some of them humbled themselves to visit him in his rooms here in London. Weren't they kind to treat him like he was one of them?"

Saxton's disparaging tone told me he didn't think much of Pickett's new friends.

"They went to his rooms?" I asked. Such gentlemen might have carriages at their disposal, ones that could transport the dead Pickett across the city without getting him wet.

"So he boasted," Saxton answered. "But no, he gave us no

names. I wagered they were simply country gents he met at his new digs in Bedfordshire."

Possibly. Grenville's friend Langley had also mentioned Pickett becoming acquainted with Bedfordshire men. *Gentlemen of the area who'd known his cousin, I believe,* I recalled Langley telling me. "Did any of you see Mr. Pickett on Monday?" I asked.

They took their time to think about it, but there was much shaking of heads and mumbles of "Not since last week," and the like.

"We meet one Wednesday a month," Mr. Saxton said. "He were here at the last Wednesday meeting, but I've never seen him outside this room. Think that's true for most of us."

There were nods of agreement. Cudgeon didn't answer, but I'd already known he'd had an appointment with Pickett on the night of his death.

"Pickett held himself above the rest of us," stated one of the better-dressed gentlemen. "He inherited a cottage in the country and gave himself plenty of airs for that." The man looked amused as though he knew Pickett's circumstances were less than lucrative.

"Why did he join these gatherings?" I asked. "If he held himself above everyone?"

"Lofty ideals," Dunwood answered. "He saw wrongs and wanted them put right. As we all do. I pegged him in a group of gents like the one you and Mr. Grenville attended tonight, coves that go on about the state of things but never lift a finger to change them. Invited him here. He was happy to sit and listen."

"And you've let *me* into your enclave," I said. "Why do you think I will not report you to the Runners?"

"Cause we ain't the Cato Street idiots," Saxton growled from the back wall. "They're a lot of fools, had spies in their midst egging them on into mad schemes of murder and mayhem. It's the Runner's men what goaded them who should have been arrested, in my opinion. And the conspirators should have checked that what the spies were telling them were true."

All good points, I agreed.

"Still, you are trusting me," I said. I sensed Brewster quivering in the corner, wishing I'd cease speaking.

"Anything we discuss here is perfectly legal," Dunwood said smoothly. "We come up with ideas for lessening the burden of those scratching for a living and present them to gents with the ear of someone in government. Hand-picked ones the MPs and Lords will listen to and not dismiss out of hand."

"Is this effective?" I asked with true interest.

Cudgeon nodded. "We've already had a petition against the Corn Laws presented to Parliament. There are other petitions as well, such as better policing on the streets of the metropolis."

"Blokes like me don't have much of a voice," Saxton said. "But here I do."

"Admirable," I said with sincerity. "I agree, there is much that the highborn are blind to." I'd seen poverty and desperation at its rawest when I'd eked out an existence in Grimpen Lane, aware I was lucky to have even the rooms I did.

"They ain't so much blind as don't want to know," Saxton said sourly. "If you own half a county your ancestors got for looking the other way at some king's carryings-on, you want the laws to favor you selling your grain for great profit, don't you? Or keeping your sheep on hills where small farmers used to grow enough for their families to eat."

I couldn't argue. The ways of the world were very uneven. I commended these men for trying to better it in the small way they could.

"Why do you think Pickett was murdered?" I asked the room at large.

Again, they took their time answering. "He wasn't a rude bloke," a man who hadn't spoken before said. "Didn't make enemies. Talked a bit too much, but many a gent does that."

"Knew something he shouldn't?" Dunwood suggested.

"Or someone thought he did," Saxton said.

"I am inclined to agree with you, Mr. Saxton," I said. "Perhaps Pickett believed he had important information, and someone else believed him as well."

There were nods, but no one suddenly betrayed guilt. A few more offered more theories, such as what most who didn't believe Denis had done it thought—a footpad who'd seen a mark and taken a chance.

After a time of this discussion it was clear they could tell me no more, or at least they'd decline to in this collective setting. I set aside my tankard and rose. "Thank you, gentlemen, for an instructive conversation. If I learn anything more about Mr. Pickett's death, I will send word to Mr. Cudgeon."

Cudgeon, who'd heaved himself to his feet, gave me a nod. "I would be obliged, Captain. And please understand that anything said in this room is spoken in confidence. Whether by us or by you."

I bowed. "I am grateful to you for your trust. Good night."

I took up my hat and moved to the door, Brewster materializing to open it for me. He hustled me down the stairs before I could say a farewell to any of the gentlemen personally.

We stepped out into the cold rain in the inky dark passageway, but Brewster didn't give me much time to settle my coat before he herded me back to the main street.

"You believe them?" he asked.

"About knowing nothing about Pickett's death?" I pulled my coat tighter against the chill. "I think so. There is not much dangerous about wanting to repeal the Corn Laws and improve the safety of the streets."

"I mean about not harming you now that you know about them."

I shrugged, to Brewster's frustration. "I suppose that remains to be seen."

"They're following us again, guv," Brewster said as we moved along Piccadilly. "The ones who were before, I mean. Must have been lying in wait for us to reappear. Should find a hackney."

There were no hired hacks to be seen in all this rain, of course. I quickened my pace the best I could and turned up Berkeley Street, passing the great pile of Devonshire House.

Our pursuers chose to attack where Curzon Street curved toward the high wall of Chesterfield House, not far from Denis's home. Here the road was quiet, the tall houses dark, as though their inhabitants had gone piously to bed.

I had my sword out of my walking stick and used its scabbard to smack away a small cudgel that came at me. The assailant ducked from my descending blade, which I could use with deadly precision.

I counted six of them. Four tried to beat down Brewster while only two faced me.

I was growing tired of people who wanted to teach me obedience. I'd left obedience behind the day my regimental colonel had sent me on a scouting mission he believed would lead to my death. While I'd since forgiven Colonel Brandon for his perfidy, I'd not let myself blindly follow orders again.

The second man coming at me grunted and cursed as my sword met his flesh. I'd not murder these two, but I'd give them plenty of stinging cuts to remember me by. Both men danced back, realizing they needed to keep their distance, but they didn't flee.

Behind me, Brewster was fighting for his life. He'd once been a formidable pugilist, but these men were giving him no quarter. I inched my way to him, preparing to jab a few backs to give them something else to think about.

The moment I turned to help Brewster, my attackers rushed me. I could not assist Brewster until these two were down, but while they bled from my sword blows, they weren't leaving me be.

Brewster was swearing and grunting, fists meeting his body with gruesome *thunks*. He needed aid, but the men on me, realizing I wouldn't kill them outright, were not letting me near him.

A shout sounded beyond our ring of battle, and a light flashed. My two assailants glanced behind them, stiffened with alarm, and faded quickly down the street into the darkness and rain.

CHAPTER 19

The light proved to be a lantern, carried by the tall, gaunt figure of Gibbons. One of Brewster's opponents turned, saw him, and abruptly sprinted away after his fellows.

The others were too intent on subduing Brewster to take notice.

"Clear off, you lot." Gibbons' angry tones cut through the fracas. His stride was not swift, but he moved with deadly intent.

Mr. Stout and the diminutive Mr. Downie were with him, Mr. Downie also bearing a lantern. Stout had a cudgel in his beefy hand and wore an expression of grim determination.

Brewster struggled out from under his three attackers, who finally noted Gibbons and the others bearing down on them. Stark fear filled the assailants' hard countenances before they too fled.

I helped Brewster to his feet. He wiped his bloody and sweating face on his sleeve and nodded at Gibbons. "Thank ye for your timely appearance," he said good-naturedly. "Though it were a good scrap."

Gibbons gave the pair of us a once-over. "Get inside." He uttered the command then turned and stalked with the same deliberate pace back toward the house.

Stout scowled at us before he followed, but Downie shot us a grin.

"A timely intervention, indeed," I said to Downie. "Those fellows certainly seemed afraid of Mr. Stout."

Downie chuckled. "Oh, they ain't afraid of Stout. Nor me. It's Gibbons what put the wind up them."

"He is certainly menacing," I conceded. "Though I think you or Stout would have been more adroit combatants."

"Nay, Mr. Gibbons would kill them as soon as look at them, and they know it."

"Here in the street?" I asked in surprise. "So close to Denis's house?"

Downie's lantern swung, scattering speckles of light onto the wet cobbles. "No one would ever find 'em, Captain. They know that too."

"Ah."

I thought of the terror in the eyes of our assailants before they'd bolted. Gibbons might be past his prime, but I agreed with the men he'd chased away. If I wanted to find a likely murderer, I should look no further than Mr. Gibbons.

———

Mr. Downie helped patch up Brewster in Denis's kitchen. I'd never been below stairs in this house and gazed about with interest.

The kitchen was no different than those in most in Mayfair homes—a square room with a fireplace and several ovens, a worktable, and a dresser filled with crockery. Pots of gleaming copper hung from a rack near the fireplace. A fire crackled on the hearth, warming the kitchen, and roasting a large hunk of meat, even at this hour.

The cook was a large man, as hard and formidable as the others, with gnarled hands and a granite-like face. I'd once watched Denis tuck into a meal upstairs that had looked exquisite, and any morsel I'd eaten in Denis's houses had been tasty indeed. This man, as much as he resembled a troll from Scandinavian tales, apparently had great talent.

Denis was not at home, Gibbons had informed me coldly when we'd entered, which explained why the large Robbie hadn't been sent out to interfere. Robbie usually accompanied Denis everywhere.

Gibbons had sent us downstairs and said no more about the matter, but I could see he was greatly put out for having to rescue us.

Downie competently bandaged Brewster's cuts, ignoring hisses and grunts as he wiped blood and gravel from Brewster's wounds.

"They never should have struck at you here," Downie said as he worked. "His Nibs will have something to say to Mr. Arthur about it."

"You know for certain they were Arthur's ruffians?" I asked, though I'd concluded as much.

Every man in the room, including Brewster, nodded.

"He's looking to take over," the cook rumbled as he basted the roast that turned slowly on its spit. "Not that we'll let 'im." There were angry murmurs of agreement.

Denis had certainly hired a loyal bunch.

"Will they make trouble for you all?" I asked. "For coming to my aid? What I mean is, are you safe here?"

Downie let out a laugh, though the cook scowled. "They won't bother us in *this* house," Downie said. "They'd have left you alone entirely if you'd made for it instead of turning to fight them."

"Which is why Gibbons looked so annoyed," I said. "Though Arthur's men didn't give us much choice."

"Mr. Gibbons is always annoyed," the cook said. "He's a bad man to cross, Captain. I'd stay on the good side of him were I you."

I was astonished to hear Gibbons *had* a good side, but I held my tongue.

Brewster winced as Downie touched a cloth to the cut under his eye. "They were fools to put most on me and underestimate you," Brewster said to me. "Also to engage in battle right under Mr. Gibbons' nose. Mr. Arthur is going to give them a ragging, I shouldn't wonder."

The men in the room chuckled, except for the cook, who only frowned at his roast.

"All done." Downie ceased torturing Brewster and tied the last bandage. "Let your lady wife finish up. The tongue-lashing Arthur gives his blokes will be nothing to what Mrs. Brewster will do to you, Tommy." He chortled. "Want a room for the night?"

"Em understands what I go through guarding the Captain," Brewster said without worry. "'Course, *he* might want to keep clear of her for a while."

"Very amusing," I said into the general laughter. "I'll send you home in a hackney, Brewster, with some of Donata's fine tea to ease her temper."

"Em recognizes a bribe when she's offered one," Brewster said. "But she won't say no to it." He heaved himself to his feet. "Come on. Let's get you home."

———

DOWNIE AND STOUT ESCORTED BREWSTER AND ME SAFELY TO THE South Audley Street house. I heard no one follow us, nor did I note any lurkers in the shadows, but I felt better once the door had closed behind me and Brewster.

Donata had not yet returned from the theatre, though I hadn't expected she would. I gave Brewster the promised tea and had an agile footman run to bring around a hackney for him.

Once Brewster was gone, I let a concerned Bartholomew fuss over me, though the bruises I'd sustained were minor. Donata returned without mishap a few hours later, she becoming agitated when she heard my tale. She took over care of me from Bartholomew, and I happily let her.

The next morning, I rose later than usual, my muscles sore from what Brewster had called a good scrap. I'd thrown off such things as a younger man, but time's winged chariot was hurrying near, as a poet once wrote.

Even so, I fell upon my breakfast hungrily, intending to work in a ride this morning, no matter what.

My repast was interrupted by Barnstable, very much as it had been two mornings ago, to announce a caller.

"Who is it today?" I asked with annoyance. "I am becoming quite popular at this hour."

Barnstable's tones were even more freezing than when he'd announced Gibbons. "It is Mr. Spendlove, sir."

"Dear God." I briefly closed my eyes. "I am not certain I can stomach Mr. Spendlove so early in the morning."

"He has insisted," Barnstable said. "Forgive me, sir, but I could not turn him away."

"Not your fault." I munched through a piece of toast with more of the excellent marmalade from Lord Pembroke and set aside the newspaper. "Where have you put him?"

"The gold reception room."

"Good." The gold reception room was the least comfortable in the house. Unwanted guests were made to wait there so they might decide to leave instead of settling in. "I'll go down."

I rose and took up my walking stick, moving slowly to the dining room door. Not only did I ache from the fight with Arthur's men, I saw no reason to rush to speak to Spendlove.

I found my visitor standing in the exact center of the reception room, studying a landscape painting of the Breckenridge estate in Hampshire. The artist had perfectly captured the idyllic setting of the imposing house amidst rolling fields that disappeared into mist-covered hills.

The picture was meant to remind the viewer in this windowless room how powerful was Viscount Breckenridge, even if he currently was an eight-year-old boy.

I planted myself in the doorway. "It is early for calls," I stated. "I haven't finished my breakfast."

Spendlove skewered me with his accusing light-blue gaze. "Mr. Denis is at home, happily eating his."

"Not my doing," I answered. "Whatever you think of me, I do not have that sort of power."

"Oh, I know exactly who to blame." Spendlove's coldness told me he'd learned how Mr. Haywood had brought about Denis's extraction from Newgate. "The magistrates are happy to let criminals walk free if they are paid enough, or if their friends in high places threaten the right people. Meanwhile, innocent men are hanged because they're too frightened to raise their head in the presence of judge or jury. A sure sign of guilt, they say." His bitterness was acute.

Spendlove's musings on such things surprisingly matched my own. The justice system was sometimes anything but just.

"In this case, I am very sure James Denis is the innocent man," I said. "I am aware that he was released by those who owed him favors, but he never should have been banged up in the first place."

I gave Spendlove what I imagined was a severe eye, but Spendlove wasn't impressed.

"You had better hope he truly didn't do this murder, Captain.

You are going to help me learn exactly what happened one way or the other. If we prove Denis really did kill that man, I'll have you as well, for assisting him to cover it up." Spendlove motioned to the doorway in which I stood. "Shall we make a start?"

CHAPTER 20

*T*he last thing I wished to do today was run about London with Spendlove dogging my steps the entire way. I'd wanted to begin rigorously searching for Lady's daughter, but did not wish Spendlove to know anything about that, or about her.

I forced myself to think things through instead of rashly telling Spendlove to go to the devil. He was very good at pursuit, pinning down those he caught and coercing information from them. He might prove Denis's innocence in spite of himself.

Also, Arthur's men would keep their distance from me in Spendlove's presence. Spendlove didn't care about a man's dangerous connections—he'd simply arrest them and let the magistrates sort it out.

"Very well," I said.

Spendlove's eyes widened slightly in surprise. He'd expected me to argue.

"I am unworried by your threat," I went on. "Because I know we'll find Denis to be innocent."

Spendlove scowled. "You'd better convince me, then."

"I will do my best. This morning, I planned to retrace Pickett's steps on his last day. You are welcome to come along."

"I'm coming whether I'm welcome or not." Spendlove gazed at me without blinking. "As pretty as this chamber is, I am ready to quit it. Lead on, Captain."

I quelled my vexation and exited the room, Spendlove following.

Once we were on the street, a light rain pattering on my tall hat, I suggested we begin in Pickett's rooms. Spendlove agreed readily.

I insisted on a hackney, knowing I'd have a long day on my injured leg. Spendlove waited with me at the hackney stand with ill-disguised impatience but made no comment on my feebleness. He even assisted me into the coach—if a firm shove on my back constituted help.

"Pomeroy let me have a look at Pickett's clothes," I told him as we rolled off.

I wanted to know if he'd noticed what I had, or had any more intelligence from them, but Spendlove only fixed me with a narrowed gaze. "What did you make of them?"

His request for my opinion surprised me a bit, but I was happy to enlighten him. "They were too dry for a man who'd walked in the rain."

Spendlove gave me a grudging nod that almost held respect. "I thought that too. I wondered if you'd be as quick."

"Then why are you still convinced Denis was his killer?" I asked in annoyance. "Denis would hardly have a dead man toted to his front door so a patroller could find him standing over it, knife in hand."

"Mr. Denis does things for his own reasons," was Spendlove's enlightened answer.

Denis had deliberately let himself be arrested, it was true. It *could* be that he'd concocted an elaborate scheme to give Haywood a chance to act, and Pickett was the unfortunate victim Denis had decided to use. I could easily picture Gibbons doing the deed and sending the body off to Seven Dials in such a way that it would never be traced to him.

A very unlikely scenario, I told myself. Denis had seemed genuinely mystified about why Pickett had missed his appointment and turned up in Seven Dials. Then again, if Gibbons had been given free rein, Denis might have known nothing regarding Gibbons' part in it, so that he could swear to it on oath.

I frowned, uncertain whether my conclusion that Pickett was killed elsewhere exonerated Denis or landed him more firmly in it. Spendlove would choose the latter, I knew.

"Her ladyship's cook will not be happy with me for abandoning breakfast," I observed into the silence. "You might have to answer to her when I'm called on the carpet for it."

Spendlove's scowl didn't lessen at my jest. "A man should not be bullied by his servants. They work for *you*."

Thus spoke a man who had few, if any, servants. "Every person in that house was hand-picked by my wife for their expertise," I told him. "They are specialists at what they do, and we should respect them for it. One cannot simply be exchanged for another." Barnstable, with his homemade remedies, his thorough knowledge of almost every person in London, and his flashes of extreme kindness, was irreplaceable.

"A few years ago, you didn't even have someone to empty your slops." Spendlove sniffed and brushed a gloved finger over his nose. "Not even a batman left over from your army days."

I cooled. "My batman was a friend, and he was killed at Corunna. He too was not expendable."

Did Spendlove apologize for dredging up a past sorrow? No, he continued his chilly stare. "Now you have a butler. Who had no intention of letting me near the silver. And a valet, courtesy of Mr. Grenville."

He knew much about our household, but then, Spendlove was thorough. "I am grateful to my friends for their aid. But her ladyship's staff work for *her*, not me. Barnstable would fend off the devil himself for her ladyship."

Spendlove only sniffed again—perhaps he had a cold coming on—and stared out of the window.

Not long later, we trundled along Piccadilly and turned down St. James's Street, quiet at this time of the morning. The coachman passed Brooks's club and let us off at the entrance to Park Place.

We strode in silence through the misty rain to the Arlington. Spendlove stepped up to the house next to the club and pounded on its front door.

"We should ask for the key at the Arlington," I told him. "Though this early, I imagine no one is there."

Spendlove ignored me. His gloved fist beat the door once again.

A few sash windows scraped open above us and heads poked out. One man wore a nightcap.

"What the devil do you mean, making all that noise?" the one in the nightcap called down.

"Open up," Spendlove shouted back. "Or I'll have all of you for obstructing the law."

Two of the heads instantly withdrew. Nightcap remained. "The law?" he bellowed. "I'll have the law on *you* for disturbing the peace."

The black door of the Arlington flew open, and Mr. Hawes, the manager, trotted out. He was fully dressed, but by the smear of butter on his mouth, he, like me, had been having his breakfast.

"What is the meaning of—oh." Hawes halted when he saw

me, whipped out a handkerchief, and dabbed the butter from his face. "Captain Lacey. What on earth?"

"This is Mr. Spendlove," I said, letting my disapproval of the man ring in my voice. "He is a Runner and wants to see Mr. Pickett's rooms."

"A Runner?" Hawes's voice rose in volume, probably to warn those in the flats that one of the famed Runners was demanding entry. "But Mr. Pickett is dead and gone. I'm about to have his chambers cleared, so another gentleman can take up residence."

"Good thing we came today then," Spendlove growled. "Open it up, you."

"His name is Mr. Hawes," I told Spendlove. "He is the manager at the Arlington."

"I don't care if he is Christ himself. Open the bloody door."

I shot Hawes an apologetic look. He heaved an aggrieved sigh and dragged keys from his coat pocket.

"Please search quietly," Hawes begged, though he must know such a request was futile. "There are gentlemen sleeping."

"Or trying to," Nightcap yelled down.

Spendlove ignored him. He speared Hawes with his cold stare as Hawes finally managed to unlock the door. Hawes pulled it open, and Spendlove shouldered his way past him.

Hawes panted up the staircase in Spendlove's wake. "I must unlock upstairs as well."

I quietly closed the front door behind me, shutting out the rain. I ascended more slowly, taking in the peaceful hush of the stairwell, broken now by Spendlove rumbling at Hawes to hurry.

I half expected Nightcap to burst out of his room on the first floor as I passed it, but no one appeared. I wished him a pleasanter sleep for the rest of the morning.

By the time I reached the third floor, Hawes had Pickett's flat open. I removed my hat as I entered the outer room and set it on a table next to the door.

Hawes tried to slip past me in retreat. Spendlove immediately swung around and pointed a gloved finger at him.

"No. You, stay. Sit there."

Hawes's eyes rounded. He took another step toward the hall but then swallowed and moved to the settee Spendlove indicated, lowering himself to its edge.

Spendlove went immediately to the wardrobe Grenville had searched and yanked open its door. While Grenville had carefully brushed fingers over the coats' fabric, Spendlove thrust his hands into pockets and dragged coats out to rip into their linings.

"Steady on," I said in indignation. "Have some respect."

"The man is dead, and I want to know who killed him," Spendlove snapped. He swung on Hawes. "Was it *you*?"

Hawes flushed heavily. "No, no. I could never. Pickett wasn't a bad sort. I had no complaint with him."

He breathed hard, his eyes showing their whites. He'd never last against a skilled prosecutor, but I believed him. His indignation rang true.

Spendlove moved into the bedchamber and the bureau there, throwing the clothes inside to the bed before he tore into them. Hawes' expression turned from fear to pain. No doubt he'd planned to sell the clothes Pickett had left behind.

I didn't know what Spendlove was hunting for—a letter from Denis vowing to end Pickett's life? A missive from the true killer confessing to the murder?

I remembered Pickett's scrawled note to visit his bookmaker and began examining the torn coats for any information regarding wagers he'd made. I also searched through the clothes Spendlove had dumped on the bed but found nothing.

Next, I turned to the bedside table I'd explored previously. Its drawer was empty, as I'd taken the diary and letters, but I noted this time that the drawer rattled a bit when I tried to close it.

A thought struck me, and I removed the drawer entirely, flipping it over. Its bottom was loose, and I pried it away.

"Ah, here we are."

Spendlove was across the room in an instant. Hawes left his post in the sitting room to see what I'd found, but in curiosity, not worry.

"Vowels," I said, placing a dozen slim pieces of paper on the bed. "For what he owed. And these." I laid out four small squares cut from cork, each about an inch square. They all bore a smudge of blue paint on one side and had letters and numbers on the other. *AW 2-12*, I read on the first of these. The second was marked *HmD 4-20*. The other two had similar incomprehensible letters and numbers.

Spendlove scooped them up. "What are they?" he demanded of me.

"I have no idea." I touched the vowels, which had large sums written on them. "But if these were unpaid, Pickett had fallen deep indeed."

Was his death a simple matter of a shady creditor tired of waiting for him to pay? Making an example of Pickett to keep his other clients tame?

He'd had an appointment with his bookmaker the day before his death. To pay what he owed? Or to collect some meager winnings? Langley had mentioned Pickett had won a guinea or two in the past, though if these vowels were any indication, they'd have gobbled up that money in a trice.

"Did Pickett have much luck at the races?" I asked Mr. Hawes.

"Rarely," Hawes answered with conviction. "Mr. Pickett was always optimistic when he went to race meetings but usually came home resigned. Never downcast—he was positive the next time would be a sure one."

Spendlove let the cork squares fall back to the bed. "Maybe he won and didn't tell you."

"Mr. Pickett never was flush with cash," Hawes said. "I'm certain he'd have boasted of it. He was never very discreet." Hawes concluded this apologetically.

No, he hadn't been. He'd burst out to Grenville that he feared he'd inadvertently helped the Cato Street conspirators, though the men I'd spoken to last night had not struck me as the type to start riots and assassinate people. Rather, they button-holed MPs and presented petitions against the Corn Laws. I doubted any of them, including the large Mr. Saxton, could have feared exposure from Pickett.

Cudgeon was confident that Pickett had purchased the guns for hunting, not for leading a revolution. Both Saxton and Langley had mentioned a group of country gentlemen Pickett was proud to have joined. I agreed that the guns had been for them.

Why, then, had Pickett grown concerned that he'd somehow played a part in the Cato Street debacle?

"Mr. Hawes." I kept my tone gentle. "Did Pickett host gather-ings in these chambers? Of gentlemen he knew from Bedford-shire, perhaps?"

Hawes's confused frown cleared. "Ah, them. Not in these rooms, but in the club next door. Mr. Pickett invited them, yes. Mostly to talk about shooting in the country or some such thing."

"What gentlemen?" Spendlove demanded. "I need their names."

Hawes spluttered. "Really, sir, that is most irregular."

Spendlove abandoned the vowels and cork squares, which I gathered up, and advanced on Hawes. "You tell me the name of every single person who visited Pickett here, or I'll bang you up for thwarting my investigation."

Hawes, on his feet, dithered. "I don't remember names. I would have to consult the Arlington's guest book."

Spendlove waved him to the door. "Do it now. There's nothing here."

He herded Hawes out the door, leaving me alone with Pickett's belongings scattered over the bed, the drawers in the bureau sagging from Spendlove's brusque search.

I collected the clothes and folded them as neatly as I could, finding nothing further inside them. Pickett had been conscientious about cleaning out his pockets, it seemed. I often left scraps of paper, letters, bits of string, and other things I'd come across in my pockets. Bartholomew often shook his head over what he found— half a loaf of bread once that Mrs. Beltan had pressed upon me.

Pickett had cleared his with thoroughness and stashed anything he didn't want found under the false bottom of the drawer.

If Pickett had hidden these odd pieces of cork, he must have had a good reason. I gathered them up, along with the vowels, and slid all into the pocket inside my coat.

I closed the wardrobe, sent a silent word of sympathy to the deceased Pickett, and left the chamber.

When I reached the first-floor landing, a man strode down a short hall to me. "Is the noise finished?" he demanded.

It was Nightcap, now dressed and minus the cap. The man's dark hair was slicked with pomade, his suit well-tailored.

I gave him a polite bow. "I apologize, sir. Yes, we are finished."

"What's a Runner doing here at this hour of the morning, anyway? Trying to decide who did for Pickett? He needs to look no further than the nearest race meeting. Pickett was always getting up everyone's nose because he couldn't win on a horse if God himself chose it."

"Did you happen to see anyone visiting him on Monday?" I asked, keeping the question businesslike. "Or late in the week before that?"

Nightcap looked me up and down. "Why are you interested? I thought you were one of Pickett's friends, dragged here by the Runner."

"I never knew Mr. Pickett," I admitted. "I am trying to bring his murderer to justice."

The man's snort was worthy of Brewster. "Some robber in the street most like. Pickett didn't have many visitors. Only the gents he'd meet in the club. They gabbed about sport—shooting, boxing, and racing. Nothing very profound."

"Not politics, then?" I asked.

The man brayed a laugh. "Oh, they mentioned it now and then, pretending to be reformers. The only reform they wanted was a way to bring windfalls to themselves. Weren't grand landholders, you understand. Minor gentry, I'd say, looking to feather their nests. The next swift horse or the best boxer were their grandest plans."

His cynicism shrouded him like an impenetrable cloak. But perhaps he was right—Pickett had started to strike me as someone who believed himself more involved in the world than he truly was.

"The noise should cease now," I assured the man. "We will take ourselves away."

He gave me a grudging nod. "See that the Runner doesn't come back."

I fervently hoped he would not.

———

"WE NEED TO FIND HIS USUAL BOOKMAKER," SPENDLOVE SAID AS we climbed into the hackney he'd commanded to wait for us. "That Hawes fellow didn't know it." He clutched a hastily scribbled list, its ink smeared, which I assumed contained names and addresses of Pickett's shooting friends. "He'll have a stall at

Tattersall's, I'll make a guess. You can get me in there—you go enough with Mr. Grenville."

"Finsbury Square," I corrected him.

Spendlove glared at me as the coach jerked forward. "How do you know?"

"It was in Pickett's diary," I said.

"His what?" Spendlove's lip curled. "Where did you find that?"

I moved uncomfortably in the seat. "In Pickett's rooms, when I searched them before. I planned to turn it in to Pomeroy." Once I'd gone over it to my satisfaction, but I saw no reason to include this detail.

"You should have brought it strait to *me*, damn you."

"I am trying to prove Denis innocent," I said coolly. "There was nothing significant in the diary apart from Pickett's appointment with Denis on his last night. I did not wish you to use that fact as another nail in Denis's coffin."

"I'll have it from you anyway." Spendlove turned his surly gaze out the window, as though the pile of St. James's Palace we passed displeased him. "Take it to Bow Street when we're finished today."

As I'd not gotten much more out of the diary, I didn't mind, but Spendlove's command irritated me. I said nothing, neither agreeing nor disagreeing.

Spendlove banged on the roof and curtly told the driver to take us to Finsbury Square. The coachman muttered something and slammed the trap door closed.

As the coach left St. James's, it passed Carlton House, the elegantly columned building with fantastic rooms inside, which I'd had the privilege to view. It had been all but abandoned now by the new king, Grenville had told me. King George had moved to Buckingham House, where his mother had lived, with plans to expand that edifice and redecorate it to his taste.

The glories of Carlton House would be no more. A pity, I thought, and a waste.

Spendlove said not a word as we rattled on through Cockspur Street to the Strand, nor did he read the list of names crumpled in his hand, reflect on them, or share them with me. I tried to glimpse what was on the paper, but he held it too tightly in his fist for me to see.

Finsbury Square lay north of the ancient City wall, developed out of the old Moorfields area. Moorfields had once been an open green—the moor drained long ago—used by dyers for drying cloth and around which notorious highwaymen had taken residence. Now Moorfields held a circular convergence of streets, one leading north to Finsbury Square.

"A balloonist lifted off there," I said, gesturing to a gate that led to artillery grounds just before we reached the square.

"Eh?" Spendlove stared where I pointed, as though believing Pickett's murderer was ready to launch himself away to safety. "What balloonist? Where?"

"Thirty-five years ago, now. He went all the way to Hertfordshire. Quite the sensation."

I'd been a boy at the time, ready to take up ballooning as a profession. My father, of course, tore up the newspapers that printed the balloonist's story, lectured me on what a fool I was, and forbade me from ever speaking of the matter again.

Spendlove curled his lip at my explanation and then ignored me. He had much in common with my father, I reflected, though Spendlove possessed a bit more intelligence.

We rolled into the square, passing Lackington's Library—referred to as the Temple of the Muses because of its many tomes within. I'd brought Gabriella here, and she'd been enchanted with the multitude of books in glass cases, the long windows looking out to the square, and the comfortable nooks where we could read to our heart's content.

The bookmaker's establishment we sought was a few doors

down from Lackington's. The house appeared to be respectable enough, with a front door neatly painted in dark green, one curtained window beside it. Double windows rose two more stories, each as orderly as the ground floor.

"Please refrain from terrifying everyone inside," I said when we climbed from the coach. "Like you did with Hawes. He was lying to us, I believe, though I'm not certain about what."

CHAPTER 21

*S*pendlove slammed the coach's door once he was on the street. "'Course he was lying. Everyone lies to the Runners. They are all guilty of something they don't want found out."

A cynical outlook, and one that was hardly helpful. "Perhaps *I* should speak to the bookmakers," I suggested. "By myself, I mean."

Spendlove's expression told me what he thought of that idea. "You're not going in there on your own. What's to say *you* won't lie to me about what they tell you?"

He had a point, but so did I. Potential witnesses were more likely to open up to a guileless and somewhat ignorant army captain. A Runner landing in their midst would hardly coax the truth from them.

Spendlove had already turned away and pounded on the door of the house, rendering my argument null.

I asked the hackney driver to wait. He nodded with ill grace, as fed up with Spendlove as I was.

A slim man in a well-fitting suit and a thick shock of dark

hair opened the door and gazed out at us with a neutral expression.

"Good morning, Mr. Spendlove," he said smoothly, as though unsurprised a Runner had decided to visit. "Please, gentlemen, come in."

While he'd recognized Spendlove, he glanced with curiosity at me, clearly unsure who I was.

"Captain Gabriel Lacey, at your service, sir." I removed my hat as I stepped inside the small square foyer. "We have come to inquire about the gambling habits of one Mr. Bernard Pickett."

The man offered his hand. "Jonathan Christie. Please enter, Captain Lacey."

His politeness was studied, a man who knew how to deal with many sorts of clients. Mr. Christie's suit resembled any Grenville would wear, but though his accent was meant to put him above the working classes, I could tell it had been carefully cultivated.

Mr. Christie led me to an office into which Spendlove had already stormed. Three clerks turned uncertainly from standing desks, looking to Mr. Christie for guidance.

This seemed to be a perfectly ordinary clerk's room at any business establishment. Glass-fronted bookcases lined the walls, with a large desk and chair in front of them for Christie. A fire crackled in a paneled fireplace, lending warmth to the chamber.

The clerks regarded us respectfully, but I detected a hint of apprehension beyond surprise at being interrupted.

"These gentlemen want to ask about Mr. Pickett," Christie announced. "Could I have his book, please?"

One of the clerks obediently walked to one of the bookcases, opened its door, ran his finger along a row of ledgers, and withdrew one of the tall tomes. He quietly closed the glass door and carried the book to Mr. Christie.

Christie set the ledger on a reading stand and opened it, flipping unhurriedly through pages. Spendlove stepped up to peer over his shoulder, but Christie continued to leaf through the book without worry.

"Ah, yes, Mr. Pickett." Christie scanned the entries as though he was unfamiliar with them. "He placed quite a lot of wagers over the years. None of them very fruitful, I am afraid." He looked up at us apologetically. "He died owing us several hundred guineas, actually."

Christie swept a slender hand across the ledger as though telling us the pages didn't lie.

"I found a number of vowels in his rooms," I said. "Along with these." I removed the cork squares from my pocket. "Can you tell me what they are?"

Spendlove was nearly breathing down Christie's neck. Christie professed not to notice as I laid the squares onto the ledger.

I felt the scrutiny of the clerks, as though they held their collective breath. A quick glance at them showed me they were staring at Christie, intent on his composed movements.

"These are a little invention of mine," Christie said calmly. "They are how I keep track of my clients' wagers. We have so much business, we sometimes need a little prompt to remember who has wagered what." He turned each square over. "The blue mark means the bet is for the horse to place. Red is to win. On the back, my men at the track note the odds at the time the wager was made."

I regarded the markers with rising interest. "The letters presumably tell you which horse each was for?"

"They do, indeed. *AW* is Apollo's Wish—one of Lord Featherstonehaugh's stud, and a poor runner indeed. *HmD* is Heimdall, who is only marginally better."

"Mr. Pickett made these wagers at the race meeting," I said, understanding. "If he'd won, he'd turn them in to one of your assistants at the track or to you here for his winnings, correct?"

"That is true." Christie laid the squares tidily on the ledger and ran a fingertip along until he stopped at entries for *AW*, *HmD*, and the other two. "I am afraid none of these horses won or even placed, as you can see." He moved aside so Spendlove could study the entries. "Apollo's Wish came dead last, and this one scratched at the last minute, after wagering was closed." His finger rested on the initials *QD*.

Spendlove frowned at the entries for a time before he stepped away.

"Did you kill Pickett because of the several hundred guineas he owed you?" he demanded. "You followed him to Seven Dials, and when he wouldn't pay up, one of your ruffians stabbed him to death. Yes?"

Christie blinked in horrified surprise. "Good heavens, no. Even if it wasn't against all civilized laws, killing a debtor would be very bad for business."

The abject fear Hawes had showed Spendlove was absent on Christie's face. I perceived contempt from him instead, which he hid beneath unruffled politeness.

"Then you lose your money." Spendlove lifted the markers and dropped them on the book's page.

Christie shrugged. "I will appeal to Mr. Pickett's heirs, as will all his creditors."

"Pickett had no family," Spendlove informed him. "No wife or children, no brothers or sisters, that I've found. Only a deceased cousin, who left him a house in Bedfordshire, but the taxmen will likely take that property."

Christie lifted the markers and closed the book. "Ah, well. Sometimes we do not profit. It is a risk we take in our profession."

He appeared resigned, but like his accent, I believed Christie's expression was artificial. I sensed relief from him more than frustration that he was out a few hundred guineas. The clerks had also relaxed and turned back to their desks.

If Spendlove noticed any of this, he made no sign. "More

fool you," he said to Christie. "Keep that book near to hand, in case I need it as evidence."

Christie blenched, this reaction true. "There is confidential information in it, sir, on clients who have nothing to do with Mr. Pickett."

"Just those pages then," Spendlove conceded ungraciously.

"Evidence of what?" Christie handed the book back to the clerk, who hurried to return it to its shelf. "That Mr. Pickett enjoyed a flutter? Many gentlemen do. It is what allows me to remain in business."

"Evidence he didn't have a pot to piss in," Spendlove said. "That a man wouldn't have murdered him for his fortune. He'd have had other motives." He swung his hard stare to me, silently indicating that his badgering of Mr. Christie didn't mean he thought Denis in the clear.

I shrugged, keeping my countenance as bland as Christie's.

"I thank you, Mr. Christie, for answering our questions," I said, then continued in a casual tone, "Why do you suppose Mr. Pickett was so unlucky? I'd think, since he wagered often, that the odds would let him gain more than the very little he did. I know he won on occasion."

"Extremely rare occasions." Christie sounded amused. "Gentlemen will take tips from those who believe they know about horses when they do not. Or they choose based on a horse's name, or the pattern of raindrops on a windowsill, or other things highly unlikely to affect the outcome of a race."

Spendlove leaned dauntingly toward Christie. "Does anyone *ever* win? Or do all the horses your clients back come up lame?"

Christie's indignation was unfeigned. "If you believe we run a corrupt shop, sir, you are wrong. Plenty of my clients— gentlemen and ladies both—win fair and square. Those clients are paid, sometimes handsomely. This is a *business*, a service to those who wish to place wagers safely and have them paid back honestly."

His resentment that Spendlove would accuse him of cheating rang from him. The clerks likewise looked affronted.

Spendlove skewered him a glare, but Christie met his gaze without wavering. Christie would do very well on a witness stand, I mused, or in the dock. I wondered if he'd ever found himself in the latter.

Spendlove grunted. Without a farewell, he strode from the room, his tread sounding heavily in the uncarpeted hall.

I made Christie and his clerks a bow. "I thank you, sir. Gentlemen. Good morning."

"Good morning to you, Captain." Christie's goodbye was cooler than his welcome had been, but Spendlove could unsettle even the most composed of men.

The clerks nodded to me in return, and I clumped out after Spendlove.

Instead of heading for the coach, where Spendlove waited, I turned my steps in the other direction.

"Where are you going?" Spendlove barked.

"A moment." I reached Lackington's and stepped inside its front door, breathing a sigh as the bookroom's calm atmosphere surrounded me.

I approached a clerk with my question, and he guided me toward books on ballooning. I purchased one, had it wrapped up for delivery to the South Audley Street house, and only then rejoined the impatient Spendlove.

———

Once we were settled in the hackney, Spendlove shouted at the coachman to take us to Bow Street. I'd ceased directing the hunt, I understood.

"What do you intend to do next?" I asked with impatience.

"Interview these friends of Pickett's." Spendlove pulled the squashed list Hawes had given him from his pocket. The ink had dried now but had been smeared further while residing in his coat. "Two of them lease houses in London. The others have residences in Bedfordshire."

"Are you going to interview all of them? Today?" I asked in true dismay. Clearly he planned to drag me all over London with him.

"Runners have authority to pursue fugitives anywhere in England," Spendlove answered with as much irritability. "So, yes, all of them."

"I will not be going with you," I stated firmly. "I have a family and other commitments."

"Yes, I do know your lady wife will have my head on a platter if I don't return you home when you're expected." Spendlove's tone held derision. "You've given me enough to go on, I'll grant you that. I'll clear them all, whittling down the list until only Mr. Denis remains on it."

"Do as you like." I was finished being cordial. "Let me out anywhere, and I'll make my own way home."

Spendlove banged on the coach's roof. The trapdoor snapped open, and the coachman peered wearily down on us.

"Stop here," Spendlove commanded. "You have the conveyance, Captain. I'll walk." The coach halted once the driver found a space to guide it out of traffic, and Spendlove pushed open the door. "Mind you bring that diary you pinched from Pickett's rooms. And anything else for that matter."

I'd already decided I would, and the reminder to obey him grated.

Spendlove jumped down and slammed the door. I wasn't certain if his abandoning the carriage was a sneer at me for being unable to walk the distances he could, or simply a way to stick me with the fare. Spendlove never looked at my leg or walking stick, and he tossed a coin up at the coachman once he'd climbed down, so perhaps neither was the case. Spendlove could be disagreeable without trying very hard.

We were in Cheapside, near the heart of the City. Spendlove strode westward down the thoroughfare, soon lost among the carts and carriages that choked the road. His absence was like an unpleasant murk lifting.

"Where to, guv?" the hackney driver asked me with a little less belligerence.

"Curzon Street," I said. "Number 45."

CHAPTER 22

$\mathcal{I}$ pondered what we'd learned as the coach made its slow way to Mayfair, passing Newgate Prison on the way. Let Spendlove pursue Pickett's friends and discover why he'd bought the guns for them. Being fixated on Denis, Spendlove wasn't convinced the Bedfordshire men had anything to do with it, but he would want to cover every contingency so he could poke holes in any defense in court.

I no longer thought the guns were important, nor were the gentlemen Mr. Pickett had purchased them for.

From what everyone I'd spoken to had told me of Pickett, he'd been excitable and melodramatic. Possibly, after the Cato Street men's arrests and the subsequent tales the newspapers had poured out about them every day since, he'd convinced himself that one of his friends had a connection with them. Perhaps he'd feared that one of the Bedfordshire gentlemen had promised one or more of the shooters Pickett had ordered to them.

If one of them truly had, Spendlove would pry that information from him, but I knew in my heart that none of the men on the list had anything to do with the Cato Street Conspiracy.

No, I believed the purchase of the guns at all was the most significant event. Spendlove should be talking to Cudgeon, the gunsmith, instead, but I'd leave him to discern this for himself.

I tipped the driver well for putting up with Spendlove once we reached Curzon Street and approached Denis's front door.

Gibbons opened it before I could knock. "He can't speak to you now," was his greeting. "He has another visitor."

"I will wait." I removed my hat and tried to enter, but Gibbons wouldn't budge. "It is important," I said in irritation.

Gibbons regarded me with his usual stoniness but at last stepped back and admitted me. "Reception room," he said curtly.

I knew where that was but before I could make for it, I heard a light voice above me. I halted in surprise.

Denis, in a neat suit, with every hair in place, stood on the first landing, contemplating the painting of the milkmaid. Next to him, in a modest brown gown and a plain white cap—a little like the one the milkmaid wore—was Lady.

"I do see," she was saying. "The light from the window is almost a character itself, a fitting illumination for a scene of strength. I once had occasion to travel to the Low Countries and was fortunate enough to view his painting of a lady reading a letter. He used a similar technique with the window and light for that one as well."

"He enjoyed quiet, domestic scenes," Denis stated. "I have tried to acquire more of his works, but they are rare, almost unknown."

"The one I was shown belonged to a wealthy gentleman in Delft. Perhaps you could persuade him to sell it to you."

"I would be very grateful to him if he would," Denis said with the barest hint of keenness, which I'd learned meant he was avid to act right away.

"Excellent. I will provide his address. Though I warn you, it was many years ago. He might have moved his residence or passed away."

Denis shrugged minutely. "I will make inquiries."

Though I longed to continue observing this tableau, Lady glanced over her shoulder at that moment and spied me watching, openmouthed, below.

"Captain Lacey," she said in surprise. "How delightful to see you."

Denis turned but did not appear in any way delighted at my arrival. "Captain."

He did not invite me upstairs. Every line of him told me he wished I'd go away.

"I would not have come were it not important," I said by way of apology. "I am close to discovering who truly killed Mr. Pickett, but I need to ask a question."

"Then I will depart." Lady continued to smile at me, but regret showed in her eyes.

I might have taken myself away and told her to enjoy Denis's art collection a while longer, but for two things. One, I did want this puzzle cleared up so Spendlove would cease pestering the both of us and return to terrorizing the everyday criminals of London.

Second, I was not certain that Denis was the sort of gentleman I wanted Lady to spend time alone with. She and Denis were of an age, and Lady was charming and lovely. Denis, I supposed, was handsome enough, and possessed good manners and a large quantity of wealth, if ill-gotten.

He also kept a houseful of dangerous men and rivals who'd jump at the chance to have any sort of hold over him. An alliance with Denis, I knew from harrowing experience, could be perilous.

I was also uncertain what sort of connection Denis would want if he was indeed succumbing to Lady's natural appeal. A

liaison had hurt her before. I would become his direst enemy if
he caused such a thing to occur again.

"Thank you for your kindness," Lady was saying to Denis.
"And for the tea. It was excellent."

Denis bowed to her in acknowledgement, then offered his
arm to escort her down the stairs. Lady rested her fingers in the
crook of his elbow, as she had when he'd taken her into the
bakeshop, and they descended together.

"Mr. Denis is proving quite resourceful," Lady said to me as
they reached the ground floor. "You were good to ask him to
help on my behalf."

Gibbons, his expression wooden, produced Lady's mantle.
Denis took it from him and held it as Lady wrapped herself in
its warmth.

Gibbons opened the door, as stiffly proper as any Mayfair
butler. I was about to dash out and find Lady a hackney—mine
had already departed—but Denis's own coach pulled forward
before I could. One of his lackeys must have run for it the
moment she'd declared she'd depart.

"Thank you, Captain," Lady said as she passed me. "I antici-
pate good news of my daughter soon. And I do hope things go
well for you and Mr. Denis. The Runners can be overzealous,
can they not?"

He'd told her, I realized, the entire tale of his incarceration
and Spendlove's determination to have him convicted of
murder.

I wasn't certain how to respond. "Perhaps there will be
happy endings for us all," was the best I could produce.

Lady's smile broadened, the young woman, as usual, amused
at my expense. "Happy endings only exist in stories, I have
discovered. Happy times in the present are to be treasured, so
we can remember them with fondness during the sad ones." Her
soft eyes twinkled. "Enjoy yours, Captain. Good day."

She glided down the few steps to the street and the waiting

carriage. Mr. Downie opened the coach door for her and handed her in, for which she thanked him prettily.

The coach rolled away, and we gentlemen stood in silence for a time, as though breathing in the last sweet air of summer.

Downie winked at me and disappeared down the outer stairs, making for the kitchen. Gibbons pointedly held the door for us, and Denis, without a word, walked back into the house and straight up the stairs.

I followed. Gibbons closed the front door and completely ignored me as he made his way to the back of the house.

I climbed in Denis's wake, pausing at the painting on the landing. I understood what Lady had meant about the pleasing way the artist had the light slanting in from the window, illuminating the woman's bright garments and one side of her face. The picture held serenity, and I knew it to be Denis's favorite of his collection.

Denis was already at his desk when I walked into the study. I seated myself in my usual chair, guessing that I would not be served any brandy or coffee today.

"You invited her to take tea?" I asked before Denis could speak.

He regarded me with more iciness than usual. "I had news of Lady's daughter and sent my coach for her so she could learn of it in comfortable surroundings, ones in which we would not be overheard. I thought it polite to offer her a repast in the drawing room downstairs. She was interested in my paintings and had seen the Vermeer on her way in. She asked to look at it, and I saw no reason not to allow this."

And, I suspected, Denis had been pleased to discuss the picture with someone who understood and appreciated art.

"What news?" I asked. "Of her daughter?"

Denis twined his hands together on the empty desk. "I located the family called Redding. When Mr. Redding died, his widow indeed sold the business, and she departed to stay with relations in Northampton. I have sent agents there to inquire about her children and whether Lady's daughter is still with her. And, if not, what became of her."

I relaxed. "Thank you. I intended to do more about it, but I have been running all over London trying to make sure you stay off the gallows."

"You *did* do something about finding Lady's daughter," Denis said. "You turned the problem over to me. I have resources for this sort of thing."

"That is true," I acknowledged. "Whereas I, who am supposed to have gained skill at catching murderers, have come up with all sorts of motives for Pickett's death, none of them the correct ones. I've been distracted by his worry about secret societies and the Cato Street arrests."

"You said you wanted to ask me a question," Denis prompted before I could begin too many musings. "What is it?"

I pulled my thoughts together. "You told me you answered Pickett's appeal for your help because he could pay your fee. How did you know he could?"

Denis's brows rose. "Because I inquired about him. I learned he'd recently inherited a house in Bedfordshire and money with it. I was reasonably certain he could pay me, even if he had to offer me the property in lieu of cash. Of course, if he could not produce the fee or proof he could obtain it at our first meeting, I would have turned him away."

"And why did he miss his meeting with you?"

"You have now asked two questions," Denis said dryly.

"I might be forgiven the second, because I am simply thinking out loud. What if Pickett missed the appointment because he was trying to get his hands on the funds with which to pay you and for some reason could not?"

Denis gave me a nod. "It is possible."

"I have been hearing ever since I first became aware of Mr. Pickett that he was unlucky. He habitually lost money on the races, did not have a family or other support to fall back on, and could rent only cheap if respectable rooms while in Town. He recently inherited the house in Bedfordshire, which I have been told is modest rather than being a grand estate. He bought furnishings for it and ran up other personal debts, according to the vowels I found, but then he ordered half a dozen shooters from Mr. Cudgeon. Even *one* of his expertly made guns would set a man back a long way. So." I paused significantly. "Where did he get the money for them?"

Denis looked interested despite himself. "His legacy?"

I shook my head. "The cousin apparently left him only a hundred and fifty guineas, along with the house. I found dunning notices from a furniture maker, which tells me he made only a partial payment for anything he purchased for his household . Even if he used a portion of the legacy to order the guns from Cudgeon, he'd never have enough to pay the for rest. Why did he believe he'd be able to make a final payment for those, settle his furniture bill, and pay you as well? I imagine your services are not inexpensive."

Denis did not answer my last supposition. "Perhaps he truly was involved in one of these fiery political societies, and someone paid him to keep quiet about it."

"That is a possibility, but not a likely one. The trouble with secret organizations is that they are not very secret. I was welcomed into Pickett's without threat—in fact, they were happy I was looking into the circumstances of his death. I do not believe Pickett knew anything at all about the Cato Street men or any other conspiracy. That was his vivid imagination."

Denis sent me an impatient look. "Very well, then, what is your solution? You have one, I can see. You are simply letting me propose others, so you can refute them."

"Yes, forgive me. Grenville and I often debate like this, which helps us both to think." I leaned forward, resting my weight on my walking stick. "My idea is this: What if Pickett *did* win at the races? Finally, after many tries. Won so much he could order guns, pay what he owed for his furniture and other debts, and promise you a hefty fee to help him flee to France in his overblown concern about his safety?"

Denis's annoyance began to dissolve. "You could be correct."

"The bookmaker I visited today swears up and down that Pickett lost almost every time, only winning a small amount on the exceptional occasion." I thought of the quiet Mr. Christie and his unruffled demeanor, even with Spendlove at his shoulder. "I propose that when Christie heard of Mr. Pickett's death, he conveniently erased this wager from his books—or possibly never logged it at all. If Pickett's estate came calling, he could claim he knew nothing about it, and in fact, Pickett had owed *him* money. The heirs could try to take Christie to court, but the courts usually conclude that if a man loses money to a corrupt bookmaker, it is his own fault for being a fool. When Spendlove informed Christie that Pickett had no heirs, I swore that every man in the room breathed a sigh of relief. I did not understand at the time, but it fits."

Denis's hands twitched, a sign of his interest. "You believe he did not yet have the winnings when he wrote to me but assumed he'd be able to fetch them and bring them to the appointment."

"And then for some reason he could not. Which is why he missed his meeting with you. Maybe he went to Finsbury Square to hand in his betting token and collect his cash, but found the place shut. Perhaps Mr. Christie saw him coming and decided to pull down the shades and not answer the door. If my speculations are correct, it must have been a powerful lot of money."

"For which one man might kill another," Denis said.

He and I regarded each other in perfect agreement.

"I must pose yet another question," I said. *"What became of the betting token?"*

CHAPTER 23

*D*enis fixed his entire attention on me, which would have been unnerving any other time. "Any number of people might have it," he said.

"From Pickett's Bedfordshire friends to his downstairs neighbor." I thought of my encounters with the nightcap-wearing man. "The neighbor eager to know what we were doing in the house. I need to speak to him again."

"The bookmaker will not be keen on paying out even if the token it is found," Denis said. "If someone already tried to hand it in, he might have taken it and destroyed it. I know Christie. He's taught himself to be well-spoken to deal with his gentlemen clients, but he is a ruthless man." That Denis believed so meant Christie was formidable indeed.

"It must have been a spectacular win if it was truly the motive for killing Pickett," I said. "I admit, I haven't kept up with the racing news."

"Robbie," Denis said to the large man at his post near the window. "Please fetch Mr. Stout."

Robbie nodded and departed. Denis offered no explanation

for why he needed Stout but continued to study me as I pondered.

"I could question Christie again, without Spendlove's interference," I said, growing uncomfortable with his intense gaze. "Though I doubt he'd tell me anything more."

"He is adept at keeping secrets," Denis answered. "A better idea is to have your friends watch the premises and alert you when one of Pickett's associates attempts to claim the money."

"If it hasn't been already. Maybe Pickett collected the cash and was killed for it when he crossed the city again. We've wondered why nothing was taken, but perhaps the robber found so much money that he didn't need to bother with the man's watch or handkerchief."

"Unlikely, as you have already reasoned," Denis said. "Christie would have told you, with genuine sorrow, if he'd paid out to Pickett. Keeping that information quiet would not benefit him—he'd prefer you and Spendlove to look elsewhere for whoever took the winnings from him. Christie doesn't fear the Runners—he fears losing money."

"Then Christie himself might have murdered him."

"Possibly, though that would be out of character for him."

I moved to the edge of my chair. "We had better act at once." I wasn't certain whether Denis would lend me a few men to help watch the place, but no matter if he did not. I'd recruit Brewster and Grenville, and find others who could assist.

Robbie returned with the prickly Mr. Stout in tow.

Stout gave me a scowl but his stance before Denis was respectful. "Guv?"

"I need information on recent horse races," Denis said. "Point-to-points or flat races, even informal ones. Have any had an unusual win?"

"Aye, one did," Stout answered promptly. "Last week, out Dunstable way. Horse came in at thirty-to-one, odds against. Gents tried to claim the rider cheated, but there was no sign of it. Bookmakers wept but paid out. Not many wagered on that horse, though, because he was way outside."

I rose with animation. "So, if Pickett made a reckless bet, say a hundred guineas ..."

"He'd have won three thousand, plus his original stake." Stout lost his churlish expression for a moment of reverence. "A fortune."

"You are proposing he put most of his legacy on a horse?" Denis brought us down to earth with his disbelieving tone.

"From what I understand of the man, it would be just like him," I said. "He might have taken out fifty guineas for his furniture order and for Cudgeon, but Pickett was a habitual gambler. Could he resist using the rest of it to have a flutter? Even if he wagered only half of his inheritance, that would have brought him ..." I tried and failed to do quick calculation in my head.

"A little more than twenty-three hundred," Stout supplied.

"Still quite a lot of money." I gave Stout an acknowledging nod. "He's given a payment to Cudgeon, with the promised balance when Cudgeon finishes the order. Same to the furniture maker. Pickett then attends the race—his Bedfordshire house is probably not far from Dunstable—and decides to place the rest of his money on the long-odds horse, an action apparently typical for him. He makes the bet with one of Christie's men, receiving the token with a red mark to win, and the odds plus the name of the horse on the back. To his amazement, he wins."

"Why didn't he take in the chitty right off?" Stout demanded. "I'd have been at that bookmaker so fast I'd have churned up the turf in me haste."

"I'd do the same," Robbie put in.

"Something prevented him." I paced as I mused. "Pickett had a bee in his bonnet about the Cato Street Conspiracy. Perhaps he feared that if he was suddenly flush with cash, the Runners would haul him before a magistrate to answer awkward questions. He decided to wait—or someone convinced him to wait."

"Then murdered him and stole the betting token," Denis finished.

"Possibly. Was the killer indeed the person who convinced him to wait? Or one of the gentlemen who recommended you as the person to help him leave the country? If any of those three needed a quick influx of cash, and here is Pickett asking their advice on how to flee …"

"That, we will have to discover," Denis said.

"Yes." I knew I was wildly speculating. "The field is still broad. Was it one of his new Bedfordshire friends? Or Mr. Cudgeon, or one of Cudgeon's assistants? One of Christie's clerks or even Christie? Though you say it is not in his character, he might have been desperate not to pay out such a sum. Or was it someone at Pickett's lodgings? They would have the best opportunity, I'd think. Mr. Hawes, for instance."

Hawes was of a timid disposition and not very large—Pickett could have overpowered such a man coming at him with a knife. Unless, of course, Hawes took him by surprise, giving him no time to defend himself. Nightcap, however, was athletically built, blunt, and unafraid. Blustering about being awakened could have covered his nervousness at a Runner's abrupt intrusion into the house.

I still hadn't ruled out the Honorable Mr. Haywood, the man who'd paid off his debt to Denis by casting doubts on Spendlove's arrest and freeing Denis from Newgate. Haywood could have murdered Pickett—or paid someone to—to give him the perfect task he could perform for Denis.

If Haywood were the killer, then Pickett's death would have nothing to do with a win at the races, crumbling my theory to dust. Though Haywood or his accomplice could have found the token and pocketed it, I supposed. They might simply destroy it, not realizing what they had.

I let out a sigh. "I have much to do."

"I agree." Denis glanced at the desk's surface as though he

longed for papers to appear on it. "I will interview the gentlemen Mr. Pickett named in his letter to me. If any of them stole the token while he consulted with them, they will tell me. Likewise, if they murdered him."

The quiet way Denis declared this chilled me.

I ceased my agitated pacing, realizing I'd left my walking stick leaning against the chair in my frenzy. I seized it, my knee aching. "I will put a watch on Finsbury Square for anyone attempting to collect Pickett's winnings. I'll try to narrow the field as well, in case the man—or woman, I suppose—decides to wait weeks before approaching Christie. Is there a time limit on when a successful wager can be collected?" I asked Stout.

"Before the bookmaker closes his doors and hies to another country," was Stout's optimistic response.

"I see. Well, then, I will bid you good day, gentlemen. I hope when we meet again, the murderer has been arrested."

"Or turned himself in," Denis said. If Denis caught the man, he would probably hurry to Bow Street for his own safety.

None of the three in the room moved to escort me out, so I made my own way downstairs, regretting that I'd rushed about on my bad leg.

Gibbons was heading toward the front door as I descended. From his expression, he was still displeased with me for interrupting Denis's chat with Lady.

"Mr. Gibbons," I addressed him as I resumed my coat. "What time was Mr. Haywood's appointment on the night before Mr. Pickett's murder?"

"One o'clock in the morning." Gibbons' lips pinched. "Mr. Haywood wished to attend a supper ball first."

His expression told me his opinion of Haywood was even lower than the one of me.

"Thank you, Gibbons. Good morning."

"Afternoon." Gibbons swung open the door to show a much lighter sky and no rain.

"Ah, yes. Good afternoon, Gibbons."

Gibbons said nothing as I stepped outside. He slammed the door behind me, shutting me out of Denis's house with finality.

———

I MADE MY WAY HOME ON FOOT, SCARCELY NOTICING THE COLD wind or even where I walked, so thoroughly did my whirling thoughts blot out my surroundings.

If I was correct about Pickett winning so large a sum, I'd have to proceed swiftly. Spendlove and I had alerted Christie that we were investigating Pickett's affairs, and he might fear that we'd return with pointed questions. Christie could very well have doctored his ledgers to remove the record of Pickett's wager, as I'd suggested to Denis. After all, the man was dead. If any heirs came calling, Christie could sadly show them the ledger he'd shown Spendlove and me.

I could be absolutely wrong about my conclusions, which was another thought that kept me from noticing the weather. Pickett might have lost his money on the race as usual, or not put down a wager at all. But a long-odds horse, the sort Pickett liked, running in a race so close to his new home, and then Pickett writing to Denis about coming into "good fortune" had to be connected. The good fortune to which he referred was not his legacy but his splendid win.

I nearly walked past my own house, so deep was I in contemplation. Only the footman calling out in puzzlement made me swing around and march inside.

I went straight to the library and dashed off a few brief letters. One to the magistrate, Sir Montague Harris, asking him what he could tell me about one Jonathan Christie. If Christie had a history of fraudulent behavior, Sir Montague would either already know about it or be able to discover it.

Second, I wrote to Grenville, asking if we could speak to his friend Langley again. Langley might know, even if he hadn't attended the same race, whether Pickett had wagered a stake on the outside horse at Dunstable last week.

Third, I scribbled a brief note to Brewster, who'd gone back home after I'd run off with Spendlove, telling him I needed to set a watch on Christie's establishment in Finsbury Square, what I'd be up to in the meantime, and where to meet me.

I hurried downstairs, instructing Barnstable to have the letters sent immediately, and prepared to set off to Pickett's rooms again.

As I'd instructed Brewster to go elsewhere, I asked Bartholomew to accompany me. He was a stout fellow, good to have at my side if I encountered a man reluctant to admit he'd stolen a very lucrative betting token.

The hackney Bartholomew fetched took us through traffic to St. James's and Park Place.

The Arlington was a little more lively on this warm and dry afternoon. Men came and went, some leaving the flats next door for the club or the other way about.

I descended in time to see Nightcap exit the club and stroll the short way to the door of the flats.

"Sir." I called to him as I approached, my walking stick striking the pavement. Behind me, Bartholomew handed the hackney driver a coin and asked him to wait.

Nightcap man turned to me, his expression annoyed. "It's you again, is it? The army officer poking about Mr. Pickett's business? The poor man is dead. Leave him be."

"How do you know I am an army officer?" I hadn't given him my name, much less my history.

The gentleman waved a gloved hand at my frame. "It is written all over you, sir. Injured fighting Bonaparte, leathery face from marching in the sun, standing at attention. I avoided the whole sorry show, I am pleased to say."

"I am Captain Gabriel Lacey," I said. "Of the Thirty-Fifth Light Dragoons."

"Of course you are. Francis Taylor." The man held out his hand. "Forgive my testiness, but you woke me from a sound sleep this morning."

I shook a hand that was steady and strong. Yes, he could very well have driven a knife into Pickett's chest. "You never answered my question."

"Eh?" The man's scowl deepened. "What question?"

"I asked if Mr. Pickett had any visitors on Monday night. You evaded the answer."

Mr. Taylor scanned the narrow lane behind me. "Is that Runner bloke with you?"

"Mr. Spendlove? No. And I will not necessarily tell him anything you say to me."

"*Not necessarily,*" Taylor repeated. "I see. I suppose you mean you will not unless I turn out to be Pickett's murderer. Yes, someone came to call on Pickett very late Monday night. You might say early Tuesday morning. They must have thought they were being quiet and discreet, but no. Pickett's friends are always noisy."

"So this visitor kept you awake?" I asked.

"Indeed. Swearing and arguing, he and Pickett were. Couldn't make out any exact words, which might at least have been interesting. I was glad when things quieted down."

"What time was that?"

Taylor shrugged. "Must have been gone two. I checked my watch at quarter 'til. Maybe another quarter hour had passed before they ceased."

"You didn't happen to notice *who* went upstairs to argue with him?" I asked without much hope.

"I did not." Taylor's gaze held true regret. "I didn't know Pickett would be murdered the next morning, did I? 'Course that happened in Seven Dials. He must have met someone else he argued with."

"No," I corrected him. "I believe Pickett was killed in his flat. In this very house."

Taylor's mouth popped open. "Good Lord, you are not joking, are you?" He cleared his throat, unnerved. "Well, do not tell Hawes. The man will faint."

"Hawes must have let the killer in," I said.

"Perhaps, perhaps not. Pickett was capable of walking downstairs and opening a door. It was very late. I imagine Mr. Hawes was in bed by then."

"I will ask him. Thank you, sir."

I turned toward the club to seek Mr. Hawes, and Taylor fell into step with me. "I say, sir, you've roused my curiosity. Let me find Hawes with you."

Bartholomew joined us as the footman opened the Arlington's door.

"Fetch Hawes," Taylor commanded the footman before I could speak. "There's a good fellow."

As the lad darted away, Taylor motioned for me to accompany him inside. Bartholomew remained in the foyer, taking the hat I handed him before I followed Taylor to a nearby anteroom.

The room was small but comfortable, with white-painted paneling, Louis XV chairs, and a lit fireplace. Paintings adorned the walls, nothing valuable, I believed, though pleasant enough to look at.

"Did Pickett ever speak to you about race meetings?" I asked Taylor as we each sank to a gilt-legged chair.

"Yes," Taylor answered without a pause. "He wagered and lost on them all the time. Couldn't *not* tell anyone about them. Tedious, it was. Where were you in the war?"

I wondered at his abrupt change of subject, but I had no objection to telling him. "I was everywhere. I volunteered at the tender age of twenty at the urging of a captain—who is now a colonel. Made a lieutenant after Mysore, then captain after Vitoria." My father had died the same year, never hearing of my promotion.

"Quite a career," Taylor observed. His interest seemed genuine. "Mysore, you say? What was that like?"

Before I could launch into any details about hot, humid Indian campaigns, Mr. Hawes opened the door.

"Captain?" Like Tayler, he glanced about as though wondering if Spendlove accompanied me. His relief when he did not see him was obvious. "How can I help you?"

"He wants to know who came to see Pickett late Monday night," Taylor said before I could speak. "Early Tuesday, actually. Did you let him in?"

Hawes shook his head, his voice becoming breathy. "I admitted no one. If a man visited Mr. Pickett, I did not see him."

"There." Taylor gave me with a *you see?* gesture. "Pickett must have let the man in himself."

Hawes calmed, liking this explanation. "I suppose he did."

"May I see Pickett's rooms again?" I asked. "I know I continue to request this, but it is important."

It was clear Hawes wanted to deny me, but with Taylor watching him so intently, he decided capitulating was the easiest option. Hawes nodded, quickly exiting. I followed, and Taylor, still curious, came with me. Bartholomew trailed us as we left the club.

Hawes did not speak as we entered the house next door and made the long climb to Pickett's rooms. Hawes's fingers shook as he unlocked the door, but he made no argument about us entering.

The flat was stuffy, the closed windows on the warming day letting no air move. I opened the wardrobe in the front room to find Pickett's coats, some still sadly torn, back on the shelves and pegs within. Hawes must have replaced them.

I knew Spendlove had searched thoroughly—he knew how to hunt for evidence—but he'd not known then what we were looking for. I removed two frock coats, feeling the linings for any telltale signs of one of Christie's betting tokens.

Finding nothing, I replaced the coats, then went to the bureau in the bedchamber and briefly stabbed my fingers through the linens in the top drawer. Nothing there either. I opened all the drawers with the same result, then closed them and eyed the bed.

I started to sink to my knees, ready to search beneath, but Bartholomew stopped me. With enviable agility, he dropped to the floor and stretched out his long body, balancing on hands and toes.

"What are you looking for, sir?" Bartholomew asked.

"Anything tucked into the mattress or beneath the bed slats," I said. "A small box. Or a folded piece of paper." The betting token could have been enclosed in that.

Bartholomew scanned the space then rolled over and scooted under the bed. "Nothing I can see, Captain," came his muffled tones.

I waited for Bartholomew to wriggle himself out and climb to his feet before I turned to the two men who hovered behind me.

"Mr. Hawes," I said, pinning him with my sternest gaze. "What did you do with the betting token?"

Hawes gaped, his confusion mounting.

Then he abruptly snapped his mouth closed, turned, and fled.

CHAPTER 24

*B*artholomew instantly sprang after Hawes, racing into the hall and to the stairs, plunging down them after his quarry. Mr. Taylor, displaying remarkable energy, charged behind Bartholomew, leaving me, cursing and hobbling, behind.

By the time I reached the ground floor and made my way out the front door, the three had already gained the busy thoroughfare of St. James's Street. Bartholomew's golden head bobbed like a beacon in the sea of carts and carriages.

I hurried forward the best I could then paused at the end of Park Place to catch my breath. Hawes was nowhere in sight and neither was Mr. Taylor. Bartholomew, towering above the crowd of men in greatcoats and high hats, saw me and shrugged. He'd lost them.

Hawes, damn him, must know exactly what had happened to Pickett, whether he'd killed the man or had simply been a witness. Either way, he'd been afraid to come forward. Spendlove showing up on his doorstep must have terrified him.

A carriage nearly ran me down as I stood gazing about, its coachman shouting invectives. Once it had moved on, I spied

Hawes. He quivered on the other side of St. James's Street, silhouetted against the stone edifices there.

I put my head down and charged across the road, willing the Almighty to make certain I wasn't struck down by waggoners or impatient coachmen. Hawes saw me coming and ran.

The bloody man. I yelled to Bartholomew but had no idea whether he'd heard me. He'd spot me, I trusted, as he scanned the street. What had become of Taylor, I couldn't say.

Hawes vanished. I willed myself to ignore the pain in my knee as I hurried to where I'd last seen him. I was rewarded when I found a small passageway between two buildings, down which Hawes was now speeding. These lanes sprang up in London now and again when houses that had been built in different eras didn't quite connect. Or, the developer had deliberately left a space for night-soil men and necessary maintenance.

Hawes scuttled down the passageway, the space so narrow two people would not be able to walk abreast. The lane curved around into the shadow of the close-set, tall buildings, the spring sunshine not penetrating here.

Hawes reached a door. He banged on it, frantically rattling its handle as I bore down on him.

The door jerked open, and a man I didn't recognize stepped out. He had a knife in his hand.

That knife went into the back of Mr. Hawes.

I shouted and ran toward them as the man lugged the falling Hawes across the threshold.

I felt a draft behind me, then something heavy landed on my neck. I fell to my knees, hard stones scraping them. Strong hands grabbed the back of my coat and hauled me unceremoniously into an inky dark space, where I knew nothing more.

————

I DRAGGED MYSELF AWAKE, AT FIRST TOO GROGGY TO comprehend where I lay. It was dark, which meant it was night, but what had awakened me?

The hard surface beneath me was not my bed. For a fleeting moment, I believed myself in a tent in Spain, taking a few last moments of sleep before I'd rise and prepare my men for the next battle.

Was I truly back on campaign, and my life since leaving the army a hazy dream? A profound sense of loss wrenched me. Was marrying Donata, reuniting with my daughter, starting a second family, and finding friends and a purpose all a lie?

I vowed I heard the bluff tones of Colonel Brandon, my erstwhile mentor, outside my tent, but as consciousness eased back to me, I realized the voice belonged to another man entirely.

"Will 'e live?"

I peeled open my eyes, expecting to find menacing ruffians standing over me, but no one lurked in my dark corner. I then realized the speaker wasn't talking about me.

I pushed myself up from a stone floor, climbing sickeningly to my knees. I knelt there, holding myself steady on a damp wall beside me, simply breathing and trying not to collapse.

After a while, I forced one foot underneath me and used the wall to pull myself up. I rested again, hugging the wall, waiting for my dizziness to abate.

When I could finally stand without support, I left my sanctuary and staggered toward a circle of light. I no longer had my walking stick. Either I'd dropped it outside, or my captors had taken it from me.

The light proved to emanate from a single candle held aloft by a beefy man. Here were the ruffians, two of them, hovering over a table where Hawes lay face down. Hawes was breathing, albeit raggedly.

"Why'd ye stick him?" the speaker I'd heard before was saying to the man with the candle.

"He was going to bring the law down on us, weren't he?" his compatriot replied, somewhat fretfully.

They both swung around as I scraped my way forward, unable to be silent limping across this floor.

"Where the hell am I?" I demanded. "If you thought I was the law chasing Hawes, you could not be more wrong."

"Who are you then?" the man with the candle asked in puzzlement.

I halted a little way from them, mindful of how handy the candle-wielding gent had been with his blade. "A fine way to greet a guest. I am Captain Lacey. This is Mr. Hawes, the manager of the Arlington." I pointed at him. "Where are we? Under one of the lavish palaces of St. James's?"

The first man ignored my questions. "If you're a military bloke, you'll know about wounds." He jerked his chin at Hawes. "Patch this one up. We don't need 'im dying."

I hobbled toward them, keeping a wary eye out for weapons. "I'm hardly a surgeon. Why do you care if he lives?"

"None of your affair," the first man said. "Help 'im."

They'd removed Hawes's coat and waistcoat, revealing a lawn shirt soaked with blood. "You need to cut that away," I commanded.

The man in charge produced a knife that glinted in the candlelight. I half-expected him to turn it on me, but he lowered the blade and competently slit Hawes's shirt lengthwise down the middle.

"Don't toss it aside," I said as he slid the garment from under Hawes. "Tear the clean parts into strips. His only hope is a good bandaging." Without the tools to sew him up, or the knowledge of exactly how to do so, this was the best I could devise.

Hawes's wound lay in his lower back. It was not deep, but it didn't have to be. If the blade had penetrated one of his organs, he'd perish, and there was nothing we could do about it.

If he were lucky, and the knife had only torn flesh and

muscle, he would eventually heal, if the wound didn't take sick. He'd be in agony for a while but live.

I used one of the cloths the man had ripped from the shirt to wipe the blood, now drying, from the wound. I folded the cloth into a pad and then bound it tightly to the gash with the other strips.

The man helped me, lifting Hawes's body so I could pass the strips beneath him. The man with the candle held the light steadily and competently. They must have performed such tasks before.

Hawes woke during the procedure and began to wail in pain. By the time we were finished, he'd subsided into an exhausted whimper.

"My walking stick," I said to the lead man. He resembled Mr. Stout, with a hard face, thick body, and wiry hair, though I doubted they were related. Of a similar type, I'd say, being raised to a similar life. "Where is it?"

"I've kept it safe for ye," he told me. "What did you want with Hawes?"

I remained stern. "To ask him a question. Hawes already knows the answer, which is why he ran from me. Was he seeking sanctuary here? The poor fellow got more than he bargained for, didn't he?"

"Mr. Hawes ain't your business," the man told me.

"No? Whose business is he, then?"

The man with the candle glowered at me. "The one who don't want you on his patch."

"Ah." I wondered if these two had been part of the gang who'd fought Brewster and me in Curzon Street. It had been too dark to distinguish anything but fists. "You mean Mr. Arthur."

"My friend talks too much," the first man said. "But it so happens, he has the right of it. Leave Hawes to us."

"Very well." I dropped the remaining makeshift bandages onto Hawes's back. "Then I'll take my walking stick and go."

"No, you'll wait."

I regarded him impatiently. "If Mr. Brewster finds me before whatever I'm waiting for occurs, you'll not be happy, I think."

I spoke with confidence I did not feel. I had no way of knowing exactly where I was, if Bartholomew had noticed where I'd disappeared to, and if he or Brewster would reach me before Arthur decided to kill me.

The lead man was not impressed. "We wait."

I assessed my chances of fighting my way free without my walking stick and finding my way out of this place in the dark. They were not good.

I moved to the head of the table, where Hawes lay groaning. "In the meantime, Mr. Hawes, perhaps you will answer my question."

"I don't have the bloody token," Hawes croaked. "He took it, didn't he?"

"The man who killed Mr. Pickett?"

"Yes."

Neither of the toughs appeared astounded that Hawes had witnessed a murder, but they frowned when Hawes mentioned the token.

"Did these gentlemen assist you that night?" I went on.

"Not *them*." Hawes twitched his fingers at the pair. "But yes."

"Mr. Arthur came to your aid." I clarified.

"Yes."

The lead man grunted. "'Course he did. Hawes is one of ours."

"I see."

I thought I truly did see now. The dark dankness of this cellar had cleared the murk from my mind.

"Did you assist in killing Mr. Pickett, even if you didn't

strike the fatal blow?" I asked Hawes. I did not think so, but I needed to be certain.

"No." Hawes's answer was adamant if strained. "I found him dead on his carpet. What was I to do?"

"Send for a watchman, perhaps?" I suggested.

"A watchman," the man with the candle sneered. "They'd have arrested 'Awes for the deed, wouldn't they? 'E'd even now be in the dock or dancing on the wind."

"Probably so," I agreed. "Night watchmen haven't much imagination, and even Runners would rather have an easy solution. They'd claim Hawes stabbed Pickett in order to steal his winnings, and I'm certain any judge and jury would believe it. But you say you don't have the token, Mr. Hawes?"

"No." Hawes's angry disappointment convinced me he told the truth.

I filled in the gaps. "You sent for Mr. Arthur to help you. The Arlington is on his patch, as he calls it, and you, or its owner, pay him to keep thieves away. He dispatched a few of his lackeys to assist you in smuggling Mr. Pickett out of the house, bundled in blankets, perhaps, into a waiting coach. Then Pickett's body was taken to Seven Dials." I regarded Hawes in curiosity. "Why Seven Dials?"

A new voice answered me. "Because I knew His Bastardness was there that morning. Why'd ye think?"

CHAPTER 25

illiam Arthur stepped from the darkness into the candlelight. He was alone, gazing at me as affably as he'd done outside the opera house in Covent Garden.

I'd been speaking with his two ruffians somewhat fearlessly, because I'd realized they'd not been ordered to kill me. If they had, I'd already be dead.

But here was the man who gave the orders.

"You seized the opportunity," I told him, pretending my heart wasn't pounding with renewed apprehension. "Why not leave a dead man on Denis's doorstep and maybe get him arrested for it? What a stroke of luck to have Denis find him at the right moment," I finished without inflection. I was very certain now that Arthur had engineered everything.

"Not entirely luck." Arthur confirmed my theory. "I knew Denis had gone to Seven Dials that night for an appointment—I know everything he does. We took the body there, wrapped in lap robes as you've guessed, and waited until his visitor was finished and things quieted. Then I had the dead bloke moved in front of his door. Denis came out very soon after—maybe he heard a noise, or maybe he sensed I was nearby. He's like a cat, that one. He nearly tripped over this Pickett fellow, and a patroller appeared to catch him. Poor Denis has a lot of people following him, don't he?" He chuckled.

"One of your lackeys alerted the patroller?" I asked. "I doubt they like to venture any further into Seven Dials than absolutely necessary."

Arthur shrugged. "That is true—they avoid the place with pleasure. Took my man a few minutes to convince him to have a look. What is this token you're going on about?"

"Mr. Pickett had won well at the races," I said. It scarcely mattered now what Arthur knew. The betting token was beyond his reach. "He wanted his winnings so he could pay Denis to help him flee the country. But the token he got from Mr. Christie's betting establishment hasn't turned up. It was stolen from him by the murderer. Whom you saw, Mr. Hawes, am I correct?"

Hawes was silent for so long that I feared he'd lost consciousness. "Mayhap," he answered at last.

"Which was another reason you sent for Mr. Arthur, wasn't it? If the killer knew you'd seen him, he might come back for you."

"Yes," Hawes wheezed. "But he never did."

I turned to Arthur as though we conversed in a drawing room at one of Donata's soirees. "You didn't go after the killer yourself, Mr. Arthur? In case he threatened Hawes?"

Arthur shook his head. "I don't know who it was, and I don't much care. Hawes is under our protection. We look after him. Don't mean we go chasing murderers for the Runners."

"Your men looked after Hawes so well that he needs a surgeon," I pointed out.

"They were mistaken," Arthur said easily. "He'll be taken care of." He assessed me slowly, the amiability in his eyes fading to something flinty. "The question is, what am I going to do about *you?*"

"A dilemma for you, I'm certain." My mouth was dry, but I would not let myself moisten my lips. Betraying my fear would gain me nothing. "My wife comes from a very powerful family, and her first marriage was into another one. She will make certain that neither takes my death lightly."

"I am pleased to hear they are so fond of you," Arthur said. "I remember telling you, I make it my practice to deal only with those who have annoyed me. I don't play petty games with their ladies and children. I can arrange things so none ever know what happened to you."

I believed he could. Donata, Grenville, and Brewster would search for me, and perhaps even Pomeroy or Denis would too. Even if they found my body, none but Denis might tumble to who'd actually killed me.

I hadn't heard of Mr. Arthur until a few days ago—I imagine he kept himself well in the shadows. Denis would realize what he'd done, and Brewster likely would as well, but they might both believe it prudent not to expose Arthur to the magistrates. They could always take private vengeance on him, but that would scarcely help me now.

"Mr. Hawes will be a witness," I tried.

"Mr. Hawes will say nothing."

Hawes made a feeble noise of agreement. He'd kept the secret of Pickett's murderer, I had to acknowledge, letting Arthur fit Denis up for it. He'd do what Arthur told him.

"Then I will have to defend myself the best I can," I said, as though resigned.

Arthur chuckled. "It is a happy day, Captain. I have decided *not* to kill you. As you say, your friends could make trouble for me, and I wager Denis himself would realize that I'd rid the world of you. He can be a bit testy about such things."

"I am glad to hear it." I kept my tone mild, but my limbs went watery with relief.

"However, I cannot simply send you out the door with my

compliments." Arthur removed his hands from his pockets. In one he held a cudgel. "I do want to give you something to remember me by. Perhaps it will teach you to stay well out of my business."

Both men at the table advanced on me. The fellow with the candle had stuck it into a holder, and he too produced a cudgel. The other man already had his knife.

Mr. Hawes made a squeak of fear, but I doubt it was on my behalf. He must be wondering what they'd do to him once they were finished with me.

All three rushed me at once, giving me no time to run. If I could find my walking stick, I could perhaps hold my own, but the odds of me stumbling across where it had been hidden were small.

I did know how to fight without a weapon—I'd had to batter my way free of sticky situations on battlefields after I'd lost carbine, pistol, and saber. I'd also taken lessons in boxing in the last few years in Gentleman Joe's rooms and learned a more brutal version of pugilism from Brewster. However, I'd not had to fight three armed men from the back streets of London, in the dark, with a knee still weak from a long-ago injury.

Blows rained down at me. I blocked them the best I could, feeling the knife blade cut through my greatcoat to my forearm. I dove under reaches to punch, balancing on my good leg to kick. I managed to stomp on one man's foot—mostly by accident—but I increased the pressure on his boot, making him dance away with a curse.

But it was a most uneven battle. I ended up simply trying to shield my face and take the worst of the hits on my shoulders and back. One blow caught my bad knee, and I went down in an ungraceful heap.

I knew they'd not kill me, as Arthur had promised. But they'd beat me until I could barely crawl away. I might not be able to find my way out of this cellar at all and die here anyway.

A burst of light stabbed my eyes, and shouting echoed from the stone walls. I remained on the floor, my knees drawn up, head down.

The blows mercifully ceased, and I heard the thump of boots fading into the darkness.

Then came Brewster's voice, shouting invectives that would make the most jaded soldier flinch. More heavily tramping feet went after the first set.

Wax dripped to my skin, stinging. Someone had brought the candle over to me.

I looked up to see the gaunt features of Gibbons brushed by candlelight against the shadows behind him.

"Get him on his feet," Gibbons barked.

Hands reached for me. One set belonged to Downie, who peered at me in worry. The other pair was Bartholomew's.

"Thank you, Bartholomew," I said, my voice a faint rasp. "Mr. Downie. Mr. Gibbons. Most timely."

Downie and Bartholomew heaved me up but had to hang onto me so I didn't fall again.

Bartholomew took in Hawes on the table and the remains of his bloody shirt. "What happened to him?" he asked in shock.

I strove to catch my breath, my body throbbing. "He was stabbed by his mates. Let that be a lesson about what friends you trust."

Neither Downie nor Bartholomew laughed, but I suspect they could barely understand what I was saying.

"We'll help him, don't you worry," Downie assured me.

"I have something to ask him first." I hobbled, with Bartholomew's and Downie's aid, over to the table.

Hawes raised his head, his face colorless in the wavering candlelight. "You all right, Captain?"

"I will be, no thanks to you." I heard the snarl in the words and reined in my temper with effort. "You can make it up to me by doing me a favor."

"Of course," Hawes whispered.

"My friends will get you patched up." My voice was cracked, but I forced it to work. "Then you will send a message to Pickett's murderer and instruct him to meet you at Mr. Christie's shop in Finsbury Square."

Hawes regarded me in abject terror. "But he'll kill me."

"We will be there to prevent that," I assured him. "Tell him you want your share of the winnings, or you'll be off to reveal all to Mr. Spendlove. Which you will be if you do not undertake this for me. Do you understand?"

I was amazed my demand held the strength it did, but my resoluteness came from anger at Arthur, Hawes, the man who'd killed Pickett, and Pickett himself for being such a fool.

My adamance reached Hawes. "Yes," he croaked.

Then his head slumped forward, and he collapsed into a dead faint.

———

BARTHOLOMEW HAD TO ASSIST ME UP THE STAIRS OF THE CELLAR I'd been imprisoned in and out into a lane I didn't recognize. The light was failing, not because the hour was late, but because of rainclouds rolling in. Spring weather in London was fickle.

Denis's coach waited at the mouth of the lane, and Bartholomew bundled me into it. Gibbons, who'd followed us, called up to the driver a direction I couldn't hear, and then he strode away, going I knew not where.

The road we rumbled down was unfamiliar to me but then the carriage turned, taking us into Jermyn Street.

"Where the devil was I?" I asked Bartholomew. London-born, he had the layout of the metropolis embedded in him.

"Bury Street. Or rather, rooms under a house there."

"Whose house?" Bury Street was in the heart of St. James's,

which had once been the area of utmost fashion, before Mayfair rose to take its place.

Bartholomew shrugged. "Who knows? Most have been turned into clubs or flats. I doubt the gents in the rooms above even know that cellar is there. It was walled off, as though separated from the house long ago."

Interesting. Likely Arthur had discovered the hidden space and commandeered it for his own purposes. Hawes had known to run there in attempt to escape me.

I'd hoped the carriage was taking me home, but Gibbons must have ordered it to Curzon Street. We halted before Denis's house, and Downie and Bartholomew helped me from the coach and inside.

I was taken to the kitchen again, where Downie began to doctor my wounds. Denis was nowhere in evidence.

Brewster arrived as the large cook had one hand on my head to steady me, while Downie stitched up a deep cut on my face.

"Should have waited for me, guv," was the first thing Brewster growled as he entered.

"I did not believe Mr. Hawes would pose me any trouble." I grimaced as Downie tugged painfully at the threads. "I wasn't aware he was in league with Mr. Arthur."

"Found this." Brewster held up my walking stick, which I was grateful to see. It had been a gift from Donata, and I was very fond of it. "Next time, use it."

"Thank you," I said gravely. "I will try to remember." Downie snorted a laugh, but Brewster's scowl deepened.

"We couldn't catch the blokes," Brewster informed me. "They have their secret routes. Hideaway's too close to His Nibs' territories for me comfort."

"His Nibs will have to attend to that without me," I said. Downie tied off the stitching with patient fingers, and I winced again. "What has become of Mr. Hawes?"

"Upstairs." Brewster pointed above our heads. "Surgeon sent for."

If he meant the quiet, bald surgeon who was rather a genius, then Hawes would be well looked after. The fact they hadn't waited for the surgeon to tend me meant they knew I'd mend without trouble. Many of Denis's men were former pugilists used to wounds, knowing which were serious and which were minor.

"I need to speak to him," I told Brewster.

"Finished." Downie broke the last thread and stepped back, the cook releasing me.

I rose, my legs wobbling—I was grateful for the walking stick to steady me. I thanked Downie, who took my words cheerfully, and made my way upstairs, Brewster following.

Bartholomew hovered in the hall. I gave him an instruction, which he leapt away to fulfill, and then I continued up the stairs. Brewster stayed close by my shoulder as though ready to catch me if I fell.

Another of Denis's large men guarded a door at the end of the landing on the second floor. He admitted us into a chamber where Hawes had been tucked into a bed. Hawes regarded me with red-rimmed eyes over the covers, his cheeks ashen.

"Am I done for?" he rasped.

"Not at all." I took a brisk tone. "A very competent surgeon will soon arrive to put you right. But you must write your message first, in case he pours laudanum down your throat and renders you senseless."

Hawes looked as though he'd welcome a hefty dose of the opiate on the moment. "I can't travel to Finsbury Square, Captain. I can't even walk."

"You won't have to. I will go and intercept the man myself."

Hawes nodded in agreement, though he was not happy. "What will become of me?"

I sank my weary body to a straight-backed chair next to his

bed. In this house, even that was comfortable. "If you help me apprehend the murderer, I will ask Mr. Denis to be kind to you. The killer will be arrested, so there will be no more reason to fear him. You might reconsider trusting Mr. Arthur, however."

"I have no choice," Hawes said. "Once you are indebted to him …" He shrugged weakly.

"I understand." At one time I had been indebted to Denis, who'd trapped me with the one bit of knowledge I'd been seeking for years.

The errand I'd sent Bartholomew on was to fetch a pen and paper, and he now entered with those. Mr. Gibbons came behind him, carrying a lap desk fashioned so a man might scribble letters in bed.

Bartholomew helped Hawes to a half sitting position, propped on pillows, and Gibbons set the desk on his lap, not gently. Bartholomew arranged a blank paper on the desk, and I dipped the pen in the ink and handed it to Hawes.

Gibbons hovered while Hawes scratched out words I dictated. Hawes signed the note, then I blotted the paper for him and folded it when the ink was dry. I passed the missive to Bartholomew, telling him where to deliver it.

Bartholomew's eyes widened, but he nodded. "Will you be going home right off, sir?" he asked me.

"After I visit Finsbury Square," I said. "I'll have Brewster with me this time, never fear."

Bartholomew did not appear pleased with the arrangement, but he did not argue. I told him to deliver one more message for me, this one in person, and he departed as I instructed.

"Thank you, Mr. Hawes." I rose stiffly, wondering how many bruises would decorate my body from the thorough beating. "You rest and recover. I will inform those at the Arlington that you'll be laid up for a time."

Hawes didn't answer. He dropped back to the pillows and closed his eyes, as though penning the letter had exhausted him.

Gibbons retrieved the ink, pen, and paper, tucked all inside the desk, and carried it out without a word. Brewster and I came behind him. My inquiry as to where Denis had gone only resulted in Gibbons turning disdainful eyes to me and bathing me in silence.

Denis's coach was no longer present when we stepped out of the house, so Brewster found a hackney to take us to Finsbury Square.

"How do you know this bloke will rise to the bait?" Brewster asked as we bumped across the city. I'd related the tale of what I'd discovered on my adventure, which Brewster had taken in with a scowl. "He could sit on this betting token for weeks until he thinks it safe enough to hand in."

"Which is why I told Hawes to write that the Runners were close to the correct solution, and that Hawes expected payment from him to keep quiet. I believe that will jolt him to act."

"I've heard of this Christie gent," Brewster said. "He'll do anything to get around paying off a wager. Claim the token is forged, or if Pickett is dead, it's null unless a legitimate heir, with his solicitor, is there to claim it."

"That scarcely matters," I said. "I only want the man to make the attempt. Christie will not have to part with any of his hoarded guineas this day."

Brewster regarded me doubtfully but said no more. Nor, surprisingly, did he give me a long lecture about putting myself into a perilous situation through my own impetuousness. I had the feeling he was saving that for later.

I asked the hackney driver to let us down in Wilson Street, the road just outside Finsbury Square. From there, we walked to the square, keeping a cautious eye out for our quarry.

Lackington's Library provided a prime place to wait. We entered it as though we were any other gentleman and his servant coming to shop. Benches had been set before the wide windows, so a person could peruse a book while basking in the view of the square.

My swollen and bruised face gained startled looks, but the clerks there recognized me and kept their questions to themselves.

I found another tome on ballooning and leafed through it, glancing up at the street from time to time. Brewster only folded his arms, leaned against a wall near me, and waited.

An hour after our arrival, a carriage pulled up in front of Christie's shop, but not one I'd expected to see.

I set the book hastily aside and rose, joining Brewster at the window. We both stared in astonishment as Lucius Grenville descended the coach and approached Christie's place of business. He paused on the doorstep, waiting for another man to descend, before he rapped smartly on the portal with his walking stick.

CHAPTER 26

*B*rewster and I departed the bookshop, both of us moving quietly but swiftly toward Christie's. Jackson, Grenville's coachman, recognized me and opened his mouth to call out, but I signaled him to silence.

One of Christie's clerks answered the door and admitted Grenville and his guest. I caught the door before it could close behind them and strode inside past the startled clerk, Brewster at my heels.

Christie rose from behind his large desk, brows lifting in inquiry as Brewster and I entered the clerk's room. "I do not believe any of you have an appointment," he said in his silken tones. "Do *you*, Captain Lacey?"

Grenville swung around at Christie's question, lips parting when he saw me. The other man also started, though whether because of my presence or the state of my face, I could not decide.

"Mr. Langley," I greeted him. "Good afternoon. Have you come to retrieve the winnings you murdered Mr. Pickett for?"

Langley gaped at me, color rising in his face. He spluttered.

"I beg your pardon? What a thing to say, Captain Lacey. What do you mean by it?"

"I mean that Pickett told you all about his win in great excitement, did he not?" I said with a calmness I did not feel. "He'd have been quite thrilled by his good turn of luck, wanting to share the news with a man he considered a friend."

Christie's smooth countenance, for once, cracked. He stared first at me then at Langley then Grenville in astonishment.

"Did he announce this one day when you saw him at Tattersall's?" I went on to Langley without remorse. "Or perhaps not until you visited him in his rooms on Monday night. He must at some point showed you the token. Worth thousands, I believe. What stake had he put on that very outside horse, at thirty-to-one odds against?"

Langley looked as though he might be sick. "Two hundred guineas," he whispered. "His legacy plus some of the money his Bedfordshire friends had given him to purchase the fowling pieces."

"At thirty-to-one?" Grenville said in shock. "Two hundred would return a great deal of money for the poor chap."

"Indeed." I leaned on my walking stick. "Too much of a return for Pickett to resist making such a wager. Did you try to talk him into sharing the winnings with you, his friend who enjoyed race meetings as much as he did? Or did you simply try to take the token from him?"

"He held onto it like grim death," Langley said, his voice hoarse. "I only wanted to look at the bloody thing, but Pickett suddenly behaved as though he feared I'd rob him. He fought me. I'm not sure why I pulled out my knife, but the next thing I knew, it was between his ribs. He fell and expired in the space of a moment."

Langley gasped for breath as he finished, a gloved hand at his heart. Christie's men watched him in amazed alarm, Christie more cynically. Christie had regained his composure by now and regarded Langley with detachment.

A direct hit to the heart would explain the lack of blood on Pickett and his clothing. A man could die of a small wound like that, the bleeding happening inside him, with little seeping out.

However, such a blow, with the victim expiring in an instant, was unlikely to occur by chance. Nor would the knife simply appear in Langley's hand at the opportune time.

I decided not to argue with Langley—I'd leave the whys and wherefores for a clever magistrate like Sir Montague Harris.

"You took the token and ran?" I asked.

Langley nodded. "May God forgive me."

"That will be up to God," Grenville broke in. "On the other hand, I doubt your friends will pardon you. A duel over a dishonored debt is one thing. Quite another to commit murder to collect on another man's wager." Grenville put a few paces between himself and Langley as though he did not want to be soiled by the man's proximity.

Langley reached into his coat. I tensed, as did Brewster and Christie, but he only retrieved a folded and soiled piece of paper. Opening it, he revealed a single square of cork with a bright red mark on one side, the indication that the wager had been for the horse to win.

"It is worth six thousand guineas," Langley said faintly, as though we'd understand and excuse his actions.

Christie darted forward before I or Brewster could stop him and snatched the token from Langley. He moved quickly out of reach and thrust the piece of cork into the fire that burned in the paneled fireplace, dropping it into the heart of its flames.

"Now, it is worth nothing," Christie announced. "Captain, please remove this man from my shop."

Langley stared at Christie in horror. I feared Langley would lunge for the man, ready to kill a second time. Instead, Langley abruptly turned and sprinted for the door.

He found Brewster there to stop him. Langley swiftly produced a knife, the movement more practiced than what he'd claimed he'd made when he'd faced Pickett. Brewster, in one deft motion, relieved him of it.

Brewster then grabbed the fiercely struggling Langley by the collar and half-dragged him out of the chamber and the house itself. Langley fought like the very devil, and Grenville and I hurried to aid Brewster.

Our assistance proved unnecessary. Langley went suddenly still when a tall man with a head of pale hair and a ruddy face stepped squarely in front of them outside the front door.

"Brought me the murderer of Mr. Pickett, eh, Captain Lacey?" Pomeroy bellowed to every house in the square. "I think I'll have this conviction for myself, and Spendlove can sing for it. Thank you kindly, Captain. I won't forget it."

———

WHEN I AT LAST REACHED HOME, DONATA CRIED OUT WHEN SHE viewed my battered and stitched-together face. She ordered me to bed and hovered while Barnstable doctored my wounds with his minty-scented ointment, the man clucking with disapproval at my state.

Donata was not one to sit at a sickbed, but once Barnstable was finished, she ordered her lady's maid to send her excuses for whatever engagements she'd promised to attend and remained in my chamber. Once Jacinthe had gone, Donata slid off her peignoir and climbed into the bed with me.

She settled against my side, being careful not to jostle my injured limbs, and demanded the entire tale. I told her all, from what I'd learned since we'd spoken last, ending with luring Langley to the betting shop.

"Grenville told me he was at Langley's lodgings when Langley received Hawes's note," I said as I finished the tale.

"Grenville had gone to set up the interview I'd wanted. When I made that arrangement, I believed someone at the Arlington had done in Pickett, and I only sought Mr. Langley's opinion on whether Pickett had wagered on a long-odds horse. I realized when Hawes sincerely denied killing Pickett that though he'd covered up the murder, he hadn't committed it himself. That made Langley a strong possibility. He shared Pickett's love of the races, and if Pickett had crowed to anyone about finally winning on a horse, it would be Langley."

Donata had propped herself on one arm to listen. "Grenville knew none of this?"

"I did not have time to inform him. But Grenville is astute, and he might have already suspected Langley. When Langley received Hawes's note to meet him at Christie's, Grenville encouraged him to answer it and even offered his carriage to take him there."

"Let us bless Grenville and his keen perception." Donata's soft hair brushed my shoulder as she lay down again. "You could have let Mr. Pomeroy and Brewster apprehend the man while you returned home and rested."

"I suppose I could have." I tried to shrug, and flinched at my soreness. "But I'd have been restless and pacing until they sent me word of the outcome, which would have done my injuries no good."

"You find any excuse to be in the thick of things, Gabriel."

I rested my hand on hers where it lay on the blanket. "I am afraid I'm not the sort of man who will sit tamely in a chair perusing his newspapers for the rest of his existence. Reading about life instead of experiencing it."

"Good." Donata's word held warmth.

We ceased speaking then, which was to my satisfaction.

———

THE NEXT MORNING, I RECEIVED A MISSIVE FROM DENIS THAT politely requested my presence in his home directly after breakfast.

I was too stiff and aching after my battle to walk, so I finished my repast and let Barnstable call the carriage for the short distance to Curzon Street. Brewster, who'd accompanied me home and spent the night, came with me.

Before departing, I'd written a note to Mr. Taylor, apologizing for abandoning him yesterday and explaining that Hawes was resting from an injury. I also told him that Pickett's true killer had been caught—though I imagined the entire sordid tale would soon be revealed in the newspapers.

Bartholomew had told me he'd lost Taylor in the crowd when we were chasing Hawes and never saw him again. I speculated that Mr. Taylor had gone back to the Arlington to drink brandy and wonder what had become of us.

I finished the letter asking if Taylor would be willing to meet me to ride in Hyde Park the following morning, if he was still curious about the whole affair. Taylor had a hard-headed sense I'd liked, and I hoped we could speak again.

I was kept waiting when I reached the Curzon Street house, even though I'd arrived in answer to Denis's summons. Eventually Gibbons fetched me from the reception room and guided me up the stairs to Denis's study.

Gibbons had restored himself to his butler's persona, erasing the man who'd helped me against Arthur's thugs. In keeping with the early hour, he set a cup of coffee on the small table instead of brandy and departed.

Denis continued to write on the paper before him, his pen scratching in the silence. I took a noisy sip of my coffee, pretending not to care that he didn't deign to notice me.

After about a quarter hour of this, Denis finally laid down his pen.

"The matter of Mr. Pickett was resolved satisfactorily?" he asked, as though he did not already know.

"It has been," I answered. "Pomeroy sent me word this morning that Langley broke down before the magistrate and confessed, though Langley maintains he never meant to kill Pickett and was striking out to defend himself in a fight." I shrugged. "Langley has no criminal past. The jury might believe him."

"I wish him luck."

I heard no compassion in Denis's voice, but I could not blame him. Langley had nearly sent him to the gallows for a crime he did not commit. Denis had won free, of course, but it had been a close-run thing. A disappointed Spendlove had made it clear he was still keeping a sharp eye on Denis.

"What will you do about Arthur?" I asked. "He has a hideout not far from your doorstep, and he's not above letting his ruffians attack those in your sphere."

"You have no cause to worry about Mr. Arthur and his men," Denis said calmly. "I will see to that."

The finality of his declaration told me Arthur had better look over his shoulder from now on.

Denis's gaze strayed to the letter he'd finished writing, and my patience ran out.

"Is that why you brought me here?" I demanded. "To ask me a question you already knew the answer to?"

Denis slid the letter aside. "Not at all. I wished to tell you that the business with the young woman you call Lady has also concluded satisfactorily."

My irritation fled, and I sat up with interest. "You found her daughter?"

"I did. As I told you, Redding's widow sold the business, pocketed the proceeds, and departed London. I now know that she has leased a cottage in a village near Epsom, in Surrey, and her children are with her."

"Vicky as well? Is the girl all right?"

Denis gave me a nod. "Miss Redding appears to be in good health. From all accounts, she is treated as a member of the family and not a servant, nor given any sort of lesser status. I have arranged for Lady to take a short journey to Epsom so she can see her daughter, if only from afar."

I breathed out in gratification. "Thank you. It was kind of you do to this."

Denis's brows rose a fraction. "It was a business arrangement. I made these inquiries for you while you made inquiries about Pickett's murder on my behalf."

"That is true," I conceded. I had my own ideas about Denis's motives, but I decided not to give voice to them. "Will you accompany her on this short journey?"

"If I am able. I have many other things that require my attention."

As usual, Denis gave an answer and did not at the same time.

I lifted the cup to sip more coffee then abruptly clicked it down again. "A moment. You referred to her as *the young woman I call Lady*. Is that not how *you* address her? Do you know her true name?"

Another nod, this one infuriatingly cool. "I did discover her identity, which was not difficult once I'd heard what she would tell me of her story. Details tend to stick in my mind."

"Who is she?" I blurted out, too curious to still my tongue.

"That, I promised not to reveal. But I can tell you she is the daughter of an Irish peer. Or, at least, that is how her parentage is recorded in the parish registry of her village. Her mother had a reputation for promiscuity, and rumor has it that several of Lady's siblings have different fathers."

"Ah." I did not have a list of the peerage running through my head, though Donata would likely know whom he meant. "I understand why Lady would want such a thing kept quiet. People might say that she is the product of her mother."

"They did say such things, which is why she departed her home near Galway, once she found herself in her unfortunate predicament. She traveled to London, to put distance between herself and her past."

"The poor woman," I said with feeling.

"She was quite resourceful, ensuring she had enough funds for the journey as well as finding a house to go to once she reached London."

Denis sounded indignant that I'd think of Lady as a pathetic waif. Also admiring that she'd not simply fled, penniless, to waste away on the streets.

"Even so, to be forced to cut all ties and begin a life in the slums of London must have been a terrible thing," I said.

"Her home life was not all that happy, she admitted," Denis said. "Her father suspected she was not truly his—whether she is or not will remain a mystery, as her mother is now deceased. He was not the most tenderhearted of fathers, and her mother had little time for her. She confessed that she committed her indiscretion because the gentleman in question was kind to her. At first, of course."

"Then abandoned her." My voice hardened. "I long to search for this gentleman and explain why he made a mistake."

"She will not name him, but I have begun making inquiries."

Denis's gaze met mine, the two of us in perfect accord.

"Lady will not thank you for it," I said.

Denis shrugged. "The man might be dead and already beyond my reach. Life is perilous for those with close ties to the English government in Ireland. It is a restless place."

Rebellions had happened in that country before, and I suspected they would again. Local men risked death if they opposed their overlords, but that did not stop them from trying.

"Will you share with me who it is if you find out?" I asked.

"I *will* find out, and no, I will not reveal the information," Denis answered with finality. "You are too rash, and she does not need to face any more shame. You will let me take care of the matter."

I subsided. I knew that if Denis did not want to tell me a fact, I'd never pry it out of him even to save his life.

I also knew that Denis would indeed, as he put it "take care of the matter." What Lady would do if she found out, I did not know. Or perhaps he would tell her. Denis could be painfully honest when he thought it best.

He'd never reveal all to me, however. It was Lady's business, and Denis was a master at pigeonholing every aspect of his life.

I eyed him sternly. "She is paying with her life and her heart for one mistake she made with a careless gentleman. Do not let her make another."

Denis regarded me without expression. "I am pleased that you worry about her welfare. However, do not assume that I would rush to exploit her weakness—a trait she does not possess, by the way. I am not as iniquitous as you assume me."

"Then you will not see her again?"

Amusement entered his blue eyes. "I will certainly see her again. As I said, I might accompany her to Epson. I will also remain informed about the welfare of her daughter, which I will report to her from time to time. I enjoy speaking with her. She has a quick and appreciative mind."

I recalled the two chatting—if Denis could be said to chat— about the painting on the landing. At that moment they'd simply been two people with a common interest in art.

"She knows that you've discovered her real name?"

"Yes." Denis stated, as though explaining to a simpleton. "I address her thus. Likewise, she knows mine."

"I see." I did not relent. "If I have not yet made myself clear— if you hurt that courageous young woman, you will answer to me."

"I am aware of your concern, Captain," Denis returned. "You have no cause to worry."

We studied each other for another moment.

I decided, after forcing my gallant tendencies to calm, to believe him. I recalled the way Denis had beheld Lady when she'd exclaimed about the light in Mr. Vermeer's painting. His gaze had not been on the picture, but on Lady herself.

I'd never seen Denis look at a living soul in that way before. I realized he understood what a rare being she was, and I suspected he'd take as much care with her as he would his price-less artworks.

I lifted my coffee. "By the way," I said, as though my interest in Lady and her welfare was a passing thing. "Why *did* you hire Mr. Stout? I admit his knowledge of the horseracing world proved useful, but I doubt you brought him back from Rome to tell you the race results. Satisfy my curiosity in that quarter at least. Had he done you a good deed in the past?"

Denis did not betray any surprise or irritation at my inquiry. Likely he was happy I'd ceased badgering him about Lady. "I had never met Mr. Stout before I offered him employment."

"Then why—?"

Denis lifted a hand. "As you will continue to pry into the question, I will tell you. I hired Mr. Stout as a favor to Mr. Gibbons. They have some connection in Mr. Gibbons' past."

I digested this answer in surprise. "One you do not know?"

"I did not make it my business to ask."

I was not sure Denis could astonish me more than he had this morning. "You certainly are trusting Stout," I said. "To hire him without knowing him, or why Gibbons asked you to—"

"Mr. Gibbons' reasons are his own." Denis pulled the letter back to himself and took up his pen. "I'd trust Gibbons with my life. Good morning, Captain."

I would get no more from him, that was clear. I set aside the coffee with some regret—it was excellent—and rose. I made a bow to Denis, which he did not acknowledge, nodded to Robbie in his usual place by the window, and left the room.

Gibbons waited pointedly at the bottom of the stairs, ready to show me the door.

I studied the man while I took my coat and hat, wondering if Gibbons was a relation to Stout. I'd dismissed the idea that Stout had a family connection to Denis, but the ages of Stout and Gibbons were such that *they* could be father and son. I had much to ponder.

I bade the silent Gibbons good morning and departed the house. The door closed firmly behind me.

CHAPTER 27

Though I thought to ride that morning, I was still too sore, and rested for several more hours once I returned home. Early in the afternoon, Gabriella, who'd been staying with Lady Aline, burst into the house in a rush, calling up the stairs when she saw me.

"Father, Emile has arrived. Is this not a happy event?"

Emile was to have joined us in another week, but it seemed he'd journeyed to England early. He must have called at Aline's first, knowing Gabriella often resided there while in London. Also, I suspected, he hesitated to face me right away.

Through the open front doorway I saw Emile descend Aline's coach, politely hand out that lady, and escort her into the house.

I greeted Emile somewhat less enthusiastically than Gabriella had announced him, but I watched my daughter, not her fiancé, as he shook my hand then gazed about the foyer.

Gabriella's entire demeanor had brightened, her smiles not dimming as she swept her arm upward, showing off Donata's elegant house.

While Emile did not fall to his knees in awe of its grandeur, I could see he was intimidated by it. A month ago, this might have given me satisfaction, but as I regarded the way Gabriella tried to put him at his ease, I realized she was a better person than I.

Gabriella radiated happiness. In my opinion, no man in the world would ever be good enough for her, but it was clear she loved the quiet young Frenchman at her side. When I finally pulled my gaze from Gabriella and observed Emile, I found it obvious that he adored her.

He'd do everything in his power to make her happy, his expression told me as she tucked her hand into the crook of his arm. I also understood he could not do that in London, with me standing over him every moment of every day.

I had to let them return to Lyon, to settle there, where Emile had his family, and Gabriella had lived her entire life. The fact that Gabriella wanted to include me in this life had pulled me from the despair that used to haunt me, and I would be forever grateful to her for that.

But it meant I had to release her. A few days ago, I'd briefly wished she'd have chosen one of the dull young gentlemen Lady Aline and Donata had vetted for her, so she'd always be within reach. Watching her now, I realized I could never pen her in. I'd lost her once before, but this time, I had to choose to let her fly.

Gabriella pulled Emile upstairs to the first-floor drawing room, and Aline followed good-naturedly to chaperone.

I could have retreated to the library to write letters, make final notes on the Pickett case, or sulk into a glass of port. I made the decision to join the others in the drawing room, to sit down with Emile and become better acquainted with my future son-in-law.

He would be my family, whether I wished it or not. I did not want the years ahead to be filled with resentment, anger, and loneliness when my daughter avoided me or anticipated my visits with dread.

For Gabriella's sake, I would keep the peace. One look into her eyes and feeling the grateful smile she beamed on me, told me doing so would be worth it.

———

When Donata rose later and began her toilette, I entered her dressing room, took my usual chair, and relayed to her what Denis had discovered about Lady and her daughter.

Donata's eyes lit with interest when I reached the part about Lady's past, and I imagined that by supper, she'd conclude exactly who Lady was and be able to put together all her family connections.

I also knew Denis had been correct in his estimation of Donata's character—she could be amazingly discreet. I had no doubt she'd keep the secret of Lady's identity and her situation from the rest of the world.

Emile accompanied us to the opera that night, and I found, to my surprise, that I appreciated his company. His witty observations on the theatre and the glittering elite around us amused me.

When Grenville joined us, he and Emile greeted each other with delight—Emile had taken to Grenville during our Roman sojourn. The two began a conversation in fluent French, while I leaned back, closed my eyes, and enjoyed the music and the sound of my wife's and daughter's voices as they chattered away behind me.

———

In the morning, I went to the mews, had my horse saddled, and rode to Hyde Park.

Brewster, though I'd told him to take some days to spend

with his wife, ambled in my wake, ready to station himself beside a tree and watch for any enemy.

"Good morning, Mr. Taylor," I called when a rider on a fine gray hunter approached me. I'd received his reply to my letter yesterday afternoon, accepting my invitation to meet in Hyde Park today at this hour.

Mr. Taylor touched the brim of his hat in greeting. "Do you always ride this bloody early?" he demanded.

"The park is quietest now," I answered. "And it's a fine day." The sun had broken free of its confining clouds, the weather deciding to welcome spring at last.

"You have a point." Taylor pulled his horse beside mine, and we moved at a slow pace along the Rotten Row. "Can't get up more than a sedate trot in the afternoons with all the dandified fools clogging up the way, showing off to ladies in carriages who can't be bothered with them. Now, what the devil happened to Mr. Hawes? It's being put about the Arlington that he's gone off to Cornwall to nurse his ill health. Evading arrest for covering up the murder of that Pickett fellow, more like."

Not so much evading arrest as hiding from Mr. Arthur, I believed. I saw Denis's hand in Hawes's flight—he'd have seen the opportunity to pull Hawes into his net in return for his safety. Denis hadn't said a word to me about Hawes, but I knew this in my heart.

"Indeed," I agreed. "I doubt we'll see Mr. Hawes again."

"Tell me what befell you when you went haring off after him," Taylor said impatiently. "I lost sight of you, and you apparently met with some adventure." He gestured with his crop at my still-bruised face.

As I readily began my tale, I caught a movement on the road bordering the park. I glanced over to see a man standing on the other side of it, nearly hidden among the early risers roaming up and down Knightsbridge.

His greatcoat was open on this warm day to reveal an ordinary suit, and his low-crowned hat was tipped back on his head. He lounged congenially near the corner of a brick barracks, hands in his pockets.

He gazed back at me without concern and without belligerence. Taylor, intent on the ride and my story, didn't notice him. Brewster, on the other hand, did notice him. He came alert, ready to defend me, but I motioned him to remain still.

Mr. Arthur and I studied each other for a long moment, neither of us giving way. Then Arthur gave me a nod, sketched a salute, and faded from sight.

ALSO BY ASHLEY GARDNER

A Mystery at Carlton House
Murder in St. Giles
Death at Brighton Pavilion
The Custom House Murders
Murder in the Eternal City
A Darkness in Seven Dials

The Gentleman's Walking Stick
(short stories: in print in
The Necklace Affair and Other Stories)

Kat Holloway "Below Stairs" Victorian Mysteries
(writing as Jennifer Ashley)
A Soupçon of Poison
Death Below Stairs
Scandal Above Stairs
Death in Kew Gardens
Murder in the East End
Death at the Crystal Palace
The Secret of Bow Lane
The Price of Lemon Cake
(novella)
Mrs. Holloway's Christmas Pudding
(holiday novella)
Speculations in Sin

Mystery Anthologies
Past Crimes
A Below Stairs Mystery Collection

ABOUT THE AUTHOR

USA Today Bestselling author Ashley Gardner is a pseudonym for *New York Times* bestselling author Jennifer Ashley. Under both names—and a third, Allyson James—Ashley has written more than 100 published novels and novellas in mystery, romance, fantasy, and historical fiction. Ashley's books have been translated into more than a dozen different languages and have earned starred reviews in *Publisher's Weekly* and *Booklist*.

When she isn't writing, Ashley indulges her love for history by researching and building miniature houses and furniture from many periods, and playing classical guitar and piano.

More about the Captain Lacey series can be found at the website: www.gardnermysteries.com. Stay up to date on new releases by joining her email alerts here:

http://eepurl.com/5n7rz

Printed in Great Britain
by Amazon